# BEAR BONES
## MURDER AT SLEEPING BEAR DUNES

# BEAR BONES

## MURDER AT SLEEPING BEAR DUNES

### A BURR LAFAYETTE MYSTERY

## Charles Cutter

MISSION POINT PRESS

MISSION POINT PRESS

Published by Mission Point Press
2554 Chandler Rd.
Traverse City, MI 49686
(231) 421-9513
www.MissionPointPress.com

ISBN: 978-1-950659-56-2
Library of Congress Control Number: 2020908457

Manufactured in the United States of America
First Edition/First Printing

Cover design: John Wickham
Interior design and layout: Bob Deck

*For*
*Charlie, Tom and Kathryn*

*Was this the face that launch'd*
*a thousand ships*
*And burnt the topless towers of Ilium—*
*Sweet Helen, make me immortal with a kiss*

Christopher Marlowe
"Doctor Faustus"

# PROLOGUE

Years and years ago, in the great forest that covered the place that is now named Wisconsin, lived Mishe Mokwa (Mother Bear) and her two cubs. One day, a raging fire swept through the woods, burning everything in its path. It drove Mishe Mokwa, her cubs and all the animals before it. Soon they came to a place where they could go no further, the great Lake Michigan.

Mishe Mokwa knew there would be no food after the fire was spent. Like all bears, Mishe Mokwa and her cubs were powerful swimmers. They plunged into the lake and swam east, keeping the light and smoke of the fire behind them. They swam through the day and the night.

Late the next day, Mishe Mokwa saw the tall white dunes on the lake's eastern shore. When she reached the place now called Michigan, her cubs were nowhere to be seen. She called to them with no answer, finally climbing the dunes to look back. As the sky turned red with sunset, she saw her cubs struggling far offshore through the cold waters. Her heart broke as first one and then the other slipped beneath the waves.

Heartbroken and exhausted, she lay upon the dune for days and days, watching the place where her cubs had perished.

Gitche Manitou, the Great Spirit Manitou, saw Mishe Mokwa watching. He was moved by her sorrow and faithfulness. While Mishe Mokwa watched for her cubs, Gitche Manitou slowly raised two beautiful islands, North and South Manitou, to mark the watery graves of the cubs.

Knowing that the Mother Bear's heart would never mend, Gitche Manitou laid a slumber upon Mishe Mokwa and drew the sand over her like a blanket, creating a solitary dune that marks the place where she keeps her eternal vigil.

# CHAPTER ONE

*Achilles* crept down the Leland River, past the shanties, the charter boats and, finally, the ferry. At the mouth of the river, *Achilles* left the breakwater to port and nosed into Lake Michigan, on her way to Sleeping Bear Bay. There was weather in the forecast, but Helen Lockwood wanted to look up toward her orchards from the lake before heading to South Manitou.

She had gotten up at first light, and by the time she put the top down on her cherry-red Benz, Tommy was already out in the orchards. She drove up M-22 to Leland in the early morning sunshine, parked on the north side of the river and walked down to her boat.

She climbed on board, went down below, lit the alcohol stove and made coffee. She lit a cigarette from the blue flame and smoked it while she waited for the coffee to perk. After her second cup of coffee, she lit the other burner and scrambled eggs. After breakfast, she went up to the nav station, checked the logbook, ran the blower and started the engines. Twin Gray Marine diesels.

After she cast off the bow line, the current caught the bow and pushed it downstream. She cast off the stern line, put the engine in gear and headed downriver. When she passed the shanties, she saw gulls circling and heard them crying, waiting for the fishmongers to finish cleaning the whitefish. She passed the ferry and nosed into the big lake. The wind blew about fifteen knots from the southwest, right on the nose. The sun was gone, and the seas were building.

Helen stood at the helm, both hands on the wheel. The waves broke over the bow and sprayed the windshield. The single wiper beat back and forth but didn't keep up with the spray.

*It's going to be a rough ride.*

Twenty minutes later, she was halfway across Good Harbor Bay. The wind had picked up, and now there were whitecaps and rain. The windshield wiper tick-tocked back and forth. She couldn't tell the difference between the spray and the rain on the windshield.

Helen reached into the hanging locker and pulled out the foul weather jacket that had been her grandfather's. The coat hung down to her knees, and she had to roll up the sleeves. The musty smell of the oiled canvas reminded her of him.

Helen Lockwood, at forty-six, was striking, even in her grandfather's raincoat. She was a tall woman with long legs and moved like a dancer. She had straw-colored hair that hung past her shoulders. In the summer, her skin was the color of wheat just before the harvest. She had blue eyes that could look right through whomever she was talking to. If her lips were a little too full and her nose a little too long, no one noticed.

The boat slowed when it crawled up a wave and wallowed when it came down the other side. She gave the engines another 200 RPMs, and the boat pounded through the waves.

*Achilles* was a forty-foot sedan, long and narrow, built at the Chris Craft factory in Holland, two hundred miles south. Oak ribs, Honduran mahogany planks and teak decks. White hull, varnished cabin. *Achilles* cruised at fifteen. She could plane but didn't like it. Helen's father had given it to her when she was twenty-five, when he knew the cancer was going to take him. Tommy didn't like boats and that was just fine with her.

She looked behind her and saw the ferry running the rhumb line to South Manitou. It ploughed through the waves, spray blowing all the way to the stern.

Off the port bow, Pyramid Point towered out of Lake Michigan, a massive dune that marked the southern entrance to Sleeping Bear Bay. The lake got choppier when she reached the point, the waves upset and confused by the shoal water. When *Achilles* rounded Pyramid Point, she was broadside to the seas and started to roll. Helen heard glass break down below.

*I hope it wasn't the gin.*

Once the boat was in Sleeping Bear Bay and in the lee of Sleeping Bear Point, the seas flattened out. Five minutes later *Achilles* was abeam of Port Oneida, where her great-grandfather had built the dock that once jutted into the lake. The steamers had stopped there for firewood for their boilers and for lumber to build Chicago. The waves and the ice tore up the dock every year, and every year he rebuilt it. But that was almost a hundred years ago. All that was left of the dock were a few rotting pilings, broken off at the waterline.

She saw what was left of the pilings in the troughs of the waves. She passed the ruined deck, came around and headed for South Manitou.

She lit another cigarette and looked back at the waves rolling on the beach at Port Oneida. When the timber ran out, her great-grandfather, Lars Erickson, had tried farming farther up Port Oneida Road, over the dunes toward M-22, long before M-22 became famous. The ground had been clear cut, and he bought a section. Almost four hundred acres were tillable, the rest of it, marsh and cedar swamp. But the soil was too sandy, the crops failed, and the land went for taxes during the Depression.

After Lars died, Helen's grandfather Carl found a way to buy it back. As wild as Lake Michigan could be, it moderated the temperatures and kept the frost away in the spring and the fall. Carl tried fruit trees, starting with ten acres of apples, but there was more money in tart cherries.

Port Oneida Orchards made good money in cherries. Carl ran out of help and brought in migrant workers to pick his cherries. He built cabins for them behind the barns.

When Helen's father, Robert, took over the orchards, he bought the first shaker in Leelanau County. That was the end of the cherry pickers. Port Oneida Orchards added more trees. Robert and Marjorie had three daughters.

When Robert died, Helen, the oldest, took over the farm with her husband, Tommy. She was going to keep it going no matter what the Park Service tried to do.

She took one last drag on her cigarette, slid back the starboard window in the steering station and flicked it out into the lake. She closed the window, brought *Achilles* around through the wind and made for South Manitou. When the boat came out from the lee of the point, it started rolling again.

*Tommy won't be able to work outside in this weather.*

Helen looked off the stern at the dunes towering almost five hundred feet above the lake. She pictured the mother bear at the top of the dune, watching for her cubs, forever waiting and watching. The trees and brush did look like a bear lying down, especially in the rain.

*It's beautiful, but that doesn't mean the Park Service can take my orchards.*

She turned back to the bow. She couldn't see South Manitou through the rain and the spray, so she set a compass course, correcting for the drift. A half-hour later she saw the lighthouse at the southern tip of South Manitou.

The wind gusted to twenty-five and blew *Achilles* off the waves. A wave broke over the side and flooded the cockpit, the scuppers washing the water over the side. When a wave rushed underneath *Achilles,* the boat rolled to starboard then lurched to port. Helen had to turn the wheel to port then back to starboard to keep her boat from broaching. The compass, mounted on gimbals, was the only thing that stayed even with the horizon.

Forty minutes later, Helen passed the abandoned lighthouse. The seas flattened, and she motored up into the crescent-shaped harbor at South Manitou.

*Achilles* passed the ferry tied up at the Park Service dock, headed into the wind and anchored in twenty feet of water.

Helen opened the lazarette and took out the inflatable. She pulled the cord and the $CO_2$ cartridge inflated the rubber raft. It took up most of the cockpit. She launched it, then mounted the two-horse outboard.

Helen retired to the main salon and poured herself three fingers of Tanqueray over ice.

*Thank God it didn't break.*

She sat on the settee and looked out the plate glass windows at the ribbon of beach and the forest beyond. There were swells in the harbor, but the anchor was holding. She thought about putting out a second anchor but decided she didn't need one. She poured herself a second three fingers and lit another cigarette.

* * *

The storm blew through the night. By morning the wind died. The sky was a clear, deep blue, and the lake was starting to lay down. By afternoon, a light wind had come up from the north, and there were catspaws on the lake. An old wooden powerboat drifted about two miles off Sleeping Bear Dunes, drifting broadside to the wind.

The boat was still there the next day.

And the day after that.

Finally, a charter boat trolling for lake trout off Manitou Shoals pulled her lines and took a look.

There was no one aboard.

Not a soul.

# CHAPTER TWO

Burr Lafayette tap, tap, tapped his yellow, Number 2 pencil on the defense table in the Federal District Court for the Western District of Michigan. David C. Powers, an assistant U.S. attorney, droned on. And on. Fifty-five years old. Five-ten with a slouch and a belly that hung over his slacks. Burr couldn't see Powers' belt. Powers had a pasty face and two chins. Burr thought he looked like forty pounds of air in a thirty-pound tire.

But Powers was a good lawyer. Dogged. Powers was dogged. He stayed with it and he paid attention to the little things, which was important in a condemnation case. Which Powers was doing at this very moment. Droning on and on about a fine point that Powers was convinced would have a bearing on the fate of Port Oneida Orchards.

Burr stopped tapping and yawned. He had driven from East Lansing to Grand Rapids early in the morning. Much too early. He knew Powers had filed his emergency motion just to make Burr get up before dawn. Burr hated to get up early, except for duck hunting, which was still three months off. Whatever this motion was about, it surely wasn't an emergency. He started tapping again.

Powers looked over at him. "Mr. Lafayette, would you please stop that tapping."

"Not if it bothers you."

"I beg your pardon."

Burr smiled at Powers, tapped with a flourish, then stopped. He had been fighting with Powers and the Department of the Interior for three years, all of it here in the Federal District Court in downtown Grand Rapids. Burr thought that was about to change.

Powers started up again, but the judge stopped him. "I've heard enough. Motion denied. And, Mr. Powers, this was surely not an emergency. In the future do not take advantage of this court with frivolity. Is that clear?"

"Yes, Your Honor," Powers said.

"Merciful heavens," Burr said under his breath. He started to gather up his papers.

"Not so fast, Mr. Lafayette," Judge Harold G. Cooper said. In his late 60s, tall, thin and tough, Cooper did not suffer fools gladly. "Approach the bench."

Burr stood before the judge.

Judge Cooper took off his glasses. "Having disposed of Mr. Powers' emergency motion that wasn't, I turn my attention to your pending motion to stay this proceeding."

Burr nodded.

The judge folded his hands in front of him. "I am not going to grant a stay in these proceedings while you fiddle-faddle around because you can't find one of your clients."

"Your Honor…"

The judge raised a hand and cut Burr off. "To review, the federal government began acquiring land for the Sleeping Bear Dunes National Lakeshore about 1970. Some years after that, the National Park Service through the Department of the Interior tried to purchase your clients' property. When that failed, the Park Service brought a condemnation action to acquire the subject property, which you have most ably opposed. For almost seven years." Judge Cooper paused. He took off his glasses and tapped them on his desk. "So far. And if your current motion is a harbinger of things to come, it will take at least another seven years to dispose of this case." The judge folded his hands together and cleared his throat. I am not going to let this case become your life's work." He paused again. "Or mine."

Burr looked down at his shoes. Cordovan loafers with tassels. Italian. They needed polishing, and the soles were worn.

*I love these shoes. I wish I could afford a new pair.*

Burr looked up at the judge. "Your Honor, my client has been missing for over a year. According to the terms of the partnership agreement, she is the manager and the only person who can make decisions when it comes to this condemnation action. We are powerless to defend ourselves without a manager."

The judge peered down at Burr. "Mr. Lafayette, for all I know, you have her in hiding just to create such a stalemate."

Burr pulled down the cuffs of his baby blue, button-down, pinpoint oxford shirt, which did not need pulling down. He straightened his red foulard tie with black diamonds, which did not need straightening. He unbuttoned the one button on his thousand-dollar charcoal suit, slightly threadbare. "Your Honor," he said again, "Helen Lockwood has not been seen or heard from since she took her boat to South Manitou Island."

"I read your brief, Mr. Lafayette."

"Of course, Your Honor, but the partnership agreement calls for the spouse of a deceased member to succeed, but we don't know if Mrs. Lockwood is deceased. She's missing and we can't act."

Judge Cooper wagged his finger at Burr. "If you'll forgive my cynicism, this is all too convenient. Especially for the most contested condemnation case I have ever had the misfortune to preside over. Surely you can find a way to name a successor."

"Your Honor…"

"Mr. Lafayette, if you have a missing client, I suggest you find her. There will be no stay."

"Your Honor…"

The judge waved his glasses at Burr. "Mr. Lafayette, our own Senator Philip Hart sponsored the legislation that created the Sleeping Bear Dunes National Lakeshore. It's over thirty-two thousand acres, and there's over fifty miles of shoreline on Lake Michigan. It is a very special place. It is altogether fitting that the public good outweighs the property interests of a few in-holders."

"Your Honor…" Burr said again.

The judge waved his glasses at Burr again. "Surely a lawyer as clever as you can find a way to overcome this deadlock."

Burr ran his hand through his hair, front to back, which he did when he was flummoxed. He had too-long, acorn hair with a few gray hairs mixed in. Whenever he found a gray hair, he pulled it out. He had clear, sky blue eyes. A hawk nose. At one time he had been six foot. Late forties. Medium build. A handsome man who knew it.

He took a step toward the judge. "Your Honor, Port Oneida Orchards are two miles up the road from Lake Michigan. It's not on the water. You can't even see the water from the orchards. They are the most successful orchards in Leelanau County. They have nothing to do with the Sleeping Bear Dunes National Lakeshore."

"Mr. Lafayette, there is nothing I'd rather do than have a trial on the merits. Shall we begin right now?"

Burr took a step back.

*We can't have that.*

A trial was the last thing he wanted right now. What he wanted to do was what he had been doing. Delay, obfuscate and wear out Powers and Cooper. Which hadn't happened yet. "Your Honor, as much as I'd like to start the trial this very moment, I don't have a client who has the authority to act."

Judge Cooper picked up his gavel. He studied it. Then he stared down his nose at Burr. He started tapping his gavel, ever so softly.

*This can't be good.*

"Here's what you do, Mr. Lafayette. You go and get yourself a death certificate. That's what you do. Go get yourself a death certificate and bring it back to me. Then you'll have a client who can act, and we'll have ourselves a trial. Is that clear?"

Burr nodded. *I was afraid he'd think of that.*

"Take a drive up M-22. It's the prettiest road in the state."

M-22 began just north of Manistee and ended in Traverse City. It followed the shoreline for over a hundred miles, all the way around the Leelanau Peninsula. It was one of the most scenic roads in Michigan and famous in its own right.

"Do I make myself clear?"

"Yes, Your Honor."

"Good. And be quick about it. We are adjourned." The Honorable Judge Harold G. Cooper slammed his gavel and walked out.

\* \* \*

"Is she dead? Or isn't she?"

"Yes, Your Honor, she is dead," Burr said.

"That's why we're here. Because she's dead. And because this is a probate court." The judge paused. "Because we deal with dead people here. In probate court." The judge paused again. "Among other things."

"Yes, Your Honor."

Judge Bill Weeks peered over his reading glasses, which put his chin almost on top of the worn-out desk in his courtroom. He was a short man who could barely see over his desk even when he was sitting up straight. He sat on the leather cushion from the chair in his office and that helped. Weeks had a bald, round head that was almost as big as the rest of him. He had black, bushy eyebrows that looked like squirrel tails, a pushed-in nose, a large mouth with bright white teeth framed by ruby red lips. All in all it looked like his face had been painted on an ivory-colored bowling ball, which was why he was known as Bowling Ball Bill, behind his back, of course. That and the awe that the local lawyers had because not only had he managed to graduate from law school, he had also been elected probate judge in Leelanau County, over and over again. At sixty-nine, he showed no signs of slowing down. Or speeding up. Or becoming the slightest bit competent.

Judge Weeks smiled. "Counsel, now that we are in agreement that poor Helen Lockwood is, in fact, deceased, please present the death certificate and I will open her estate for probate."

"Your Honor, we don't have a death certificate."

"Don't waste my time, young man. Come back when you have it." He banged his gavel. "Case dismissed." If the Federal District Court in Grand Rapids was near the top of the legal pecking order, the Leelanau County Probate Court was surely near the bottom, from the courtroom to the furniture and, most importantly, to the judge.

"Your Honor," Burr said, "the very reason we are here is to ask you to issue a death certificate."

"I'll do no such thing. If Helen Lockwood is dead, the medical examiner will issue a death certificate. If he hasn't issued a death certificate, then she's not dead, and I will not be the one to declare her so. I am a powerful man, but not that powerful." Bowling Ball Bill took off his glasses and waved them toward the heavens. "Only God has that power. Now, shoo."

"Respectfully, Your Honor, you have more power than perhaps you think you have."

"I said shoo." The round-headed judge paused again. "I do?"

"Yes, Your Honor. Indeed, you do," Burr said.

This clearly piqued Judge Weeks' interest. Burr had made a career of flattering judges. When it suited his purpose. Most of the time he argued, fought, persuaded, cajoled and did whatever he had to do to get what he wanted from whomever was in his way, but he flattered when he needed to.

Even so, he could not quite fathom how he found himself in the Leelanau County Probate Court. He had been head of the litigation department at Fisher and Allen in Detroit. Two hundred lawyers strong and Burr one of the finest litigators in the city. But he had been a knight of commerce. He saved rich companies on behalf of his rich clients. But he had given it up or lost it all, depending on the day, over a younger woman who happened to work for his rich client. He thought he loved her. Maybe he had, but it cost him his practice not to mention his wife.

And here he was in the Leelanau Probate Court arguing about whether Helen Lockwood was dead. Or not.

"Continue, Mr. Lafayette. About my power."

Burr approached the bench. "Your Honor, as I pointed out in my brief, Helen Lockwood has been missing for over a year. She disappeared without a trace. Not a soul has seen her."

"Is that so?"

Burr looked down at his shoes, the same cordovan loafers he had worn in Judge Cooper's courtroom. They still needed polishing.

*The old fool hasn't read my brief, and he must be the only person in Leelanau County who didn't know that Helen Lockwood had disappeared.*

Burr looked up at the judge. "Your Honor, the settled law in Michigan provides that if a person has not been seen for one year, the probate court may declare the person dead and issue a death certificate."

"I see," said Judge Weeks, who didn't. He opened the file in front of him, which Burr assumed was his unread brief. He shuffled through it. Then looked at down at Burr.

"Your Honor, the legislature codified the common law which favors the living over the dead and the need to get on with the business of living."

"Of course, it does." The judge nodded knowingly. "And what business of living would that be?"

"Your Honor, the deceased…"

"I didn't say she was dead yet."

"Yes, Your Honor." Burr pulled down the cuffs of his charcoal suit, still his favorite suit and slightly threadbare.

"Helen Lockwood, the missing person, is – was – a principal in Port Oneida Orchards. The Park Service is trying to condemn the farm. I represent the family in federal court in Grand Rapids and I…"

"Would you please get to the point?"

*Save me from fools.*

"Your Honor, it has become impossible to represent my client with Mrs. Lockwood's status in limbo. We need a death certificate in order to proceed."

"Young man, you seem to have made it this far without me."

"Your Honor, the law makes provision for just this sort of eventuality."

"Just who is it that you represent, Mr. Lafayette?"

"Today I am here on behalf of Helen Lockwood's husband, Thomas Lockwood."

"Is that him?" Judge Weeks pointed to the lean, fiftyish man sitting at the plaintiff's table. Burr walked back to his client. Tommy Lockwood had jet black hair, a tan face, lined from a lifetime spent outside. He had soft, black eyes and a smile that made you want to give him all your money.

"Yes, Your Honor."

"And what do you want, young man?"

"I want my wife back. I hate the thought that she might be dead."

"And how is her being dead going to help?"

"Your Honor," Burr said, "the affairs of the farm are impossible to manage with Mrs. Lockwood's status unresolved."

"Mr. Lafayette, while I am sympathetic to the problems faced by a lawyer in a thousand-dollar suit, I don't give a hoot about what happens in the Federal District Court for the Western District of Michigan."

*If only I could still afford thousand-dollar suits.*

"Your Honor..."

Weeks pointed a stubby arm at Burr, chubby palm out. "Mrs. Lockwood is either dead or she isn't. Which is it?" The judge folded his hands on the desk in front of him.

Burr looked to his right, where his opponent would normally be sitting. Today, though, he had no opposition. Except Judge Bill Weeks, who was supposed to go right along with what Burr wanted.

"Which is it, Mr. Lafayette?" Judge Weeks said again.

Burr looked down at his shoes again. He put his hands in his pants pockets and pulled up the cuffs of his slacks. His socks matched.

*That's something.*

Without Eve here to check on him, he was never quite sure what was going to happen with his socks. "We're right back where we started. This old fool hasn't heard a word I've said," he said to his shoes.

"What did you say?"

Burr took his hands out of his pockets and looked up at the judge. "Your Honor, I said, please don't make a decision until you've heard the proofs."

"The proofs?" The judge laughed. "You actually have something to support your case?"

Burr walked back to his table and rummaged through his files, his back to the judge.

*This would have been a good time to have Jacob here.*

"Turn around and look at me, young man," the judge said. "Your backside is not particularly compelling. Although, so far, it makes more sense than your front side." The judge laughed.

Burr ignored Weeks. He looked up at Helen's two sisters sitting in the back row. He had told them they didn't need to come today, but he was glad to see them. It was looking like he could use all the help he could get. He nodded at them and turned around to face the cranky judge whose word was law at least as far as the Leelanau Probate Court was concerned.

"May it please the court, Your Honor," he said in his most supplicating voice, a voice he used only when he didn't think anything else would work. Like now. "Your Honor, the petitioner would like to present its proofs."

Judge Weeks shook his fingers at him, like he was shooing a cat off the dining room table.

Burr took that as a yes. "Your Honor, we submit four files. The missing-person report filed by the petitioner on June 12th of last year, the report of the Coast Guard search, the Leland County Sheriff's report and the petition of Thomas F. Lockwood, Mrs. Lockwood's husband, asking that Mrs. Lockwood be declared deceased."

"You mean dead."

"Yes, Your Honor."

*Surely Weeks knows what 'deceased' means.*

"Let me see those." Burr handed him the files. The judge made a show of studying them, but Burr didn't think he was actually reading. The judge put the files in a neat pile in front of him. "So, what exactly happened?"

"Your Honor, Helen Lockwood was last seen leaving Leland Harbor on the morning of June 9th. She piloted her boat, *Achilles*, a forty-foot cabin cruiser, to the anchorage at South Manitou. There was a storm that day and into the night. For the next two days there were reports of a boat matching *Achilles* off Sleeping Bear."

"*Achilles*?"

"*Achilles* was the name of Mrs. Lockwood's boat, Your Honor."

"Funny name for a boat." Weeks shooed at Burr again.

Burr gritted his teeth. "On the third day, a commercial fisherman near Manitou Shoals pulled up alongside *Achilles*. He said the boat was adrift."

"Adrift?"

"Drifting in Lake Michigan. The engines were off."

The judge leaned toward Burr. "And?"

"There was no one aboard. The key was in the ignition, but the engines were off. The gas tanks were half full." Burr paused. "There was no sign of Mrs. Lockwood."

"Anything suspicious?"

"Your Honor, I'm not sure if this is suspicious, but there was a half-empty bottle of Tanqueray rolling back and forth across the cockpit."

"That's expensive gin."

Burr gritted his teeth again. "Your Honor, the Coast Guard and the sheriff both concluded that Mrs. Lockwood fell overboard and drowned."

"Where's her body?"

"It hasn't been found."

"Maybe she ran away."

"Your Honor, her purse was on board. Her car was where she left it."

"What kind of car?"

"A Mercedes."

"What model?"

"A 150 convertible, Your Honor."

"She was pretty well fixed for blades," the judge said.

Burr was tired of the round little judge and his obsession with the wealth of Helen Lockwood. "Your Honor, Mrs. Lockwood's bank accounts have been untouched since she went missing. There have been no financial transactions and no one has seen her." Burr looked back at the two sisters, over at Tommy and then at the judge. "Your Honor, in light of the disappearance of Helen Lockwood for over twelve months, and in compliance with the state statutes, we respectfully request that you declare Mrs. Helen Lockwood deceased."

Judge Weeks fumbled around with his gavel. "As much as I don't like you, you are convincing." He picked up his gavel. "I grant the petitioner's motion and declare Helen Lockwood to be deceased…"

"Your Honor," said a voice from the back of the courtroom.

Weeks stopped his gavel in midair. It slipped out of his hand and landed at Burr's feet.

"For the love of Mike, who said that?"

"I did, Your Honor." This from one of Helen's sisters in the back of the courtroom.

"Don't you know better than to interrupt a judge?" Weeks looked around for his gavel. Burr bent over, picked it up and set it in front of the judge.

"I lost my grip."

"I should say so." Burr turned around. "In more ways than one."

"I heard that," Judge Weeks said. He picked up his gavel and pointed at the two women, one standing, one sitting. "And who might you be?"

One of the sisters stood. "My name is Lauren Littlefield and this is Karen Hansen. Helen is our sister."

"Was," Burr said.

"Be quiet," Weeks said to Burr. "Until this gavel comes down, Helen Lockwood still 'is'." He looked at Lauren. "What would you like to say, Mrs. Littlefield?"

Lauren Littlefield smoothed a wrinkle in her dress, a black knit knee-length cotton dress with a scooped neck, three-quarter length sleeves and a thin black belt. An altogether appropriate dress for a visit to a probate court. She had on two-inch black heels. If Helen Lockwood was tall, her sister was not. Five-four in heels and too round for Burr's taste. But curvy in a pleasant way. She had mousey brown hair pulled back in a bun that didn't do much for her, but she had a pretty face, green eyes, a small nose with full lips. She didn't wear any makeup.

"Your Honor, my sister and I don't believe our sister is dead."

"Why ever not?"

Burr gritted his teeth for a third time.

"She's missing, not dead. We know she's going to turn up."

"Your Honor," Burr said, "all of the family, Mr. Lockwood and Helen's two sisters, agreed that it would be best to have Helen declared dead. I ask that you rule on my motion."

Weeks ignored him. "What about you young lady?" The judge pointed at the sitting sister.

She stood. How the three of them could be sisters was beyond Burr. Karen Hansen was medium height and rail thin. Burr had never seen her eat. She had wild black hair that covered her shoulders. A long nose with thin lips and a strong jaw that made her look like she knew what she wanted.

It was Karen Hansen's turn to smooth her equally black dress. "Your Honor, we don't want Helen to be dead."

Judge Bill Weeks smiled at her. "I'm sure you don't. But no one has seen hide nor hair of her for a year. She must be dead."

"She's not dead," Lauren said.

"What could have happened?" the judge said.

The two sisters didn't say anything.

"Your Honor," Burr said. "This is upsetting for all of us, but we must move on. This is what the family decided they wanted to do."

"It doesn't seem that way to me." Then to the two sisters, "What could have happened?"

"I don't know, but that doesn't mean she's dead," Lauren said.

"Maybe she fell overboard?" the judge said.

"Helen spent her whole life around boats. She would never fall overboard or drown," Karen said.

Lauren nodded.

"Maybe she ran away," the judge said. "What do you think, young man?"

"Helen would never run away. She loved the orchards too much," Tommy said.

"Well then, where is she for God's sake?"

"I don't know." Tommy bit his lip. "I think she must have fallen overboard and drowned."

"Your Honor," Burr said, "this is an upsetting time, but the wheels of justice must grind forward."

"Mr. Lafayette, I'm not sure that's what your clients want."

"They want you to issue a death certificate. We can keep looking for Helen, but we simply must move on." Burr said. "This is what they all want, Your Honor."

"No, it's not," Karen said.

Bowling Ball Bill rubbed his bald head.

Burr leaned down to Tommy. "What is going on?"

Tommy shook his head. "I don't know."

"Come back when you've made up your minds."

"Your Honor, this has nothing to do with making up our minds. This has to do with the facts."

Judge Weeks crashed his gavel. "We are adjourned."

# CHAPTER THREE

Burr, Tommy and the two unhappy sisters sat in the breakfast room at Morningside, the farmhouse at Port Oneida Orchards. Burr thought only those with too much money had the luxury of naming their houses. Until Helen had disappeared, this was every lawyer's dream, rich clients with a big problem. The Erickson family fit the bill. But it wasn't such a dream now. Helen had run the business end of the orchards, and she was the one Burr had dealt with. She knew what she wanted. She made up her mind, and she didn't back down. She would never, ever agree to sell the orchards to the government.

Tommy was a different story. He was certainly smart enough, but his heart was in the cherries, not the lawsuit. Karen, the middle sister, was quiet. She wanted to sell the orchards. Lauren, the youngest, didn't, and between the three of them, they couldn't make up their minds about anything. Their performance in probate court had just proven the point.

After the disaster in court, the four of them had taken M-204 west across the Leelanau Peninsula from Suttons Bay to the family orchards on Port Oneida Road. It was just past noon and the sun, almost directly overhead, lit the trees with clear, bright light. They had driven through the cedar swamps, across the narrows at the village of Lake Leelanau that separated North and South Lake Leelanau, then into the orchards, cornfields and woodlots. At M-22, they had turned south and drove along the bluff above Lake Michigan, sparkling hundreds of feet below them, then onto Port Oneida Road and the orchards. The cherry trees drooped with the bright, lipstick-red fruit, the branches bent over with their weight. The blacktop driveway, in better shape than the road, wound through the fruit trees, past a gazebo and up to the farmhouse.

They turned in the circle drive in front of the farmhouse. The driveway ran on past the house to the outbuildings, a white barn and sheds all with red trim. Just like the farmhouse, which didn't look like any farmhouse Burr had ever seen. Two stories with three gables, the center the largest, with white siding, cherry shutters and leaded windows. A stone fireplace at each end of the house. "Zeke," he said to his aging yellow lab, "there's money in cherries." Burr had been here before and had said this before, but there was nothing quite like Morningside.

They parked in the circle drive, and Tommy led them up the walk past an army of annuals: petunias, marigolds, impatiens and snapdragons lined up in rows and columns like soldiers at attention. They were a riot of color, but the orderliness of it all made Burr nervous.

They sat in the breakfast room at a maple table with spindle legs and matching chairs. The room faced east and looked out onto a lawn with forty-foot sugar maples. The window was framed with Christmas lights, C-9s, the big old-fashioned kind that didn't blink. Red, orange, blue, green and yellow.

Tommy plugged in the lights.

"No, Tommy. They remind me of Helen," Karen said.

"That's why I plugged them in."

A pair of cardinals picked at sunflower seeds from a platform feeder. Three chicks, just fledged, sat on the top of the feeder demanding to be fed.

"I don't like coming here," Karen said, "now that Helen's not here."

"Isn't it time to get the cherries in?" Lauren said. "Before they get blown off."

"They're almost ready," Tommy said. "Consuela, would you please bring in lunch?" She brought in ham and cheese sandwiches on white with the crusts cut off.

*Thank God. I'm about to expire.*

"The cherries won't do us any good if they're on the ground," Lauren said.

"We're getting the shakers out this afternoon." Tommy started in on his sandwich. Cherry shakers, a contraption that clamped on the trunk of a tree and came within an inch of shaking the tree to death, had changed fruit farming. Two men and a shaker could do in a day what a dozen pickers could do in a week. And a shaker didn't need room and board. The migrant cabins behind the barns had been empty for fifteen years, but Tommy kept them nicely painted.

"If we're going to sell the orchards, it doesn't matter when they come off," Karen said.

"We're not selling the orchards," Lauren said. "And we need to get the cherries in."

*At least she knows her own mind.*

"Unfortunately, we need to talk about getting on with the lawsuit," Burr said. He took a bite of his sandwich. Swiss cheese and a coarse, sweet mustard.

*This would be even better with a Labatt.*

"I don't want Helen to be dead," Karen said.

Burr put his sandwich down. "I'm sorry, but if we're going to stay in this lawsuit, we have to have a death certificate."

Consuela brought in a pie.

*Cherry, of course.*

"I thought the cherries weren't ready," Lauren said.

Tommy smiled at Lauren again. "I hand-picked these."

"I don't want Helen to be dead," Karen said again.

"She must have drowned. What else could have happened?" Tommy said.

*We already plowed this ground.*

"We don't know that she is dead," Burr said. "I hope she isn't. All we know is that she's missing." Consuela served him a slice of pie. He looked at it longingly, picked up his fork but paused to speak. "Just because we get a death certificate doesn't mean Helen is dead. It just means we have a death certificate."

Burr couldn't wait any longer. He took a forkful of pie. The filling oozed around the cherries and dripped off his fork. The crust was light brown. He chewed it slowly.

"I think it's bad luck to get a death certificate," Karen said.

"It is," Lauren said.

"The death certificate is a legal fiction," Burr said.

"A what?" Lauren said.

"A fiction. It doesn't mean Helen is really dead. It just means that as far as the law is concerned, she is."

"Let's not talk about her being dead," Karen said.

"Karen, this is the worst thing that could have ever happened. None of us want this, but the judge in the federal court told Burr that we had to have a death certificate," Tommy said.

*He has the patience of a saint.*

"I don't want her to be dead," Karen said. Again.

"For God's sake, Karen, you've said that three times," Lauren said.

\* \* \*

A week later, Burr sat at the walnut desk in his office and tap, tap, tapped his Number 2 yellow pencil. Jacob Wertheim, the Wertheim in Lafayette and Wertheim, sat across from Burr in a navy-blue leather wingback chair that matched the chair next to him, the blue leather matching the leather of Burr's desk chair, which also matched the leather on the couch across the room. On the couch where Zeke was napping.

"Burr," Jacob said, "as I have been telling you for the past week, the judge does not have to grant your motion."

"Jacob…"

"It is discretionary."

"Helen Lockwood has been missing for over a year. Her boat was found floating off Sleeping Bear. She wasn't in it."

"Just because you want the judge to grant your motion doesn't mean he has to."

Jacob tightened the knot on his tie, a striped tie with peach, mint and baby blue stripes. He had on a starched white shirt and a tan summer-weight linen suit. Jacob was natty. Jacob did the research and the writing for their esoteric appellate practice. He abhorred conflict and public speaking, the two most important qualities a litigator could have, so that's what Burr did. Jacob spent almost all his time in their law library. Burr thought Jacob could wear his pajamas to work and no one would notice.

Burr stopped tapping. "I want a death certificate from Judge Weeks."

Jacob ran his thumb and forefinger along the knife-sharp crease in his slacks. "I know. We all want something."

Burr stood up, walked around his desk and sat down next to Jacob in the twin of his chair.

"It is so patronizing when you do that," Jacob said. Mid-forties, shortish but not short, medium build, prominent nose, olive complexion and hair like steel wool with a touch of gray. Jacob twirled his finger through his hair.

"You always do that when you're nervous," Burr said.

"Do what?"

"Your hair."

Jacob stopped twirling. "I'm not nervous. I just know you're about to ask me to do something that can't be done."

"No, I'm not."

"We can't force Judge Weeks to issue us a death certificate."

Burr drummed his fingers on the arm of his chair. This somehow woke Zeke, who jumped off the couch. He came over and sat between Burr and Jacob. He licked Jacob's hand. "Get that cur away from me."

"I love that word," Burr said.

Jacob took a handkerchief out of his pocket and wiped off his hand. "He sheds all year round." Jacob picked an imaginary dog hair off his slacks. "How is that possible?"

Burr scratched Zeke's ear. Jacob studied his handkerchief. He started to put it in his pocket, thought better of it, and dropped it in the wastebasket next to Burr's desk. Zeke trotted back to the couch and resumed his nap.

"You hurt his feelings," Burr said.

"If only I could."

At that moment, Eve McGinty, Burr's longtime, long-suffering legal assistant, walked in from the reception area.

She was five-five, thin, with chin-length brown hair. She was a year older than Burr, which he never let her forget. She had a hint of crow's feet, which she didn't like. Burr thought she was pretty for fifty, pretty for any age. She had snow-white teeth and a smile that made Burr melt. She also had ice in her veins.

"What do you want from poor Jacob this time?"

"Just a death certificate."

*She's twice as smart as I am and three times as sarcastic.*

"I don't think that's going to be a problem," she said.

"You see, Jacob," Burr said, "there is always a way."

Eve tugged at her gold hoop earring.

*She only does that when something is wrong.*

"What is it, Eve?"

She tugged at it again.

*What could possibly be wrong?*

"Has Helen been found?"

Eve nodded.

"Where exactly is she?" Burr said.

"She's on South Manitou Island."

Burr stood. "What's she doing there?"

Eve started to reach for her earring. Burr walked over to her and touched her wrist. She pushed his hand away. "I will play with my earring if I want to."

"Eve, please. Why is Helen on South Manitou Island?"

"She's been there for about a year."

It was Jacob's turn to stand. "What's she been doing all this time?"

"She's been lying in a grave."

Eve started out of Burr's office.

"Must you be so mysterious?" Jacob said.

"How do you know all this?" Burr said.

She stopped and looked back at him. "Her sisters are in the lobby."

"Bring them in," Burr said.

"I'll bring them as soon as they catch their breath." She walked to the door and looked back at him. "The elevator is broken again."

Burr walked behind his desk and ran his hands through his hair, front to back. He looked out the window, then sat. "Damn it all."

"How can you possibly be surprised? They just had to walk up six flights of stairs." Jacob said. He ran a thumb and forefinger along one crease in his slacks.

Burr had bought the rundown Masonic Temple building, circa 1937, when he moved to East Lansing. It was a six-story, skinny, burnt-red brick building right in the middle of downtown East Lansing, with no parking. The realtor had told him it had "great bones". It just needed a little fixing up, and it would be a great investment. It wasn't.

There was a restaurant on the first floor, a few shops on the mezzanine. His offices and living quarters were on the top floor. Everything in-between was empty. The restaurant, Michelangelo's, was northern Italian and quite good, but the restaurateur was chronically behind on the rent.

"That elevator has nearly broken me," Burr said, still looking out the window.

"It has never worked right."

"We don't need the damn thing." Burr said. "It's just us up here."

"And your out-of-breath clients."

"The building inspector has no sense of fairness." Burr looked west down Albert Street, Michigan State University campus to his left, fraternities, sororities, and student housing to his right. "It's a great location," he said out loud but to himself.

Eve walked back in. "It's too bad there's no parking."

Burr turned away from the window. He scowled at Eve.

"Karen and Lauren have recovered."

"Show them in," Burr said.

"I don't think the Leaning Tower of Lafayette has made much of an impression." Eve disappeared into the reception area, then stood in the doorway and ushered in the sisters Erickson. Karen had on blue jeans, a red top and tennis shoes. Her hair was pulled back. No makeup. Lauren had on a nurse's uniform white dress, just-above-the-knees, white nylons and shoes that squeaked when she walked.

"We came to see you as soon as we heard about Helen," Lauren said.

"I'm so sorry," Burr said. He pulled an unhappy Zeke off the couch. "Please sit down," he said to the sisters. Burr and Jacob pulled their side chairs to the coffee table. "This must be a terrible shock."

"Tommy called me and I drove down to the hospital and picked up Lauren."

"I'm so glad you came," Burr said, "but you needn't have come all this way. I could easily have driven up there."

"We didn't know what else to do," Karen said.

"Would you like something to drink? Coffee? Tea?" Burr said.

"Tea, please," Karen said.

"Could I have a glass of water, please?" Lauren smoothed her dress. "You might want to get the elevator fixed."

"Eve called about it yesterday, but so far no one has shown up."

Eve shot a look at Burr, then left.

"This must be a terrible shock," Burr said again. "Can you tell me what happened?"

"I can only tell you what Tommy told me," Karen said.

"I thought Tommy would be the one to be here," Burr said.

"He had to go to the island," Karen said.

"To identify the body," Burr said.

Both sisters nodded. Lauren started to cry.

Jacob reached into his left pants pocket for his handkerchief. Then his right.

Burr leaned over to him and whispered, "You threw it away."

"Damn that dog," Jacob said under his breath.

"What's that?" Karen said.

"Let me get you a Kleenex." Jacob got up and walked out.

Eve came back with Karen's tea and Lauren's water.

"I don't want anything," Burr said.

"I didn't think so." Eve sat on the edge of the coffee table. "I'm so sorry."

Jacob came back with a box of Kleenex and set it on the coffee table in front of Lauren. Her mascara had run down her cheeks. She took a Kleenex and wiped her eyes.

"I'm sorry," Jacob said.

*As soon as we're all done being sorry, maybe someone will tell me what happened.*

"What do you think happened?" Burr cleared his throat. "This is a terrible tragedy. Do you think you could tell us what happened?"

Neither sister said anything. Karen handed another Kleenex to Lauren. "Your mascara ran."

Burr thought Lauren looked like she had raccoon eyes. She took the Kleenex and wiped her eyes. Burr thought she looked worse than before.

"Let me help." Eve took another Kleenex and wiped at the streaks of mascara.

"A box of Kleenex always comes in handy," Jacob said.

*Can we please get on with this?*

"Where were we?" Burr said.

Eve gave Burr a nasty look.

Karen started again. "The sheriff called Tommy this morning. He said a body had been found on South Manitou Island."

"Oh my God," Jacob said.

"Where?" Burr said.

"On the beach," Karen said.

"I'm so sorry," Eve said again.

"It might not be Helen," Jacob said.

"The sheriff asked Tommy to go to the island to see if he could identify the body," Karen said. She looked at Burr. "We'd like you to go with him."

"Me?" Burr said.

"We don't want him to be alone," Lauren said.

"Of course not," Eve said.

"That's right," Jacob said.

"If you leave right now, you can make the afternoon ferry," Lauren said.

# CHAPTER FOUR

Burr and Zeke led Lauren and Karen down the stairs.

*At least they won't get winded.*

He followed them to their car, then found his Grand Wagoneer a block up on MAC, across the street from St. John's Catholic Church. He let Zeke in the passenger side, then pulled the parking ticket off his windshield and threw it in a trash bin. He started up the Jeep, did a U-turn, turned right on Grand River and headed toward US-127. He had almost a tank full of gas, but he'd have to stop to fill up before Leland. He loved his Grand Wagoneer with the fake wood sides, but when he drove over 45 mph, all four barrels of the carburetor opened up and he could watch the gas gauge fall. Then there was the back window, which never did work right, not to mention the rear wiper, which he broke off before it could break on its own.

He hoped the body on South Manitou wasn't Helen's, but he was afraid it probably was. He looked over at Zeke. "Who else could it be? If it is Helen, at least we can get a death certificate."

Just north of Clare, Burr turned onto M-115. The farmland of central Michigan gave way to the woods and swamps of northern Michigan. At Cadillac, he stopped for gas, then took M-37 north. Just before Traverse City, he turned onto the back roads until he got to M-22.

Burr drove into Leland and parked at the marina, the Leland River to his left, Lake Michigan in front of him. A breakwater protected the small manmade harbor filled with slips. The ferry to the Manitous was tied up on the Leland River. Burr took his foul weather jacket from the Jeep. Zeke, afraid of being left behind, jumped out. "I don't know if dogs are allowed, old friend, but we'll give it a try."

They walked across the parking lot to the *Northern Lights*, the fifty-foot ferry with a steel hull painted blue. The ferry had a cabin with a steering station, seats for the passengers and an aft deck open to the weather. Life jackets were strapped to the cabin sides and on the orange life raft on top of the cabin. He heard the diesel pounding and smelled the exhaust over the smell of the fish shanties just upstream.

One of the deckhands, a young woman in a forest green Park Service uniform and tennis shoes, cast off the bow line. Burr ran over to the boat. "You need a ticket," said the other deckhand, a young man in need of a shave who was taking tickets at the stern. Burr started to climb aboard. "You need a ticket," he said again. "The deckhand pointed at a small building on the dock. "Over there."

"I'll be right back."

"We're late as it is."

Burr couldn't see how a few minutes to a ferry going to two uninhabited islands could matter to anyone. He turned on his heel and bought a round trip for himself. Zeke rode free.

*A minor miracle.*

Burr handed his ticket to the young man and climbed aboard. Zeke jumped on. The captain backed down the river until he had room to turn around, then motored past the breakwater and into the big lake. He opened up the throttle and the ferry picked up to about fifteen knots. She cruised through a light chop from the southwest. There were six other passengers, four of them college-age and an older couple. They all had backpacks. The afternoon sun ducked in and out of the cumulus clouds, casting shadows on the lake. Zeke sat on the port side of the aft deck. His ears blew in the wind and he bit at the spray. Burr stood next to Zeke out of the wind and the spray. He saw Pyramid Point and Sleeping Bear looming in the distance.

They came up on the lighthouse at Manitou Shoals, the graveyard of who knew how many boats. Then South Manitou, the ribbon of beach and the dark woods beyond, the abandoned lighthouse on the south end of the island, and just beyond that, the hull of a freighter that foundered on the shore forty years earlier, stripped for salvage and slowly worn away by the wind and the water.

*How long will it be before there's nothing left of her.*

*Northern Lights* entered Manitou Passage, then the crescent-shaped harbor on South Manitou. The boat slowed and Burr felt the wake catch up with the ferry to roll under the hull and lift the boat stern first. He saw the ferry dock jutting out into the harbor. A sheriff's boat, a twenty-five-foot launch with a sharp prow and cuddy cabin was tied up on one side of the dock.

The ferry docked across from the sheriff's boat and all of the passengers got off, except Burr. He walked up to the captain, a thin man with short gray hair and a Park Service uniform.

Burr stuck his hand out. "Burr Lafayette."

The captain nodded at him, shook his hand, but didn't say anything.

"I'm the lawyer for Thomas Lockwood. Can you tell me where to find the…" Burr paused. "His wife." Another pause. "His wife's body."

"No."

"No?"

The captain nodded.

"Does yes mean no?"

Another nod.

Burr leaned toward him and read the nametag on his shirt. "Mr. Sutherland."

"Captain."

"Captain Sutherland. I am here at the request of the family."

"Okay."

"Can you tell me where she…the body is?"

"No." Captain Sunderland turned away from Burr and made a show of studying the gauges on the instrument panel in the steering station.

"No, there is no body or no, you can't tell me."

"Just no."

"If there's no body here, why is the Leelanau County Sheriff's boat tied up on the other side of the dock.?"

"What boat?"

Behind them, people heading back to Leland started to board. The captain pushed the throttle in and revved the engine a bit.

"Look here, we've got to get going. If you're staying, you'd better get off."

"Listen up, Captain Queeg, I'm just about to tell everyone on this boat there's a dead body here."

Sutherland pulled back the throttle. "The Park Service don't want no trouble. No bad publicity."

Burr smiled at him. "Tell me where the body is and you won't get any trouble from me."

The captain fiddled with the throttle. Burr felt the engine run up a few hundred RPMs. "The easiest way to get there is through the island." He pointed ashore. "Up that way, then over there." He stopped. "You ever been here before?"

"No."

He pointed down the beach, toward the southern end of the island. "Follow the beach. Past the lighthouse. Past the wreck. It's past there. You can't miss the yellow tape." He nodded at the deckhand in the bow, then at the one in the stern. "All aboard."

Burr, with Zeke in tow, passed through the twenty or so passengers. He stopped at the gangway and turned back to the passengers. "There's a dead body on the island."

Captain Sunderland glared at him. Zeke trotted up the dock, Burr in tow.

They walked by a green Park Service shed, then started down the beach. The sand was loose and Burr slogged through it. Burr took off his foul weather jacket and tied it around his waist. "Zeke, it's cocktail hour and I am without a cocktail." He slogged through the sand. "That was poor planning on my part." The clouds had blown off to the northeast, and the sun was still high in the sky. The wind died. Burr smelled the cedars in the woods to his right. The smell reminded him of the cedar closet in his office. It was tough going through the loose sand. He walked down to the water's edge and traded a tiring walk with the smell of cedars for an easy walk and the smell of dead fish. Zeke ran into the lake up to his chest and drank. Then he started swimming. "Zeke, it's this way." Zeke swam farther out then, came back to the beach. He shook off on Burr. "Damn it all."

Burr tried walking at the water's edge. The walking here was much easier, but he was walking on an angle where the sand sloped into the lake, and it made his back hurt. He looked out to the channel and saw the ferry cutting through the waves. A few minutes later, its wake rolled ashore, soaking Burr's shoes and the cuffs of his khakis. "Damn it all," he said again.

They passed the lighthouse, a white brick cylinder at least a hundred-fifty feet tall, then the wreck a quarter mile off the beach, an oceangoing freighter, her superstructure midships.

They trudged on. Burr's feet chafed in his wet shoes. "If I'd known my shoes were going to get soaked, I'd have worn socks." Except for court, Burr didn't wear socks from May till November. A hundred yards further, he sat down on a log and took off his shoes. Zeke licked him on the lips.

"Thank you." Burr wiped his lips with the back of his hand. "I think."

They started out again. The beach started to get rocky so Burr moved closer to the tree line. The sand crunched under his feet and pushed up between his toes. "When in God's name are we going to be there?" He walked on. "I wonder if that damn captain sent me the wrong way."

They kept going, the trees here twisted and bent over by the wind. Zeke trotted at the water's edge.

Twenty minutes later, Burr saw the yellow tape in dune grass just off the beach. When they got closer, he saw the tape was strung around stakes about fifteen feet on a side.

"Stop right there," said a voice.

Burr looked to his right. A deputy in a dark brown uniform shirt with a gold badge, tan pants and a sidearm. He had on a brown baseball hat that said, 'Leelanau Sheriff's Department.' He raised his arm at Burr, his hand palm out. "Stop right there."

Burr started toward the yellow tape.

"Stop right there. This is a crime scene."

"I hardly think so." Burr dropped his shoes. "Tommy Lockwood asked me to come. I'm the family lawyer."

"That don't matter to me."

Burr started toward the deputy. "My name is Burr Lafayette. And you are?"

"Holcomb. Deputy Glen Holcomb."

"Thank you, Deputy Holcomb. I'd like to have a look around."

"No can do." Holcomb put his hands on his hips. "For all I know you're a rubbernecker."

Burr didn't think Deputy Holcomb could be more than twenty. He was a tall, gangly young man with the remains of acne on his cheeks. He had a mustache that wasn't coming in, underneath a long nose, above a mouth that was an orthodontist's dream. He had sunny, brown eyes that made the rest of him look just fine.

"Deputy, please." Burr smiled at Holcomb. "The sheriff called Helen Lockwood's sisters. They asked me to come over and identify the body. How could I know that if I wasn't on the up and up."

"My orders are no one gets near the tape."

Burr wiggled his toes in the sand. Burr looked down at his feet. The sand, warm in the late afternoon sun, was most pleasant. *I am surrounded by people who follow the rules.* He looked up at Deputy Holcomb. "All right then, where is Mr. Lockwood? He can vouch for me."

"He's not here."

"The sheriff?"

"He's not here, either."

Burr looked down at his toes. *Another one who believes in rationing his words.* He wiggled his toes again. "Where are they?"

"They left."

"I didn't see them."

"You took the long way."

Burr shook his head. "Deputy, is there a body here?"

Deputy Holcomb kicked at the sand with his standard issue brown sheriff's shoes, which had no business on a beach on South Manitou Island.

"Is there a body here?"

More sand kicking.

"Deputy."

The sand kicking stopped. "Yeah."

"Thank you," Burr said. "Is it Helen Lockwood?"

"Yeah."

"Where is she?"

"Over there." Deputy Holcomb pointed a long arm past the yellow tape. Burr started over.

"You can't go past the tape."

Burr stopped at the tape. He saw a hole about ten feet long and about five feet wide. It was about three feet deep. He couldn't see in it. Burr leaned over the tape, but he still couldn't see in the hole. He looked back at the deputy, then took a step back toward him. The deputy nodded and looked out at the lake. Burr ducked under the tape and ran to the hole.

"You can't do that."

Burr looked into the hole. There was a black tarp over the body.

Deputy Holcomb ran over, grabbed Burr by the shoulder and spun him around. "I said no."

"Is Helen Lockwood under that tarp?" Burr said.

The deputy looked down. He tugged at his would-be mustache. He nodded at Burr.

"Could she have drowned and washed ashore?" Burr said, hoping.

"She didn't get in that hole by herself unless she dug her own grave."

Burr jumped. "I beg your pardon?"

"Somebody buried her here."

Burr shut his eyes. "Who found her?"

"A dog."

"A dog."

"Some campers, over there." Holcomb pointed inland. "Their dog brought a bone back. They didn't think much of it until he brought back another one. They followed him here. Dug a little and found a body. They told the ranger, who called us."

"I need to see the body."

"No can do."

"Deputy Holcomb, I came all this way."

"Nope." The deputy tugged on his would-be mustache again.

"All I have to do is walk back to the dock and get permission from the sheriff."

"It ain't that easy."

"Lift the tarp. Just for a second."

"Nope."

"Then I'll do it."

"You do and I'll arrest you."

"Then you lift the tarp. It'll be our secret."

"This is not a good idea."

Burr started toward the hole.

"Stop right there."

Burr looked back at him. "How exactly do you think you're going to arrest me way out here.? And if you do, what are you going to do with me?"

Deputy Holcomb thought this over. He reached for his gun.

"You're surely not going to shoot me."

Holcomb pulled a hand held radio out of its holster.

"Deputy, please."

Holcomb looked at this radio, then at Burr, then at the radio. "You stand right there. This ain't a good idea." He walked over to the tarp. "Take a good look." The deputy pulled back the tarp.

Burr looked down in the hole. A body left to rot and decay in a shallow grave was not a pretty picture. It certainly didn't look like Helen or anything human he had ever seen. Burr threw up in the hole. He cleared his throat and spit. Zeke trotted over to investigate. Burr shooed him away.

Deputy Holcomb walked over to Burr. "Kind of makes you sick, don't it?"

Burr spit again.

"I told you this was a bad idea." Deputy Holcomb put his hands on his hips. "That's what they look like after being in the ground for a year. It ain't how they look at the funeral home."

"No, it isn't."

The deputy grinned at him.

"Are you sure it's Helen Lockwood?"

"Sure seems like it. The mister recognized the coat."

"Her coat?"

"He said it was her favorite coat. Belonged to her grandfather."

Burr looked at Deputy Holcomb. "Was it an accident?"

"I don't hardly think so."

"I thought she might have fallen overboard and drowned. Then she washed ashore."

"That don't explain the grave."

"Could the sand have blown over her?" Burr said, hoping against hope.

Holcomb looked back at the hole. "It's too far from the lake. And the hole's about three feet deep. And there's bushes and stuff around that ain't buried."

*Holcomb is smarter than he looks.*

"Still, it's possible."

Deputy Holcomb tugged at his mustache again. "That don't explain the bullet hole."

Burr jumped. "The bullet hole?"

"There's a bullet hole in her head."

"That changes the water on the minnies."

"What?"

"It's an old saying," Burr said. "My aunt says it."

"I guess so…"

"Are they done here?"

"For today."

"Deputy Holcomb, I appreciate you helping me out. This can stay between us."

The deputy nodded at him.

"I'll get going now." Burr started back to the beach.

"Let me show you a quicker way."

"Thank you, deputy."

"How are you getting back to the mainland?"

"The ferry," Burr said.

"Ferry's done for the day."

"I'll go back with the sheriff."

"They left."

"I'll go back with you."

"That'll work."

"Good."

"I get relieved at eight."

"That's not too long."

"In the morning."

Burr clenched his teeth. "What am I going to do?"

"I'm pretty sure me, you, your dog and the body are all going to be here tonight."

# CHAPTER FIVE

Burr could barely move. He tried to sit up but only managed to raise his head. Zeke came over and licked his face. "Thank you, Zeke." He put his head back down. It was only six in the morning but broad daylight. It wasn't the sun that woke him up. It was the damn birds, tweeting and tweeting like their lives depended on it. It was probably the sun that woke the birds, so maybe it was the sun's fault after all.

Without a boat back to the mainland, there was nothing Burr could have done but spend the night here with Zeke, Deputy Glenn Holcomb and the late Helen Lockwood.

The deputy had been kind enough to share a baloney sandwich with Burr, who shared his with Zeke.

Sleeping accommodations were a different matter entirely. Burr had no intention of sharing the deputy's sleeping bag with him, not that it was offered. That left Helen's tarp which Burr thought better of.

He scraped a bed into the sand and used his jacket for a blanket. Zeke slept next to him, which helped, but by morning, Burr was chilled to the bone.

And then there was his back. Burr tried to sit up but failed. He grabbed a branch on a bush and managed to turn on his side. From there, he was able to get on his hands and knees and crawl out of his bed in the sand.

"Whatcha doin' there, Mr. Lafayette?"

Burr ignored him and crawled to a cedar that had been bent over and twisted by the wind. *I am the human version of this tree.* He pulled himself up on the tree. He couldn't stand up straight, bent at the waist like a half-opened jackknife.

"Sleep well?"

Burr straightened up, mostly, the blade still not locked into place.

"Breakfast?"

Burr looked over at Deputy Holcomb and nodded.

"We got Pop Tarts. Apple Cinnamon or Chocolate."

"Apple Cinnamon, please."

\* \* \*

Deputy Holcomb's replacement showed up a little after eight. There was no one from the coroner's office so Burr saw no reason to stay.

Holcomb led him back to the ferry dock through the interior of the island. They walked through the scrub brush and into the woods. Cedars gave way to hardwood – maple, beech, ash, oak. Then to a path and finally a two track that Holcomb said would take them to the ferry.

South Manitou had been uninhabited until the late 1800s, when it was logged for firewood for the steamships. After that, settlers tried to farm it, but the soil was too sandy, the growing season too short, and the crops not valuable enough to ferry to the mainland. The farms were abandoned, and all that was left were a few summer residents and boaters who anchored in the harbor. The island stayed that way until the Park Service condemned all the private property, unpopular with the landowners, but they didn't put up much of a fight. Unlike the late Helen Lockwood.

Deputy Holcomb was kind enough to take Burr and Zeke back to Leland in the sheriff's boat. He said it was strictly against the rules. The wind hadn't come up yet and they skimmed across the lake, a sheet of glass, a soft blue in the morning light.

\* \* \*

They tied up in Leland about 10:30. Burr was tired, hungry and in need of a shower, but he had two stops first. He unwrapped the last Pop Tart and gave half of it to Zeke.

They drove past Port Oneida Road and into Glen Arbor, population two thousand, more than doubling in the summer. It swelled in the summer with the cottagers. Glen Arbor was a stone's throw from Glen Lake, one of the bluest and deepest inland lakes in Michigan and not much farther from Lake Michigan and Sleeping Bear Dunes. Burr passed the grocery store, the gas station, a diner and two bars before parking in front of a small white house. He cracked the windows for Zeke and walked into a waiting room. There were five empty chairs and a receptionist, a heavy-set woman with bright red lips and reading glasses on a chain. She looked up at him.

"I'd like to see Dr. Murray."

"Do you have an appointment?"

"No."

"Let me make you one." She put her glasses on the end of her nose and opened up an appointment book.

"It's about Helen Lockwood."

"Oh." She stood and lumbered through a door behind her.

A few minutes later, she came back in. "Dr. Murray will see you now." She pointed him to a door. "He's at the end of the hall."

Burr opened the door and walked past two examining rooms. He was sure they had been bedrooms in their former lives. He walked into the room at the end of the hall.

A thin man with white hair sat behind a small desk. He had his back to Burr and was looking out a sliding glass door.

"Goldfinches," said the man with the white hair. "Do you like goldfinches?"

"Yes," Burr said. "Yes, I do."

"They like thistle seed."

"Yes."

"Do you even know what a goldfinch is?"

"My aunt is a bird watcher." *And then there's Maggie.*

The older man turned around. He had bloodshot eyes magnified by a pair of glasses with black frames that took up most of his face.

*They look like goggles.*

"And who might you be?"

Burr offered his hand. "Burr Lafayette." The older man reached out a long, bony arm. His hand was clenched with arthritis but he had a strong grip.

"Claude Murray. So you're here about poor Helen?"

"I'm the family attorney."

"What can I do for you?"

"I'm here about the death certificate."

"The death certificate." Dr. Murray leaned back in his chair. "It's too soon for that."

"Well, Mrs. Lockwood is dead."

"She is that." Murray set his hands on his desk, fingers bent at the knuckles.

"I…the family wants to make arrangements for the funeral."

"Young man, she was just found yesterday. The EMTs and the sheriff are going back today. We don't have a cause of death yet."

"I thought she'd been shot."

"How do you know that?"

"I just got back from South Manitou."

"Did you spend the night out there?"

"I did."

Dr. Murray sniffed. "You do seem a little ripe. Why don't you go take a shower and come back in about two weeks?"

"Dr. Murray, Mrs. Lockwood is dead."

The doctor took off his glasses. His eyes sunk back in his head.

"We can't have a funeral without a death certificate," Burr said.

"And you can't get a death certificate from me until there's a cause of death. And that's not going to happen until Helen is on the table in the room next door and I do an autopsy." He fumbled with his glasses, tried to put them back on but his fingers didn't seem to work quite right.

*It's probably safe enough for him to cut open dead people, but I wouldn't want him to take out my tonsils.*

"She should have sold out a long time ago. Now somebody has gone and shot her."

"Could it have been suicide?"

The good doctor got his glasses back on, but they were crooked. "The sheriff told me there's a bullet hole in the middle of her forehead. You don't commit suicide by putting a gun to the middle of your forehead." He made his crooked forefinger into a gun and tried to point it at his forehead. "See. It's awkward. You can hardly do it. If you want to shoot yourself, you put the gun in your mouth. Like this." He put his finger in his mouth. "Or like this." He put his finger up to his temple. "Nobody shoots themselves the way Helen was killed."

"It's all the more reason to give the family some closure."

"She's been missing for a year. Another two weeks, maybe a month, won't make any difference."

"Doctor..."

"I know what you want, young man. You want that death certificate for your precious lawsuit down in Grand Rapids."

Burr started to run his hands through his hair. He thought better of it and put them in his lap.

"We get the papers here. That lawsuit is holding up a lot of important things around here. All you care about is the money." He swiveled back to the window. "The female goldfinches are the same color all year. See that bright yellow one. That's a male." He pointed out the window. "They change colors. Yellow in the summer, drab in the winter, like the females." He turned back to Burr. "Shame on you."

\* \* \*

Burr and Zeke headed back the way they had come. Burr turned at Port Oneida Road, then up the driveway, passing two men running a shaker. The tree shook, the branches whipped, the leaves blew back and forth, and the cherries fell off the tree onto a canvas apron spread under the poor tree.

*It's like a monster trying to shake the tree to death.*

"Zeke, that can't possibly be good for the tree."

Burr knocked on the farmhouse door. Consuela told him Tommy had been inside but now he wasn't, which Burr didn't think was particularly helpful.

Burr and Zeke checked the outbuildings, then started into the orchard. "Zeke," he said, "if there really are four hundred acres of cherry trees, this could take awhile." They walked through trees that had been picked, trees no more than fifteen feet tall. It looked like half of their leaves had been shaken off with the cherries. Then into unpicked tarts, the branches drooping with the lipstick red cherries. They walked up and down the rows, ankle high weeds at their feet, then through a field where older trees had been pulled out of the ground but hadn't yet been hauled away. "Zeke, my guess is these didn't produce enough fruit." Burr bit his lip. "It's tough being a cherry tree."

Then they were in the sweet cherries, black with a hint of crimson, the branches sagging with fruit. They found Tommy about two rows in. Zeke licked his hand. Tommy bent down and scratched behind Zeke's left ear. The dog groaned.

"That's his favorite spot," Burr said.

Tommy picked a cherry off the tree and popped it in his mouth. He had on a blue checked shirt, khakis and work boots. "The sheriff told me you were out at South Manitou."

Burr nodded.

"It must have been her. It was her coat." Tommy spit out the pit. "It was awful. Looking at her like that."

"I'm sorry."

"Claude called before I came out here," Tommy said.

Burr nodded but didn't say anything.

"He said you were just there."

Burr nodded again.

"Don't you think it's a little too soon to ask for a death certificate? Can't we just take a little time to get used to this?"

"I thought it would be a help."

"A help?"

"One less thing you'd have to do."

Tommy picked another cherry. He studied it then threw it away. He picked another, studied it, then ate it. He spit out the pit, then kicked at the trunk of the tree. "These trunks are too big for the shakers. We have to pick them by hand. And we have to get them off at just the right time."

Burr nodded again, relieved that they were talking about cherry trees and not the death certificate.

"I don't see why you couldn't wait for the death certificate."

Burr ran his hands through his hair. "Tommy, I'm sorry. It seemed like the right thing to do. To help you get some closure."

Tommy looked down at his boots, then up at Burr. "This isn't about money. Helen's gone. I knew she was probably dead. I knew it. But I guess I hoped she wasn't. No. I knew she was, but it really got to me. Seeing her like that. That was terrible. And now it is final. And for you it's just the money. I don't care if they do get the farm. And I don't like what you did." Tommy stared at Burr, anger in his soft brown eyes. "You're fired." Tommy spit out the cherry pit and walked away.

# CHAPTER SIX

"What do you mean, fired?" Jacob wrung his hands.

"Is there more than one meaning?" Eve said. She was sitting at her desk in the reception area with the door closed.

*She has an uncanny ability to hear everything I say, especially what I don't want her to hear.*

"What do you mean, fired?" Jacob said again, still wringing his hands.

"Would you please stop wringing your hands," Burr said.

"He does that when he's upset," Eve said from beyond the door.

Burr ignored her. After the disastrous meeting with Tommy, Burr had driven straight back to East Lansing and gone right to bed. After breakfast, he had walked out of his apartment, down the hall and into his office. Now he was at his desk, Jacob in front of him in a side chair. Zeke asleep on the couch. Just like always. Burr hadn't expected breaking the news to Jacob and Eve to go well, and so far he was right.

"We'll soldier on like we always do," Burr said.

"Soldiers need to eat," Eve said.

"Eve, would you mind gracing us with your presence?" Burr didn't hear any movement from Eve's headquarters.

"We have no other money coming in," Jacob said.

"We have other cases," Burr said.

"They don't pay like this one did," Eve said.

"Eve, please come in here." Burr reached into the top drawer of his desk and took out the sharpest Number 2 yellow pencil he could find.

"Don't tap that pencil," Eve said from the reception area.

*How can she possibly know?*

"It was the height of insensitivity to try and get a death certificate so soon," Jacob said.

"Helen Lockwood has been missing for a year," Burr said.

Eve came in and sat down across from Jacob, facing Burr. She had a letter in her hand.

"Thank you, Eve. Your offstage was a little unnerving. I felt like I was in a Greek tragedy."

"You are starring in it," Eve said.

"Stop it. Both of you," Jacob said. "We have no money coming in."

"It was a stupid thing to do," Eve said.

Burr, about to tap his pencil, thought better of it. "I was trying to make it easier for Tommy."

"You were trying not to get defaulted by the judge," Jacob said.

"That, too."

"Would another day or two have hurt anything?" Eve said.

"Who knows how long it would have taken," Burr said.

Eve reached over and grabbed Jacob by the wrist. "Would you please stop wringing your hands?"

*This isn't going well.*

Zeke woke up from his nap and looked at Burr. Burr nodded at him. The yellow lab jumped off the couch, went over to Jacob and licked his hand. Jacob jumped to his feet. He grabbed Burr's pencil and broke it in half. Then he stormed out.

"You did that on purpose," Eve said.

"We've said everything twice," Burr said.

"What are you going to do?" Eve said.

"I have a couple of possibilities."

"Here's another possibility for you." Eve handed Burr the letter.

"It's just another letter from Grace's lawyer. Maury is harmless."

"He's so harmless that Grace wants full custody of Zeke-the-Boy."

Burr read the letter.

"Grace doesn't like you seeing Maggie."

"Maggie has nothing to do with this. I didn't even know her when Grace and I split up."

"Hell hath no fury…"

*Like a woman scorned.*

\* \* \*

Burr, with Zeke-the-dog in tow, took the stairs down to Michelangelo's, Burr's tenant on the first floor.

He was about halfway through a very nice bottle of Chianti when he considered actually looking at Maury's letter. He gave Zeke another noodle from his clams with red sauce on angel hair pasta. Zeke slurped the noodle.

"Zeke, I've never missed a payment to Grace. Never." He poured himself another glass of wine and took the letter out of the envelope.

Burr read how awful he was. Drinking, guns, boats, womanizing. Chronically late in child support and alimony. "Zeke, I have never been late on child support. Alimony maybe."

Burr thought he had been a fairly good husband until Suzanne. He may have worked too much, duck hunted more than he should have, and drank too many martinis, but it was Suzanne that had ended it all. He was defending his rich ad agency client because of the misleading copy Suzanne had written. She was tall with dark hair and pouty lips. She wasn't beautiful, hardly pretty, but she was striking. He was a fool over her. She didn't encourage him, but that encouraged him even more. She never said she loved him. He loved her, at least he thought he did. It cost him his partnership at Fisher and Allen. And his marriage.

And now here he was with Maury's letter. *She wants me to keep paying, and she wants to take Zeke-the-Boy.*

It never had been the best of marriages, but it certainly hadn't been the worst. Grace tended toward melancholy, but that was no reason to ruin his marriage over a woman almost young enough to be his daughter.

The waitress came over and refilled his glass. "Mr. Lafayette, Scooter says there are no dogs allowed."

"Please ask Scooter to come see me."

She smiled and left. Burr knew full well that Scooter would never come over. Scooter would rather have Zeke sit at the table with a napkin around his neck eating linguini with red clam sauce than pay the back rent. Burr offered Zeke another long, thin noodle. Zeke sucked it in.

\* \* \*

Two weeks later, at eleven on a Saturday morning, Burr sat in the back pew of the Bethlehem Lutheran Church in Glen Harbor. The church had white wood siding and a square steeple above the doors to the sanctuary. It made

Burr nervous to sit with his back to a door, any door. It made him even more nervous to sit in the front with people and doors behind him. So here he sat in the back of the church. On the aisle. At least he could turn his head and see the doors.

He had driven in early this morning and parked underneath a fifty-foot sugar maple. He cracked the window for Zeke, straightened his tie and walked into the little church. It was packed to the gills with flowers and mourners. A matron played dreadfully morose music on a groaning organ. Burr didn't think the music was particularly memorable but he wasn't particularly Lutheran. The Erickson family took up the first two rows. Tommy sat next to Lauren and her husband, Curt, late thirties, lean and fair haired. Burr thought he looked like the boy next door. Their three children sat next to him. Burr liked Curt well enough but couldn't really say that he knew him. Then Karen and her husband, Glenn, broad shouldered and thick waisted. He looked like he could lift Karen over his head with one hand tied behind his back. Their four children sat between them. Consuela sat one row back. An older man in uniform, who Burr thought must be the sheriff, sat near the back of the church with Deputy Holcomb and another equally adolescent-looking deputy. Burr assumed the rest of the sanctuary was filled with friends and neighbors. The men looked decidedly uncomfortable in their coats and ties.

Burr hadn't been invited to the funeral, but he thought it was the least he could do. He thought there must be a death certificate if they were having a funeral. He might even get rehired.

The windows were open, but it was August and the air was still. The sanctuary was getting stuffy, a hint of sweat over the scent of flowers.

The pastor entered, sufficiently funereal. He was about sixty-five, tall and spare, thinning gray hair with a pinched face. Burr thought he looked like the archetypical Swedish clergyman.

"We are here today to celebrate the life of Helen Lockwood. She left us much too soon, but she will always be with us."

The funeral dragged on. Helen's sisters spoke, as did various nieces, nephews, and friends. There was no mention of how Helen had died. Shot in the forehead and buried in a shallow grave on South Manitou. When they all finished, Burr didn't think he knew her any better than he did before they spoke.

He had found her to be one of the fiercest, most beautiful women he had ever met. She knew exactly what she wanted and how to get it. She was damned if she was going to lose Port Oneida Orchards to the Park Service. He hadn't spent much time with her other than professionally. He knew she favored Tanqueray on the rocks, and he thought she might be a little wild. She put her hand on his knee once, and he wondered if it was a little more than friendly.

If he did manage to get rehired, Burr hadn't seen anyone who had the fight that Helen had. Certainly not Tommy

At last the funeral was over. The organist started in again with more unfamiliar but equally lugubrious church music. Tommy and the family left first, then the rest of the mourners. Tommy nodded at Burr on the way out.

Burr was the last to leave. He stood just outside the church in the heat of the day. He couldn't leave Zeke in the car much longer, shade or not.

He saw the family talking amongst themselves on the grass. Some of the mourners came up to the family and paid their condolences. Burr watched the unhappy scene play out. When the last of the mourners left, the sheriff walked over to Tommy. The two state policemen stood about ten feet behind him. The sheriff said something to Tommy. Deputy Holcomb got out of the sheriff's patrol car and walked over to Tommy and the sheriff. The sheriff nodded at his deputy, who took the handcuffs off his equipment belt. Deputy Holcomb handcuffed Tommy, led him to the patrol car, opened the rear door of the car, pushed Tommy's head down and got him into the backseat.

The sheriff said something to Lauren and Karen, then got in the passenger seat of the patrol car, Deputy Holcomb behind the wheel. He started the car, turned on the flashers and off they went.

\* \* \*

Helen's sisters and their families stayed where they were. No one moved. No one said a word. The air was still, and the sun bore down on them.

Burr, still standing off by himself, put his hands in his pockets. He rocked back and forth, heel to toe. He thought he should ask Lauren and Karen how he might help, but then again, he had been fired. But that was the condemnation case.

Burr wiped his forehead with the back of his hand and started over to the sisters, but he really couldn't leave Zeke in the Jeep any longer. He changed direction and walked to the Jeep. Zeke didn't seem any worse for wear, but Burr rolled down the windows, started the engine and turned on the air conditioner. The dog licked Burr's cheek. "I'll be right back, Zeke."

He looked over at the family, still not moving or talking. A baby cried and, as if on cue, they all came to life. Karen and Lauren got in a car and drove off. So did everyone else.

By the time Burr pulled out, the funeral posse was nowhere in sight. "Zeke, there's only one place they can be going." Burr raced across the little finger to Suttons Bay. He passed the probate court where he had failed to get a death certificate and then pulled into the parking lot of the 86th District Court. He saw Lauren and Karen's car parked near the entrance. He parked under yet another maple tree, cracked the windows and ran to the court- house. Which was locked.

"Damn it all." He pounded on the door. No answer. He pounded again. Still no answer. Burr ran around behind the building. The patrol car was parked near the back door next to a shiny, black BMW sedan and a red Ford pickup with rust on the rocker panels. He ran up to the door and pulled. It was open.

He ran past offices, conference rooms and closets. When he reached the front door, he turned around. "It must be this way." Burr took off down a hallway to his right. He skidded to a stop in front of a brass plaque that read *86th District Court. Judge Irwin Conway.* Burr opened the door, slipped in and stood in the back of the courtroom. He didn't think anyone had seen him come in.

Tommy, still in handcuffs, stood in front of a judge with a double chin and a hairline racing to the back of his head. There was a bailiff standing off to the side of the courtroom and a court reporter sitting to the judge's right. Deputy Holcomb and the other deputy stood on each side of Tommy. Lauren and Karen sat in the gallery. There was no one else in the courtroom.

"This had better be good," the judge said.

"Yes, your Honor." A tall, slender man sitting at the prosecutor's table stood. He had jet-black hair swept back behind his ears, and a tan that showed off his brilliant white teeth. He had on a summer-weight khaki suit, white shirt and a striped tie in pastels of blue, green, orange and pink.

"Mr. Brooks, you better have a damn good reason for pulling me out of my roses on a Saturday."

"Yes, Your Honor."

"If the aphids get my Abraham Lincolns, there will be hell to pay." The judge looked at his fingernails. He picked up a paper clip and cleared dirt out from under one of them. Then another. And another.

The prosecutor cleared his throat. The judge kept working on his nails.

"Excuse me, Your Honor," the prosecutor said.

The judge looked up. "Where were we?"

"We were just about to get started."

"Right." The judge looked back down at the forefinger of his left hand and worked some dirt loose. "There," he said. "All right, Peter. Tell me why you dragged me away from my roses on Saturday afternoon, and why I had to throw this robe over my jeans. And why you've got Tommy in handcuffs."

"Your Honor…"

The judge cut him off. "First, take those cuffs off. We're all friends here." Judge Conway looked at Tommy, then the prosecutor. "Well, maybe you two aren't."

"Your Honor," the prosecutor said. "Mr. Lockwood is being arraigned on an open murder charge. We're going to prove first-degree murder. He is a dangerous and desperate man. I'd like to leave the handcuffs on."

Judge Conway looked at the top of the paperclip. He rubbed off a little dirt, then blew on it. "That's the silliest thing I ever heard. Tommy, did you kill Helen?"

Tommy looked up at the judge but didn't say anything. Burr thought his former client must be in shock.

"Tommy?"

Lockwood shook his head no.

"All right, then. Deputy Holcomb, take those handcuffs off. Tommy, you go sit there." The judge pointed at a chair behind the defense table.

"Your Honor, I insist that the handcuffs be left on."

"All right. Tommy, stay right there for a minute." The judge looked back at the prosecutor. "Peter, have those handcuffs taken off. Tommy can stand between the two deputies. This better be good."

The prosecutor walked up to the judge. "Your Honor…"

*This is as good a time as any.*

Burr stood. "Your Honor…"

"Now what?" the judge said.

Burr hurried to the front of the courtroom and stood beside Tommy.

"Who the devil are you?"

"Burr Lafayette, Your Honor. Counsel for the defense."

"Tommy, is this your lawyer?"

Lockwood looked at the judge, then at Burr, then back to the judge. He shook his head no.

"Tommy, this man says he is, in fact, your lawyer. Is he?"

Tommy shook his head again. His hair fell in his face. He tried to brush it off but couldn't with his hands cuffed behind his back.

"Peter, for the last time, take those damn cuffs off. Now."

"Your Honor…"

"Tommy Lockwood is not dangerous."

The prosecutor looked up at Judge Conway. "He murdered Helen, Your Honor."

"The hell he did. Take those cuffs off. We'll be safe. There's two armed deputies here."

The prosecutor looked down at his shoes.

*They're nicely polished.*

Burr looked down at his shoes, which weren't. Brooks nodded at Deputy Holcomb. The deputy unlocked the cuffs. Tommy rubbed his wrists, then brushed the hair out of his eyes.

"That's better," Judge Conway said. "Now, is this man your lawyer?"

"He was but I fired him."

"That seems clear. Mr. whatever-your-name-is … you are excused."

"Your Honor, Mr. Lockwood needs a lawyer."

"He certainly does, but it doesn't look like it's going to be you."

"Your Honor…"

"You are excused." Conway pointed to the door. "Out."

Burr stood his ground.

"Out. Now. Or do I have the deputies put the handcuffs to a better use."

Burr turned to go. "Here we go again."

"What did you say?"

"Nothing, Your Honor." Burr started up the aisle.

"Tommy, you can stand there or you can go sit at that table." Conway pointed at the defense table.

"Your Honor," Brooks said. "It is customary for the accused to stand during an arraignment."

"Mr. Brooks, it is also customary for a lawyer to show deference to a judge."

Brooks looked down at his shoes again. "Yes, Your Honor," he said to his shoes.

"Look at me when you're talking," Conway said.

Peter Brooks looked up at the judge but didn't say anything.

Burr walked by Lauren and Karen. They looked like they were in shock, just like Tommy. Burr took advantage of the legal sparring and took a seat near the back of the gallery. He hoped Conway wouldn't see him.

Judge Conway looked at his fingernails again. "Peter, let's have it."

"Thank you, Your Honor. This is what I will prove at the trial. Thomas Morgan Lockwood shot his wife, Helen Lockwood, between the eyes on or about June 9th of last year."

The judge cringed.

*I thought Helen was shot in the forehead. Between the eyes is better theater.*

"And how do you know this?"

"Your Honor, this is what we have pieced together so far."

"I hope you've done more than pieced something together."

Brooks ignored the judge. "Your Honor, on the morning of June 9th Helen Lockwood took her boat from Leland to South Manitou."

"*Achilles.*"

"Yes, Your Honor. She anchored in the harbor. That evening, Mr. Lockwood shot her between the eyes with his handgun. Then he took the boat around to the south side of the island. He buried her in a shallow grave. Then he set *Achilles* adrift in the lake. The boat was found drifting off Sleeping Bear two days later by a charter boat. At the time, the sheriff and the Coast Guard determined that Mrs. Lockwood fell overboard and drowned. Her body was never found until…." Brooks paused and turned to Tommy. "Until three weeks ago, when two campers discovered a body in a shallow grave on South Manitou. It was Helen Lockwood."

Karen burst into tears. Lauren put her head in her hands.

The judge chewed on his cheek. "You're going to have to walk me through this step-by-step."

"Yes, Your Honor."

"Did anyone see Helen leave Leland?"

"Yes, Your Honor."

"Did anyone see her in the harbor? At South Manitou?"

Brooks nodded. "Yes, Your Honor."

"Did anyone see Tommy shoot Helen?"

"No."

*That's is a big problem for Brooks.* Burr craned his neck so he could see the prosecutor's face. *He doesn't look worried.*

"How do you know it was Tommy?"

"We found the murder weapon, Your Honor. It was Lockwood's gun."

The judge scratched his nose. Burr saw a black smudge where he had scratched. "Keep going."

"After Lockwood killed his wife, he was seen taking the ferry to South Manitou on the day Helen was killed."

Judge Conway's jaw dropped.

Burr swept his hands through his hair.

The two sisters sat straight up.

Brooks put his hands in his pockets. He rocked back and forth, heel to toe and back again, just as Burr had done after the funeral.

The judge shut his mouth. He chewed on his lower lip, then said, "This is all well and good, Peter, but why in the world would Tommy want to kill Helen?"

Brooks stopped rocking and pointed at Tommy. "Helen Lockwood and her sisters have been fighting with the federal government for the last seven years about their orchards."

"I am aware of that."

"As you know, they have refused to sell. Mr. Lockwood has been trying to get his wife declared dead for some time. As soon as Dr. Murray issued the death certificate, Lockwood began negotiating to sell the orchards."

*Tommy never told me that.*

Judge Conway chewed on his cheek again. "And your point is?"

"Mr. Lockwood murdered his wife so he could sell the orchard and pocket the proceeds. He tried to make it look like she drowned." Brooks ran a finger through his hair and tucked a stray lock behind his ear. "When the body was found, I became suspicious and pieced this together."

*This isn't good.*

Conway sighed. He looked at Tommy. Burr couldn't see Tommy's face, but he was sure Lockwood must be in shock.

"This is serious, Tommy," Conway said. "Peter, what would you have me do?"

Brooks stood up straight. "Arraign Lockwood on open murder, Your Honor."

The judge looked Brooks up and down. "How much of this has to do with what Tommy may have done and how much has to do with your family's property being tied up in the lawsuit with the Park Service?"

"Your Honor…"

"You know exactly what I mean." Conway paused and itched his nose again. His smudge was getting bigger..

"This has nothing to do with my family's property," Brooks said.

"Of course not." The judge bent the paperclip like a pretzel. "Do you have the names and addresses of your witnesses?"

"Yes, Your Honor."

"And the autopsy and ballistics?"

"Yes, Your Honor."

"All right then." The judge looked at the accused. "Tommy, I'm not sure what's going on here, but Mr. Brooks has enough evidence to arraign you on murder. If what he says is true, you have committed a horrible crime."

Lockwood didn't say anything.

"How do you plead?"

Burr jumped up. "Your Honor, Mr. Lockwood pleads not guilty."

"What the Sam Hill are you still doing here?"

Burr rushed up to the front of the courtroom. He stood in front of Judge Conway. "Burr Lafayette, Your Honor. Counsel for the defense."

"Tommy fired you," Brooks said.

Burr walked over to Tommy. "You can fire me again as soon as this is over. Right now, you need a lawyer."

"Get out, Lafayette," Brooks said. "You were fired."

"I'm in charge here, Peter." Conway looked at Tommy. "Is he or is he not your lawyer?"

Lockwood nodded at the judge.

"Very well. Mr. Lockwood, you are charged with the murder of your wife, Helen Lockwood. How do you plead?"

Burr leaned down and said something to Tommy.

"Not guilty." Tommy said, barely above a whisper.

"Enter a plea of not guilty."

"Thank you, Your Honor." Burr walked up to the judge. "Your Honor, the defense requests a personal recognizance bond in lieu of bail."

"Bail?" Brooks said. "He's accused of murder."

"Your Honor, the prosecution's story is nothing but gossamer blowing in the breeze."

"Gossamer?" Judge Conway said.

"It's so much speculation and whimsy."

"Whimsy?"

"Your Honor, Mr. Lockwood murdered his wife. There is no bail in a murder charge."

"Your Honor…" Burr said.

Conway cut him off. "Stop it, both of you. Bail is set at one hundred thousand dollars. We'll see what's what at the preliminary exam." Judge Conway crashed his gavel. "We are adjourned."

# CHAPTER SEVEN

"Bail?" Jacob said.

"Yes, bail," Burr said. He studied a piece of paper on his desk and didn't look up.

"That was a bit nervy. After the gruesome story the prosecutor told."

Burr didn't look up.

"You are a silver-tongued devil." Jacob smiled and twirled a finger in his curly hair, his own personal tic.

"And now we're back on the payroll." This from Eve.

"There is the small matter of getting a check," Burr said.

"There is always something with you."

They were all sitting in their assigned seats, Burr leaning over his car-size desk, Jacob and Eve facing him. Eve always sat to the left of Jacob, except the one time that Burr had them switch. They both squirmed and fidgeted and nothing got done. That ended Burr's experiment, not that he wasn't a creature of habit. Zeke napped on the couch, as was his habit.

"Since you asked us in here, would you please look at us?"

Burr nodded but didn't look up.

"Burr," Eve said.

"It's all right, Eve. We're getting paid again," Jacob said.

"We'll see how long that lasts." Eve tugged at her earring.

Burr looked up. "We're in this one for the long haul. It's going to be a full-blown murder trial."

Jacob stopped twirling and Eve stopped tugging.

"You can't say you don't do criminal law anymore. This is your fourth murder trial," Eve said.

"And your point is?" Burr said. He stood and turned away from them. A light summer rain was falling. He opened the window.

"It's going to get wet in here," Eve said.

"There's no wind." Burr took a deep breath. The air smelled of earthworms, car exhaust, and wet. Zeke trotted over and sniffed out the window, too.

"So, we can have the murder trial and the condemnation. All at once," Eve said.

Burr turned back to Eve. "When the trial is over, we'll negotiate with the feds."

"Why not now?" Eve said.

"If Tommy is acquitted, he, Karen and Lauren can do whatever they want to with the farm," Burr said.

"If he's convicted, he can't profit from murder." This from Jacob.

"Really?" Eve tugged again.

"State law prohibits murder for economic gain." Jacob ran his thumb and forefinger along the crease on his other pant leg.

"So, nothing is going to happen with the condemnation case?" Eve said.

"Judge Cooper issued a stay pending the outcome of the trial," Jacob said.

"This will keep you in mulch and perennials for some time," Burr said.

"We're profiting from someone else's misfortune," Eve said.

"That's what lawyers do," Burr said.

Jacob rubbed his hands together. "The sun is shining on us. For once."

"Not entirely." Burr picked up the piece of paper he had been studying.

"What could possibly go wrong today?" Jacob said.

Burr handed Jacob the piece of paper.

Jacob studied it, then looked at Burr. "This is terrible."

Eve read over Jacob's shoulder. "Now you've done it."

"How could you possibly manage to have a warrant out for your arrest?" Jacob said.

"Child support?" Eve said.

"I've never missed a payment for Zeke-the-Boy."

"Alimony," Eve said.

"That hardly warrants a warrant," Jacob said.

"Maury isn't the sharpest tack in the box, but he's a bulldog." Burr ran his hands through his hair. "He never gives up."

"Just like someone else I know," Eve said.

"Why, thank you, Eve."

Zeke walked over to Jacob and licked his hand. Jacob jerked it away.

"We're still going to get paid," Eve said.

"Not if Burr's in jail." Zeke rubbed against Jacob. "Stop it, you cur." He stood and walked out the door. "Another day ruined."

\* \* \*

It was still raining when Burr parked his Grand Wagoneer in Suttons Bay at noon the next day. The low had stalled somewhere over Wisconsin, and until something pushed it through, it was going to keep raining. Not that Burr minded. He quite liked the rain. He found it soothing, washing the balefulness out of his world. At least he hoped it would.

Burr let Zeke out of the Jeep, cracked the windows and put him back in. The Jeep was going to smell like wet dog.

Zeke loved the rain. He would sit in the rain all day, which had upset Grace. It didn't matter to a lab whether he got wet from the feet up or the head down. Burr thought sitting in the rain was a perfect use of Zeke's time.

*I have bigger problems than a car that smells like a wet dog.*

Burr made his way into the county building, past the 86th District courtroom where Tommy had been arraigned. Two hallways later, he found Peter Brooks' office. Brooks was looking out his window, his back to Burr. "It's too wet to get the cherries off," Brooks said.

"I thought they were all in."

"The sweets. Not all the tarts." Brooks turned around and took a step toward Burr. "I thought you were someone else." He walked over to Burr and shook his hand.

"Please sit down," Brooks said.

Burr took a side chair. Brooks turned the matching chair toward Burr and sat. "Yes?"

"I'd like the names and addresses of the people you interviewed before you charged Tommy at the arraignment," Burr said.

"At the arraignment," Brooks said.

"And your witness list for the preliminary exam."

"Preliminary exam," Brooks said.

*Is he deaf or just slow?*

Burr looked over Brooks' shoulder at the framed University of Michigan Law School diploma. *He can't be slow.* A Kalamazoo College diploma hung underneath. *Definitely not slow.* Burr looked around the office. A walnut desk, much like Burr's. Leather side chairs, parquet floor with oriental rugs.

*This is like the office of a senior partner in Detroit. Brooks must have paid for it out of his own pocket. He's no slouch.*

"Mr. Lafayette?"

Burr jumped in his seat.

"You were saying?"

"I'd like the list of the people you interviewed for the arraignment and your witness list for the preliminary exam."

"Tommy Lockwood should not be out on bail. He committed a horrific crime and he's dangerous."

"The judge didn't agree with you," Burr said.

"Lockwood should be in jail."

"What does that have to do with the lists?"

"Mr. Lafayette, you are not a criminal lawyer by trade, are you?" Brooks grinned.

*He's looked me up.*

"Criminal law is part of my practice."

"Not a big part and only since you…" he paused, "left Fisher and Allen."

*Definitely not a slouch. Ten years younger than me and no slouch.* "I'd like the lists."

"You are aware that the court rules do not require me to provide you any further information until the preliminary exam."

"I am not so aware."

Burr stood. Brooks stood. "Mr. Lafayette, I suggest you read the court rules."

"What exactly is your problem?" Burr said. "I can get the names from the transcript of the arraignment."

Brooks walked back to the window. "It's going to rain for another week." He turned back to Burr. "Mr. Lafayette, there is a piece of paper on my desk. I think you will find it to be of interest to you."

*Maybe I won't have to ask the judge.*

Brooks looked down his long nose at Burr. "It's a warrant for your arrest. Something about child support and alimony."

*Damn it all.*

"As an officer of the court, I have no choice but arrest to you."

Burr got to his feet. "I've never been late on child support."

Brooks walked back to his desk and picked up the warrant. "That's not what Maury Litzenburger says."

"He is overzealous."

"You can discuss that with Judge Conway. Perhaps you'll be out of jail by the time the transcript is ready." Brooks picked up his phone. "Sherry, would you please send a deputy in here. Holcomb, if he's around."

\* \* \*

As it turned out, Judge Conway was in his chambers. Brooks wanted Burr locked up, but Burr persuaded them to call Maury, who agreed to back off if Burr sent a check that very day. He said the check didn't resolve the custody issue. Burr wrote the check and then asked the judge for the transcript of the arraignment.

\* \* \*

The transcript showed up a week later. Eve came into his office and sat in her chair. Burr thought he'd try Brooks' strategy and sat next to her.

"Why are you sitting there?"

"I thought it was more collegial."

"Collegial." She laughed. "I'm your legal assistant. Go sit behind your desk."

Burr didn't budge. "I have an idea. Let me buy you dinner tonight."

Eve laughed again.

Burr looked out the window. He had a much better view from Jacob's chair.

"What is it that you want?" Eve said.

"I need the phone numbers and addresses of the names in the transcript."

"Can't you wait for the preliminary exam?"

"No."

"Why not?"

"As I recall, you're the legal assistant."

"Touché."

Burr took his usual seat. He thought Eve looked more comfortable.

"We're out of money again," Eve said.

"I'm about to bring in an appellate case."

"Goody. What are we going to do until then?" She got up to leave. "Why did Brooks do that? With Maury? And the transcript?"

"No quarter asked and none given. A man after my own heart."

\* \* \*

Burr drove up the west shore of Lake Leelanau, bright blue in the sunshine, darker when the puffy white clouds covered the sun. It was seventy-five and crisp, wind from the northwest at fifteen. Burr had his window down. The passenger window was halfway down. Zeke had his head mostly out of the window, sniffing, ears flapping.

"Zeke, old friend, this would be a great day to be on the water."

Burr drummed the fingers of his left hand on the outside of the door. "If I don't get fired again, we'll have to see about getting *Spindrift* over here."

Zeke looked over at him but didn't say anything. Burr turned north on M-22 and cruised into Leland. He parked under yet another old sugar maple in front of the Riverside Inn, a two-story bed and breakfast with white siding. He walked past the clay pots of impatiens – red, white, pink, purple, orange – and up to the screen door. He could smell the fresh paint on the siding and see the scars where it had peeled, been scraped and painted over.

He checked in, then sat by a parlor window overlooking the river. The lawn ran down to the lazy, green river, cottages on the other side.

A comely young waitress smiled at him. He smiled back. "I'd like a very dry, very dirty Bombay martini on the rocks with four olives."

She nodded. "And your dog?"

"Water. Straight up." He handed her the keys to the Jeep.

Two martinis later, Burr ordered planked whitefish and a glass of Tall Ships Chardonnay. He didn't expect much from a local wine, but he was mistaken. It wasn't too sweet and it wasn't too oaky. "We are at the forty-fifth parallel," he said. After dinner, he fed Zeke, took him for a walk, then climbed the two flights to their room overlooking the river. Zeke jumped on the bed. "Nothing like a hotel that takes dogs. That and a twenty."

\* \* \*

Burr found Tommy in the orchard not too early the next morning. He was a bit fuzzy after last night. The chardonnay had gone a little too well with his whitefish.

"Last year for these trees," Tommy said. "They only last so long. Bearing fruit is hard on them." Tommy broke off a dead branch.

No matter how this turned out, Burr was sure he'd be able to teach a course in cherry farming by the time this was all over. Tommy looked up at Burr.

"How are you going to get this dismissed?"

"There is a way. A very easy way."

"Really?"

"If you have someone or someones who can testify they were with you from the time Helen left for South Manitou until the time her boat was found. That would do it."

"You mean an alibi?"

"That's right."

Tommy bit his cheek, then he looked down at his boots.

"Someone must have seen you." Tommy kept his eyes on his boots. "How about your housekeeper?"

"She had the day off."

"Why?"

"Helen always gave her time off when she went off on one of her adventures."

"How about your farmhands?"

"I don't know. Maybe. They were out in the trees."

"Where were you?"

"I was in the shop. I ran some errands. I don't really remember."

*His memory is a bit too fuzzy.*

"Tommy, where were you and what did you do when Helen left?"

"I told you. I was in the shop. Then I ran some errands." There was edge to his voice.

"Who were you with?"

"No one."

"You didn't see anyone for three days?"

"I went down to the Betsie. Fly fishing."

*I don't want anything to do with fly fishing, rivers, or whatever the hatch du jour is.*

"Where did you go?"

"On the Betsie. Upstream from the Homestead dam. There's brookies up there."

"I'm sure there are. And who were you with?"

"I went by myself."

"Where did you stay?"

"I camped."

"By yourself?"

Tommy nodded.

"You must have seen someone. Bought some gas. A six-pack. Maybe some worms."

"I use a fly rod."

"For God's sake, Tommy, you've been accused of murder. Brooks has witnesses who say they saw you get on the ferry at South Manitou the day after Helen anchored in the bay. She was killed with your pistol, and right after her body was found, you do a one-eighty and want to make a deal with the feds." Burr broke a dead branch off one of the trees. "And there's nobody who can say you were with them?"

"I wasn't on South Manitou. I always made sure Helen had the pistol when she went by herself on *Achilles.*" Tommy grabbed the branch from Burr. "I don't have any family. Helen was the only family I had. There's no reason to keep this place without her."

Burr walked away from Tommy.

*Why is this always so difficult? Couldn't he just have an alibi?*

Burr grabbed another branch, then let it go. *That would be too easy. I could never get involved in something that easy.* He turned around and walked back to Tommy.

"Why did you pick that time to disappear from the face of the earth?"

"When Helen went on one of her adventures, that's what I did. It was a way to get away from this."

"I thought you liked it."

"Everybody needs a break."

"You picked a great time to take a break."

Tommy brushed the hair out of his eyes. "What are you going to do?"

"I suppose I'm going to have to find a suspect or two." Burr reached for another branch. Tommy grabbed Burr's wrist with one of his meaty hands, but he jerked free. Burr shook him off. He broke off the branch and walked off with it.

Back at his Jeep, Burr opened the passenger door and let Zeke out. The dog sat down and looked up at him.

"What do you want?"

The dog wagged his tail.

"What is it now?"

Zeke wagged his tail again. Burr shook his head. Then he remembered the branch he was holding. "Oh," he said. Burr threw it. Zeke brought it back. He threw it again. Zeke brought it back again. And again. And again. Finally, "That's enough. You'd bring this back until my arm fell off." He gave Zeke the stick. "Let's go."

The brothers-in-arms drove off. Burr, for his part, felt better after the game of fetch but thought he might be defending a murderer. "Zeke, I'll defend him until I'm sure he killed Helen. And until then … we need the money."

They headed back north on M-22 toward Leland. The road opened up on Good Harbor Bay. Burr looked out at the big lake. The wind had swung around to the southwest and a soft, summer wind blew in off the lake. Another mile up the road, he turned inland. Seven roads later, three of which were wrong turns, he pulled into what he hoped was Karen Hansen's home, a two-story white farmhouse with green shutters and a barn in back.

He could park in the shade of yet another big, old sugar maple, but he was tired of parking underneath big, old sugar maples. He drove past the house and parked in the shadow of the barn. He cracked the windows one more time. "I won't be long."

Burr walked around the side of the house and knocked on the front door. Karen Hansen opened the door and stepped out on the porch. She had on a blue sleeveless top, cutoffs and sandals. Her wavy, black hair was pulled back, no makeup, and a red splotch on her cheek. "I wasn't expecting anyone. And certainly not you."

Burr stared at Karen's cheek. She scrunched her nose, then felt her cheek with her finger. She rubbed at the splotch, then sucked her finger.

"You can come in but I'm at a critical point." She turned around and walked back into the house. Burr found her in the kitchen. A pot of rasp-berries cooked on the stove, bubbling ever so slightly. Burr stuck his nose over the pot and smelled the sweet, sticky, fruity smell. There were quarts of raspberries in boxes on the counter and canning jars everywhere. Karen stirred the pot. Burr walked over to the table and looked out the window. He could see Lake Michigan off in the distance.

"It's not the typical view from a farm kitchen. My father bought it for us." Karen dipped a spoon into the pot, blew on the hot jam, then carefully tasted it. "It's almost ready." She scratched her nose. She looked at Burr. Now there was a dab of jam on her nose. "What is it?" she said.

Burr touched the tip of his nose.

Karen wiped the jam off. "We're not going to get very far this way."

Karen turned around and stirred again. She wiggled a little when she stirred, which Burr found provocative in a jammy sort of way.

"It's almost ready for the pectin. That's what makes it set up."

"Of course." Burr had no idea what she was talking about.

"I'm the one who wanted to sell the orchards. Helen and Lauren didn't." She stirred something into the pot. "Here goes the pectin."

"I've just been to see Tommy. He doesn't have much of an explanation of where he was when Helen was killed."

"I was sure he didn't do it until I heard Peter at the courthouse."

"Tommy said he was fishing."

Karen stopped stirring and looked at Burr. "Really?"

"Does he fish?" Burr said.

"Not that I know of. But I suppose he might."

"Do you think Tommy killed Helen?"

"No." She turned back to the pot of gooey red jam and stirred. She turned back to Burr. "But I suppose he could have."

# CHAPTER EIGHT

Burr and Zeke wound their way back to M-22, then turned north. Three miles up the road, they passed the Happy Hour Tavern, a modest, single-story, white building at a wide spot in the road. "Zeke, I'm told the Happy Hour has the finest hamburger in Leelanau County. Maybe the whole state." Burr sighed. *Another time.* Another seven miles up the road, they stopped at the blinker, the only traffic signal they had seen all day.

Burr drove straight through the blinker into Northport, the northernmost village in the little finger. They fumbled around the village until he found 425 Maple, a white, three-story Victorian with red gingerbread trim and *de rigeur* maples in the yard. Burr cracked the windows again and left Zeke on guard. He smelled freshly mowed grass on his way up to a porch full of white wicker furniture. He knocked on the hardwood door.

Lauren's husband, Curt, the boy next door, answered. "Why, Burr, what are you doing here?"

"I was in the area and thought I'd see if Lauren was around."

"She's almost out the door. Come on in."

Curt disappeared into the house.

Burr waited in the foyer on a throw rug, the dining room to his left and old-fashioned parlor to his right.

*The Ericksons know how to live.*

Lauren rushed in. "I'm just on my way to work." She had on scrubs, solid purple pants and a flowered purple top. She had her mostly blond hair pulled back, pink lipstick, and a tiny bit of eye makeup. She looked every bit a nurse, competent and not a bit fragile. Lauren led him out to the porch but they didn't sit down. "I only have a few minutes."

"Where do you work?" Burr said.

"OB-GYN. At Munson."

"In Traverse City?"

She nodded.

"That's a long way from here."

"Curt has an insurance agency here, so we can't move. There's an apartment for us near the hospital if the weather's bad or if the babies don't come when they are supposed to." She smiled at him. "Which is most of the time."

She turned and started back where she came from. "I've really got to go."

"I'll only be a minute. Do you think Tommy could have killed Helen?"

Lauren sat down. "No, not really."

*Maybe she isn't in such a big hurry after all.*

Burr sat down next to her. "How was their marriage?"

Lauren wiggled in her chair. Burr couldn't tell if it was the chair or Helen and Tommy's marriage. Burr wiggled in his chair. The wicker made him feel like he was sitting on sticks.

*If this was my furniture, I'd burn it.*

"You've been at this lawsuit a long time. What do you think?" Lauren said.

Burr wiggled again, and it wasn't because of the chair. "I thought they got along well enough. I never saw them argue, but then I rarely saw them other than professionally."

Lauren looked straight at him but didn't say anything.

Burr was starting to wonder who was interviewing who. "As I look back on it, I think all Tommy wanted was to grow cherries and all Helen wanted was to keep the farm."

"My sister was a strong-willed woman. And probably the most beautiful woman I've ever known."

*Where did that come from?*

He thought so, too, but he wasn't going to be the one to say it. He made a point not to wiggle.

Lauren stood up. "I have to go to work."

Burr stood. "Do you think Tommy could have killed Helen?"

"Could and did are different. I suppose he could have. But I don't think he did."

"Why not?"

"He loved her." Lauren looked away from Burr, then back to him. "He wanted to make her happy. And he wanted to grow cherries. And all that was just fine with Helen."

"This would have been so much easier if Tommy hadn't changed his mind about selling the farm," Burr said.

"Without Helen, I don't think he cares that much about it."

"If not Tommy, then who?"

Lauren shook her head. "I don't know. There's plenty of people who are mad at us for holding things up."

"How would killing Helen help get the farm sold?" Burr said.

"You know as well as I do that Tommy gets Helen's vote if she dies."

"How would anyone but the family know that?" Burr said.

"This is a small place. Everyone knows everything."

"Tommy loves the orchards."

"I really have to go to work." Lauren ran into the house and came back out with a purse and an overnight bag. "I hope the babies are on time." She started down the steps. "It doesn't seem like he loves the orchards as much as I thought he did."

* * *

"Good God, man. What are you doing?" Jacob said.

Burr looked up from his clams with red sauce and angel hair pasta. "I'm having my lunch." Burr unwound a noodle from his plate and held it over the table. Zeke lifted his head from Burr's lap and sucked it in. "Will you join me?"

"I don't eat with dogs."

Burr poured himself another glass of Chianti.

"If you keep drinking that wine, you'll never stay awake this afternoon."

"I don't intend to," Burr said.

Jacob had tracked Burr down at Michelangelo's. Jacob straightened his tie, another foulard, this one with royal blue diamonds on a mandarin orange background. "What have you done this time?"

"If it's not lunch, I'm sure I don't know."

Jacob took out a piece of paper from the breast pocket inside his navy blazer. He unfolded it and set it next to Burr's clams with red sauce.

"Where did you get this?"

"From Eve."

"Everyone is a spy."

"You simply can't waive the preliminary exam."

Burr swirled his glass and drank some of the wine. "Why not?"

"We've got to see what else Brooks has."

"We know what he has. We have the names of the witnesses. I got them from the judge."

"We need to know what they're going to say."

"My dear Jacob, they're going to say exactly what Brooks said they were going to say at the arraignment."

"But you can question them."

"I don't need to have them as witnesses to question them. I'm going to go and see them."

Jacob ran a finger through one of the curls of his steel wool hair. Burr wondered if Jacob's hair was naturally curly or it was curly because of Jacob's incessant twirling tic.

"It's too risky to waive the preliminary exam. What if you could get the charges dismissed?"

Burr twirled his fork around some of the unsuspecting angel hair. "With a murder weapon, witnesses who saw Tommy on the ferry and a motive, I think not." Burr nudged a clam onto his fork. "And as you know, the standard is low. The judge only has to decide that it was more likely than not that Tommy murdered Helen. We're not at the beyond-a-reasonable-doubt stage yet."

Jacob started on another curl. "Eve and I think this is foolish."

Burr chewed on his pasta.

Scooter appeared at their table. "Mr. Lafayette, there are no dogs allowed."

"He's a seeing-eye dog."

Scooter made a show of a big sigh. "We've been through this. You're not blind, and he's not a seeing-eye dog." Scooter put on his best restaurateur's face. "Anything for you, Jacob?" Jacob shook his head. "You never order anything." Scooter walked away.

"You are outrageous," Jacob said.

"Scooter owes me four months' rent. We play out this little drama every time I come in with Zeke. He feels much better after he says there's no dogs allowed." Burr reached into his khakis. Now it was his turn to unfold a piece of paper. He set it in front of Jacob. "Look at this."

Jacob studied the paper. Burr fed Zeke another noodle.

"It's just the names of the people Brooks used at the arraignment."

"And addresses. Eve found the addresses."

"So?"

"Jacob, look at their addresses. The ferry captain has a winter address in Key West. The deckhands go to school in Alabama. The woman who found Helen's body has an Atlanta address."

"I don't see your point." Jacob twirled a third curl.

"Jacob, the preliminary exam is in two weeks. It's still summer. These people are likely still here or close by. They'll testify, and their testimony will be in a transcript."

Jacob reached for a fourth curl. Burr grabbed his hand.

"If we waive the preliminary exam, there will obviously be no testimony on the record from any of them. When it comes time for the trial, these witnesses will be far away. Some or all of them may not show up."

"Brooks will subpoena them."

Burr swirled the wine in his glass. "Of course he will. But they'll be far away and it will be difficult for Brooks to compel them to attend."

"And?"

"And, if any or all don't show up for the trial, there will be big holes in Brooks' case."

Jacob started for a curl but thought better of it. "Genius. It's genius. But it's risky."

"Not if I interview them now. While they're still here." Burr finished his Chianti and poured himself a third glass.

* * *

"Did it ever occur to you that your client might actually be guilty?" Aunt Kitty said.

Burr smelled the beach, wet sand and dead fish. He imagined he smelled suntan lotion. He squirmed in his chair. Zeke, who was curled up at his feet, looked up at Burr, then put his head back down.

"If you keep taking clients accused of murder, at some point one of them will actually have done it."

Burr squirmed again.

"What you're doing is quite different from squaring off with another silk-stockinged lawyer representing another rich company. That's just about money. This is about right and wrong." Aunt Kitty took another swallow of her martini. "Would you please stop squirming."

Burr felt like a schoolboy. He wished he hadn't stopped for cocktails on the porch of Cottage 59 on Harbor Point, a hundred-year-old, gated cottage association in Harbor Springs.

Aunt Kitty, though, was his only living relative except for Zeke-the-Boy. She lived alone in the family cottage, if you could call a three-story Victorian with wraparound porches a cottage. It was the white house with the forest green shutters, the last house on the tip of Harbor Point. It fronted the harbor on Little Traverse Bay, with Lake Michigan on the back. A million-dollar view on each side. Cottage 59 was all that was left of the Lafayettes' once considerable fortune. It was destined to pass to Burr should he outlive his eighty-year-old maiden aunt, which didn't seem as probable as the laws of actuarial science would predict.

Aunt Kitty handed him her glass. "A dividend please." Burr took the glass and started for the kitchen. "What am I going to do with you?" She shook her head and her white ponytail swung back and forth.

In the kitchen, Burr filled their glasses with ice, then poured two shots of Bombay into each.

"Not too much vermouth," Aunt Kitty said from the porch.

Half a capful of vermouth for Aunt Kitty, and a full capful for himself. *I may have been pouring from this bottle of vermouth since she taught me to make her martinis.* He finished off his martini with four olives and a generous splash of olive juice.

Back on the porch, Burr handed Aunt Kitty her glass and sat back down in one of the forest green Adirondack chairs that matched the shutters.

"Why must you insist on ruining perfectly good gin with olive juice?"

Burr knew better than to say anything. He quite liked his martinis dirty.

"As I was saying, it's one thing to fight over a rich company's money, but it's quite another to fight crimes, especially a capital crime."

"Yes, Aunt Kitty."

She pointed at him with a long, bony forefinger. "Don't 'yes, Aunt Kitty' me. Peter Brooks is a smart Michigan lawyer from a good family. He must believe he has something."

Burr started another "Yes, Aunt Kitty" but she raised her hand and shushed him. "From what you've said, there is a body, a murder weapon, means and motive."

Burr's Aunt Kitty had gone to the University of Michigan Law School when it had been barely possible for women to be admitted. She had worked at saving woods, water and marshes in Northern Michigan her entire life and knew everyone worth knowing. Burr knew it was pointless to argue with her, but he couldn't quite help himself.

"Every person accused of a crime deserves representation."

Aunt Kitty sat straight up, no easy task in an Adirondack chair, and leaned toward Burr, which was even more difficult. "Where is your moral compass?"

"It is pointed squarely at my client."

"And if Tommy Lockwood is guilty?"

"All the more reason to have a good lawyer."

Aunt Kitty sat back in her chair. "I suppose he does deserve representation." She took a big swallow of her drink. "Which brings me to my next point."

Burr started to groan but thought better of it. Instead, he buried his head in his martini.

"Look at me when I'm talking to you."

*There's a good reason I feel like a teenager when I come here.*

"As much as I appreciate your visit, I suspect the real reason you're here is to pick up that leaky sailboat of yours and sail it to Leland."

"The docks at Leland are full," Burr said.

Aunt Kitty glared at him.

Burr looked at the lighthouse on the tip of Harbor Point, out at the bay, then at the cottage to his left. Finally, he said, "There's room in Northport."

Aunt Kitty dismissed him with her hand. "Where you dock your wretched boat is not my point. My point is your cavalier attitude. You're defending a man accused of murder and all the while you're cavorting on a sailboat. A leaky old sailboat at that."

"I need a place to stay. *Spindrift* is the cheapest place to stay." Burr squirmed again.

"Stop that squirming. My point is you're having too much fun while Tommy Lockwood's life is in the balance. It doesn't look right."

*My beloved aunt is talking out of both sides of her mouth.*

Burr swirled the ice in his glass. Then he fished out an olive and chewed it slowly.

Aunt Kitty looked out on the harbor. "At least it's still floating."

Burr looked at *Spindrift,* a 1940 wooden, thirty-four-foot cutter-rigged sloop, as she swung on her mooring. She was no *Kismet,* his last boat, but then *Kismet* was about five miles due west, on the bottom of Lake Michigan in two hundred feet of water, more or less.

"How are you possibly going to run your office from a sailboat?"

"I have a car phone."

"A what?"

"A car phone."

"Do those things work?"

"Aunt Kitty, on the one hand, you really don't want me representing Tommy Lockwood. On the other hand, you don't like the way I'm going about it. Which is it?"

She ignored him. "And I suppose that girlfriend of yours is going with you."

"Zeke and I are taking the boat over." The aging lab looked up at Burr, then put his head back down.

*I wish Maggie were going with us.*

\* \* \*

Burr and Zeke spent a quiet night on *Spindrift.* At seven the next morning, after watering Zeke, Burr fired up the three-cylinder diesel. He cast off the mooring and off they went. They motored across Little Traverse Bay in a flat calm, leaving Petoskey to port. By ten, they were abeam of the channel at Charlevoix. The wind came up from the northwest. Burr hoisted the main and staysail and turned off the engine. Zeke, his reluctant first mate, wasn't much help. By four, they were tied up in the harbor at Northport.

*All is right with the world. At least for today.*

# CHAPTER NINE

Burr woke with a stiff back, one of the few drawbacks of sleeping aboard *Spindrift*. He bent down and tried to touch his toes, the only stretch he ever did. Ten seconds later and slightly more limber, he took Zeke ashore and found his Jeep in the marina parking lot, driven down from Harbor Springs at an outrageous price. He walked up the block to the Little Finger, the only diner in Northport. After poached eggs on toast and a side order of bacon for Zeke, the two of them took M-22 south past the Happy Hour Tavern. "Someday soon, Zeke."

Fifteen minutes later, he parked at the Leland marina. They walked over to the weather-worn dock that ran along the bank of the Leland River, deep green and in no hurry to reach the blue of Lake Michigan. Burr leaned against one of the pilings and looked downstream at the charter boats and past them, to the Manitou ferry. Creosote came off on his shirt. He tried to wipe it off, but it smeared and smelled like tar. "Damn it all, Zeke." Upstream, unpainted single-story buildings looked more like shacks than shops.

He was standing in the middle of Fishtown, a once thriving commercial fishing village in what would become Leland. Fishing shanties had lined both sides of the river when the lake gave up staggering numbers of white-fish, lake trout, walleye and perch. When the lake had been fished out, the shanties were abandoned. They rotted for years, until enterprising souls turned them into cheese, ice cream and T-shirt shops. Larson's was the only working shanty left.

Burr walked in and the smell of fish almost knocked him over. The smell was so strong that he was sure there must be tubs, or more likely, barrels of fish everywhere. Instead, refrigerated glass display cases lined with ice and filled with fish ran along the walls. A woman in a yellow sleeveless top and a floral Lily Pulitzer, lime-green skirt was searching her bamboo purse. Behind the counter, a 70-ish woman punched the keys on a cash register. The cash drawer opened. She slammed it shut. It dinged twice. "You got forty dollars and seventeen cents worth of smoked whitefish, but this damn machine don't work right so let's call it good at forty even."

"I can pay with a credit card or a check," the woman said.

"Cash is better."

"I'm sure I don't have that much."

The older woman punched the keys, opened the cash drawer and slammed it shut again. It dinged twice. "Don't that beat all?"

"I beg your pardon?"

"We don't take credit cards."

The woman with the flowered skirt looked like she had never heard anything so ridiculous.

"All right then, a check will do."

The woman in the flowered skirt scribbled out a check and handed it to the annoyed cashier. She opened the register again, stuffed the check in the drawer and slammed it shut. Another two dings and she handed the woman in the flowered skirt a package wrapped in brown oiled paper. She looked at Burr on her way out. "It's supposed to be the best whitefish in the state. The rest of the place, I don't know."

Burr toured the store. There was fresh whitefish, smoked whitefish, frozen whitefish, whitefish dip (with or without horseradish), whitefish pate', whitefish chowder. It looked to Burr like he could buy anything he wanted as long as it was whitefish. Although he did see about a half-dozen boxes of water crackers on the counter next to the cash register.

The cashier punched at the keys again. The drawer opened again. She slammed it again. It dinged twice. Again. "Don't that beat all," she said again. She slapped the machine. She looked up at Burr. "There's no dogs in here." She had gray hair underneath a hairnet, glasses pushed in through the hairnet and just about the deepest tan Burr had ever seen.

"Do you have any whitefish?"

The woman laughed. "All right, he can stay." She tucked a strand of hair back under the hairnet. "Until somebody else comes in."

Burr stuck his hand out. "Burr Lafayette."

She put her hands on her hips. "I guess that means you're not going to buy anything."

"Actually, I'd like a pound of smoked whitefish and some of those crackers."

"That's best with a cold beer," she said.

"Beer makes just about everything better," Burr said.

"Don't I know it." She reached into one of the glass-fronted coolers and took out three pieces of the smoked whitefish. The smoker had turned the skin a shiny acorn brown. She wrapped it up and weighed it. "Twelve dollars and forty-six cents. Let's make it twelve even."

Burr handed her a twenty.

"You got the right change?"

Burr shook his head.

She handed him the fish. "Just take it. We got more where this came from."

"Why, thank you, Miss..."

"It's Mrs." She paused. "Mrs. Larson."

"You're the Larson in 'Larson's'?"

"One of 'em."

"Actually, I'm looking for Steve Larson."

"You mean Sven?"

"I thought it was Steve."

"I ought to know my own son's name."

"Of course, Mrs. Larson. I understand that your son found Helen Lockwood's boat out in the lake."

"What do you want him for?"

"I'm Tommy Lockwood's lawyer."

"That whole family thinks they're special because they figured out how to grow cherries." The older woman started to punch the keys on the cash register again. She thought better of it and looked back at Burr. "He's on the *Emma B II*. He was just tied up here, but he moved. The customers don't like the smell much."

Burr couldn't imagine how anything could smell stronger than what he was smelling. "How can I find him?"

"Just look for the seagulls."

"Did you know Helen Lockwood?"

"Everybody knew Helen."

"And you liked her?"

"She was the most pigheaded woman I ever met. Ran that family like she was the Queen of Sheba."

*I've heard that once or twice.*

"What's the best way to get to the *Emma B II*?"

"Go up to the bridge, then walk down the other side. Unless you can walk on water. Which my late husband thought he could do."

"I beg your pardon."

"He drowned out there. The first *Emma B* caught fire out in the lake thirty years ago November. She burned to the water line. He drowned in two hundred feet of water. Thirty mile an hour wind, forty-degree water. A man can't last long in that. I hate that lake and all this damn whitefish. But a body has to make a living, and Sven won't do nothing else."

Burr reached his hand out again. "I'm so sorry."

This time she took it. "Emma Larson," she said. "Emma B. Larson."

Burr, Zeke and the smoked whitefish made their way past more reclaimed shanties, a kite shop, a bookstore, another T-shirt shop. They crossed the river at M-22, just above the three-foot dam that made Lake Leelanau what it was today. They skirted the Falling Waters, a pricey hotel and restaurant, then cut back to the dock on the south side of the river. There were no shops on this side. They passed a thirty-five-foot Sea Ray with a fly bridge, a forty-foot Egg Harbor Sedan, a vintage Christ Craft runabout with a third seat. Then a flock of seagulls swarming over what Burr thought must be the *Emma B II*. Not that she looked anything like new. She was about thirty feet long, with a fat bow and a broad stern. Her cabin covered the entire hull but was cut away for about six feet on the port side, two-thirds of the way from bow so the nets could be run in and out of the boat. The cabin jogged up about ten feet from the bow. There were windows at that point so the captain could see what he was doing.

The gulls screeched at Burr and Zeke when they reached the *Emma B*. "Zeke, sit." The dog sat. His head followed the gulls as they swarmed above the boat. Up and down, side to side. Back and forth.

*That will keep him busy.*

Burr stuck his head inside the cutaway section. The stench of fish overpowered him. He staggered back onto the dock. Burr was sure he was going to be ill. He started breathing through his mouth.

A man in his forties stuck his head out. He had short blond hair and a sunburned head that looked like a pincushion. Bright blue eyes squinted in the sun.

"Sven?" Burr said.

"Steve."

Burr decided that was a question for another day. "My name is Burr Lafayette. I represent Tommy Lockwood."

Sven, or was it Steve, nodded at him.

"I understand you were the one who towed Helen Lockwood's boat in."

"Yeah."

The fisherman climbed onto the dock. He had on a black rubber apron that ran up to his neck and yellow boots that came up to his knees. Burr thought he looked like Daffy Duck except that he had forearms the size of Popeye's and a Paul Bunyan-size chest. He looked Burr up and down with his piercing blue eyes. He gave Burr a smile full of white teeth and stuck his hand out. "Steve Larson. My mother calls me Sven because it's on my birth certificate. I don't like it much."

Burr shook a giant hand covered in fish slime. He coughed.

"You got a cold?" Steve said.

"No," Burr said.

"You get used to the smell," Steve said.

Burr desperately wanted to wipe his hand on his khakis, but then he'd have to live with the smell the rest of the day. He started to put his hand in his pocket but thought better of it. He had no idea what to do with his hand. Finally, he dropped it to his side, careful not to let it touch his pants.

"You're the one who towed Helen Lockwood's boat in," Burr said again.

"Yeah." Steve wiped his hands on his apron. Burr wished he had done that before they had shaken hands.

"I saw that boat out in the lake the day before, but I didn't think much of it. It was out in the lake all the time. The next day, I started paying attention. It was broadside to the waves, rolling in the swells. Drifting. The wind was light. I didn't think much about it." Steve scratched at his nose. Burr had an itch himself. He scratched with his right hand and immediately wished he'd used his left.

"Something wrong?" Steve said.

Burr shook his head.

"Anyway, I had nets to pull in, so I didn't think about it much. Good catch that day. I got 'em on ice and started in, but then I see her boat's drifting off the dunes. My curiosity gets the best of me, so I go over there. She's drifting all right. I hail three or four times. No answer. I start to get a little worried so I run up alongside and tie onto her. I go onboard and look around. Key in the ignition in the *on* position. Not a soul aboard. I go back to the steering station and turn the key. She started right up. Damned if I knew what happened."

"Did you see anything wrong?"

"Wrong? I don't know. There was a half empty bottle of gin rolling around, a glass with lipstick on it. Cigarette butts in the ashtray."

Burr nodded. "Any signs of foul play?"

"Foul play?"

"Any signs of violence." Burr paused. "Or anything that was missing. Something that should have been there that wasn't."

Sven shook his head no. He scratched his nose again. Burr was tempted to scratch his own nose.

*I wish he wouldn't do that.*

"Was her purse on the boat?"

The fisherman nodded.

"Did you look in it?"

"Yeah. Seemed like the right thing to do."

"Was there anything missing?"

"Not that I could tell."

"Cash, credit cards?"

"Full of credit cards. A little cash. Driver's license."

"So, nothing out of the ordinary?"

Sven looked at Burr like he was crazy. "Not unless you think finding a boat drifting in Lake Michigan with no one on board is out of the ordinary."

*Touché.*

Burr bit his lip. "Anything else?"

Steve wiped his hands on his rubber apron again. "I'm not sure I was the first one there."

Burr cocked his head. "Did you see another boat?"

"Lots of boats out there."

"Did you see any?"

"*It'll Do* was close by."

"*It'll Do?*"

"Charter boat out of Frankfort."

"Did you see her tied up to *Achilles*?"

"She was close by. Could have been before I got there."

"Is there something I should know about *It'll Do*?"

"Captain's a crook is all."

"Really? What's his name?"

"Danny, Donny, Drury. No, it's Dilly. That's what it is."

Steve scratched his nose.

*The smell doesn't bother him at all.*

"But there was nothing missing."

"Nothing that I noticed, but I don't know nothing about what was on that boat."

*Tommy didn't say anything about anything missing, but if Tommy killed Helen, he wouldn't.*

"What do you think happened to Helen Lockwood? And her boat?" Burr said.

"I think the plan was to set that boat off across the lake. It's eighty miles to Wisconsin. Good plan. Except the engine stalled out, and there wasn't much wind, so she drifted around until I brought her in." Steve, nee Sven, looked down at his calloused hands. "I think whoever killed her tried to make it look like she fell overboard and drowned. But that's not what happened, is it," Larson said, not asking.

"No, it's not." Burr's itch had come back. He used all his willpower not to scratch it.

"Drowning is what happens out there. All the time." Larson looked back at his boat, then at Burr. "That's what happened to my dad. Damn boat caught fire. There's nothing you can do when the water's forty degrees. You got twenty minutes with a life jacket to get rescued. You can't make any money unless you fish alone. Can't afford a mate. Didn't matter, though. That would have been two dead."

"I'm sorry," Burr said.

"My mother wants me to give it up. She's sure the lake's gonna get me, too." Steve climbed back on board his boat. He turned and looked at Burr. "I don't like 'Sven.' That was my father's name. I figure I got a better chance with Steve." He disappeared inside.

Zeke, still mesmerized by swooping and diving gulls, was in no hurry to leave the dock. Burr, for his part, couldn't get away from the stench quickly enough. Halfway up the dock, Burr blew the air out of his lungs and started breathing through his nose again. "Thank God for fresh air." By the time they crossed the river, Burr's appetite had returned. It was well past lunchtime and he was famished. He opened the bag with the whitefish. The smell of smoked fish drifted out of the bag, but the stench from the fish shop and the *Emma B II* drifted up with the smoked fish. Burr was sure he was going to be ill. He closed the bag and folded it over itself six times. He threw it in the trash and walked into the sandwich shop on the corner of M-22 and the bridge. He ordered roast beef on rye with horseradish, a pickle and a six-pack of Labatt.

The two of them ate the roast beef sandwich at a picnic table on the lawn by the marina. Burr drank three of the Labatts. He considered a fourth but he didn't want to dull his senses.

After lunch he took his car phone out of the Jeep. Back at the picnic table he unzipped the bag, fussed with the antenna, and turned it on. It lit up and beeped a most competent beep.

"Zeke, this is going to change our lives." He dialed his office.

Eve answered on the third ring.

"Lafayette and Wertheim."

"Eve, it's me. How are you on this fine day?"

"What?"

"It's me, Burr. Seventy-five and sunny. Not a cloud in the sky."

"Who is this?"

"It's Burr."

"All I hear is static." She hung up.

Burr looked at the phone, then dialed again.

"Lafayette and Wertheim."

"Eve, it's me. Burr."

"Who?"

"Burr. You know, Burr."

"Oh. Hello, Burr. You sound like you're calling from a tornado."

"It's my new car phone. They call this one a bag phone because it's in a bag and I can take it anywhere. Isn't it grand?"

"Grand what?"

"No, it's grand. The phone."

"I can't hear you. Now you sound like you're in a tunnel."

"Look, I need you to find out who owns a boat in Frankfort. It's called *It'll Do*."

"The what?"

"The *It'll Do*."

"It'll do what?"

"That's the name of the boat."

"Are we going to get a bill for this thing?"

"It will make us money."

"I can't hear a thing you're saying. Why don't you call me back from a pay phone." The line went dead.

Burr cradled the receiver. He zipped the bag and lovingly put it back in his Jeep. "Zeke, there's just a few bugs to work out. Then we'll have a whole new way to live. No more being tied down to an office." Zeke jumped up on the passenger seat and gave Burr a look that made him wonder if the car phone was such a good idea after all.

Burr started to the ferry. "Come on, Zeke, we're not done here yet." Halfway to the ferry, Burr stopped in his tracks. "Damn it all." Burr watched the *Northern Lights* motor down the river and out into the big lake. "That was the other reason we came down here."

# CHAPTER TEN

Burr decided he'd deal with the car phone later and take matters into his own hands about the whereabouts of the *It'll Do*. Twenty minutes later, the Jeep passed Port Oneida Road. For the next twenty miles, Sleeping Bear Dunes National Lakeshore lay to his right. The road twisted through the woods, on top of the bluff, opening up on the lake every now and then to spectacular views of Lake Michigan hundreds of feet below – and not a guardrail in sight.

"Zeke, I suppose the park is a good idea. It's just that it's not a good idea to take private property to put it together." He drummed his fingers on the steering wheel. "Although I suppose the beach property probably should be in the park. Otherwise, there's a crazy quilt of what's in and what's out. I'll be damned if I'll ever admit that to anyone other than you." Burr looked over at Zeke, who had his head out the window. "You're not listening again, but the orchard is so far away from the beach that it's silly to put it in the park. It's that damned Sleeper. If it weren't for him, we wouldn't be in court. But then if we weren't in court, I wouldn't have a client."

Burr drummed his fingers again. "I suppose all is right with the world." He looked back at Zeke, who still wasn't paying attention. "I was doing just fine defending Helen and her sisters' claims to keeping the farm. We've been paid handsomely so far, but now I wonder if I'm defending a murderer."

They left the park and, in another ten miles, drove into Frankfort. They were on the north side of Betsie Lake, near the channel to the big lake about thirty miles north of where M-22 began. Not big enough to have a stoplight but bigger than Leland and big enough to have a movie theater. He parked at the city marina and looked for *It'll Do* but couldn't find her anywhere. Finally, he asked the harbormaster, who pointed across the water. Back in the Jeep, they crossed the bridge over the Betsie and drove down the Elberta side, the poor cousin to Frankfort on the other side of the lake that lay between the river proper and Lake Michigan. They passed the Cabbage

Shed, a trendy, two story restaurant that had once been a warehouse and stored cabbage from top to bottom. It hung on to a dock that looked like it might collapse at any moment, then an abandoned car ferry tied to a dock in about the same shape, and then three or four charter boats. As luck would have it, *It'll Do* bobbed in the water. Burr parked the Jeep and, as luck would further have it, he saw a man on the dock next to the boat who Burr thought surely must be the captain.

As luck wouldn't have it, the captain had on a black rubber apron like Larson's and was wielding a knife that could have been the blade on a guillotine. He was cleaning a fish. Gulls circled and the stench pushed Burr back a step. "Not again." He took a deep breath and walked up to the fish cleaner. "Are you the captain?"

"Sure am." He stuck his hand out. "Captain Lester Dillworth. Everybody calls me Dilly." Burr clenched his teeth and shook Dilly's hand. He didn't have Sven's grip, but his hand had the same fishy smell. Burr took his hand back and fought off another almost uncontrollable urge to rub his hand on his khakis.

"You want to sign up for a charter? The cohos are coming up the lake." The fisherman nodded to the lake. Burr saw brown eyes flash under his "*It'll Do*" baseball hat. His nose stuck out from under the bill and looked like it was on at least its third peel of the summer. Burr thought Dilly must be about fifty. Broad shoulders and chest and a big belly. Dilly pulled a Stroh's from a cooler at his feet.

*That explains the belly.*

Dilly sliced off a filet and threw the carcass in the lake. Two seagulls dove after it and fought over it. Zeke couldn't take his eyes off of them.

*Here we go again.*

Dilly reached into a coffin-size cooler next to the beer cooler and grabbed another fish. "You here to book a charter?"

"Actually, Steve Larson told me you were down here."

Dilly stopped what he was doing and drove the point of his knife into the cutting board.

"You tell that Swede son-of-a-bitch that I never cut his goddamn nets." He pulled the knife from the cutting board and pointed it at Burr. "But you tell him, if he keeps setting them damn nets where the salmon get snagged up in 'em, somebody sure as hell is gonna cut them nets in a million pieces." Dilly waved the knife at Burr's Jeep. "Now get the hell out."

"I have no idea who did what to who's nets. I'm here because Steve Larson thought you may have seen the *Achilles* drifting off Sleeping Bear last summer."

"The what?"

"*Achilles*. She was a forty-foot powerboat drifting near the Manitous last summer."

"That's a long run for me. There's better fishing right here."

"You never go up there?"

"I didn't say that." Dilly turned to his boat, a thirty-two-foot Tiara with a fly bridge. "She'll run up there all right."

"So you did see a boat drifting up there?"

"Might of. But I didn't cut no nets."

"No one said you did."

"That's what Sven thinks. It's not Steve, it's Sven."

"Sure, Sven." Burr started to put his hand in his pocket. He stopped himself. "I should've started at the beginning. I represent Tommy Lock-wood. He's accused of murdering his wife."

"I heard about that." The charter captain sliced the fish just behind its head.

"Did you see the boat drifting?"

Dilly sliced the fish along its backbone, head to tail. Then he held it by the tail and sliced back the other way. The filet came off the fish. Dilly dropped it in a bucket of water and turned the fish over. "I pulled up along-side. No one on board. Didn't know what to make of it."

"Did you go on board?"

Dilly looked up at him, then drank from his Stroh's. "I tied up along-side her."

"Did you go aboard?"

"Yeah."

"What did you find?"

The charter captain told Burr what he found, which was pretty much what Steve had told him.

"What happened after that?" Burr said.

"I saw Sven coming my way so I took off."

"You left?"

"Next thing I knew, Sven was towing her."

"Did you do anything else?"

"Nothin' else to do." Dilly flipped the fish over and cut along the head.

"You didn't call the sheriff. Or the Coast Guard?"

"There was nothing to call about when Sven showed up." Dilly sliced off the second filet. He dropped it in the bucket and threw the carcass in the water. The gulls dove again.

\* \* \*

"Zeke, there's something fishy going on around here." The dog, riding shotgun again, looked over at him. "It's a play on words." Zeke looked back out the window. They drove along the shore toward the lake. In about two hundred yards, the road turned up a steep hill. Burr passed a sign for the township park. At the top of the hill – a dune, really – he pulled over, got out of the Jeep and looked out over Lake Michigan. He saw the channel below him and the white lighthouse at the end of the breakwater. At the end of the breakwater, the murky brown river water from the Betsie emptied into the lake. It flowed due west, then to the blue water of Lake Michigan, bending around to the northwest on either side until the river spread out and mixed with the lake. Burr walked back to the Jeep.

"This is perfect. Absolutely perfect."

Burr pulled out his car phone and set it on the hood. Then he turned it on and waited for it to warm up. He dialed his office and Eve answered.

"Eve, it's Burr."

"Who?"

"Burr."

"Burr who?"

"You heard me."

"Where are you? I hear a freight train in the background."

"But you know it's me."

"What?"

"Eve, I need you to find out if either Sven Larson or Lester Dillworth have any kind of criminal record."

"What?"

"Eve, I'm on top of a giant hill. You must be able to hear me."

"I know it's you because the reception is so terrible."

"What?"

Burr grabbed the Jeep's antenna. "Damn it all."

"There you are. I heard that."

"Good. Please find out all you can about Sven Larson and Lester Dillworth."

"You're breaking up again."

"Find out all you can about Sven Larson and Lester Dillworth."

The line went dead. Burr slammed down the phone.

* * *

Burr drove into Leland about 5 p.m. There was no sign of the ferry, so he kept on going up M-22. A quarter mile past the Happy Hour, he made a U-turn. Five minutes later, he had a window booth and a Stroh's. Sadly, there was no Labatt, but at least the Stroh's was on draft.

*The only thing I learned today is that car phones have a long way to go.*

He took a long pull from his Stroh's. "Yet another tribute to my over-sized ego."

"I beg your pardon."

He jumped in his seat. Somehow the waitress had snuck up on him. "I didn't know anyone could hear me."

"I hear you perfectly. You're just not making any sense."

Burr ordered another Stroh's.

"Would you like to hear about the specials?"

"Not if it swims."

"How did you know?"

"I'd like your hamburger medium rare with ketchup, mustard, pickles and onion, with fries and coleslaw. And a plain hamburger to go."

* * *

Burr woke to a rapping on *Spindrift's* cabin top, followed by Zeke barking.

"Merciful heavens."

Burr stuck his head out of the cabin. The harbormaster stood on the dock. "Call your office," he said. Burr dressed, watered Zeke, and made a collect call from the pay phone outside the harbormaster's office.

After calling his office – which had been a call about not calling on the car phone ever again – Burr and Zeke drove back the way they had come the day before, through Leland and Good Harbor. South of Good Harbor, Burr turned onto Dune Highway into a gravel parking lot. He parked in front of a very large hole, at least thirty feet by fifty feet, and ten feet deep, with an orange fence around it and signs that said "*Keep Out*" and "*Property of the United States Government.*"

"Zeke, old friend, I can't imagine why there needs to be a sign telling me to keep out of that hole." Burr cracked the windows and got out of the Jeep. He looked down into the hole, which was about half full of water. A pair of mallards swam in lazy circles. Off to his right, a dented white trailer sat under a single maple tree. "This must be the place." He walked over, climbed the single concrete-block step and knocked twice. "Anybody home?"

"We open at nine," said a voice from inside.

Burr looked at his watch. It was 8:55. "It's as good as nine."

"Come back when it's nine."

Burr knew who the voice belonged to. He turned the door knob and let himself in.

"That's supposed to be locked," the voice said.

"Hello, Dale," Burr said. "How nice to see you again."

"Get out, Lafayette. We're not open until nine and don't come back when we are open."

Burr looked at Dale Sleeper sitting at the far end of the trailer in a beat up, maroon Lazy-Boy with his feet up, near a faded blue couch pushed against the sheet metal wall. Gray filing cabinets on the other wall, then a galley kitchen and, past that, a door to what Burr thought must be the bathroom. There was a bruised desk and a swivel chair at the far end of the trailer.

Burr thought the trailer smelled like it could use a shower. "Dale, this is quite the place. For a man of your stature."

Dale Sleeper, a big man with big hands, pulled on the joystick of the Lazy Boy and sat up straight. He put his hands on the armrests of the chair and pushed himself to his feet. His green Park Service shirt had come untucked, but he made no effort to tuck it in. He had a broad face and eyes that were way too far apart. Burr wanted to push Sleeper's eyes closer to his nose every time he saw him. Sleeper looked at his watch. "We're open. Now get out."

"Dale, I just want to talk a little." Burr sat down on the couch.

"I said *out*. We're adversaries in a federal lawsuit, and you are committing a grave offense talking to me without my attorney present."

"I'm not here about the condemnation. I'm here about the murder."

Sleeper got up and stood over him. "It doesn't matter."

Burr looked up at Sleeper. "You might turn around and tuck your shirt in."

Sleeper looked down but didn't do anything about his shirt. "Out," he said.

"All I have to do is send you a subpoena and then we can have a nice long talk in my office."

Sleeper turned around, unzipped his pants, and tucked in his shirt. "If it weren't for you and that damned lawsuit, headquarters building would be done by now and I'd be out of this trailer."

"Dale, you know as well as I do that's not true."

"It is true."

"The government funds this park every now and then. When it crosses their mind. Maybe the next time they think of you, you'll get enough money to drain that pond and build your building." Burr smiled at Sleeper. "Did you know you have ducks?"

Sleeper pointed to the door. "Out. Before I throw you out."

Burr was sure Sleeper could pick him up with one arm and toss him out, but he was sure he wouldn't. The two of them had been going at this for the better part of seven years. Helen Lockwood was fighting with Sleeper long before that.

Dale Sleeper, a Cadillac native, was a career Park Service employee. He had been appointed park superintendent, the crowning achievement in his long, undistinguished career, except he couldn't quite get the park up and running. In his heart of hearts, he believed that the Sleeping Bear Dunes National Lakeshore was his manifest destiny. Helen Lockwood had been sure it wasn't and had hired Burr to make it so. Sleeper hated Burr.

Burr thought he'd been doing pretty well until Helen's body was found.

Sleeper glared at Burr, who made a point of smiling back at him. Finally, Sleeper walked back to his Lazy Boy, sat down, then got right back up. He walked to the far end of the trailer and sat in the swivel chair behind his desk. It creaked under his weight.

"I don't have to talk to you, Lafayette."

"That's right, but if you help me, you just might get your beloved park put together faster."

"How so?" Sleeper furrowed his oversized brow.

Burr walked the length of the trailer. He found a folding chair leaning against the wall and sat down facing the burly park superintendent. "As long as Tommy is being tried for murder, your condemnation case is on hold. There's no provision in the partnership agreement for a missing partner, so Judge Cooper ordered a stay."

"Helen's been found and now Tommy gets her vote."

*Sleeper has read the pleadings. Good for him.*

Burr smiled at Sleeper again. "But now there's another stay. As long as Tommy is on trial for murder, he can't have Helen's vote. If he's acquitted, he gets her vote."

"Tommy doesn't want to sell. He loves those damned cherries," Sleeper said.

"Dale, Dale, Dale," Burr said. "Tommy did call you, didn't he?"

"I don't have to talk to you about this."

"The only way he gets Helen's vote is if he's acquitted."

"So what if he's acquitted … and he votes to keep on fighting?"

"That's the risk you have to take. If he's convicted, then Lauren and Karen have a draw, and there's going to be a long fight to break the tie. It could go on for years. And the rest of the property you want will be tied up until it's decided."

Sleeper leaned toward Burr. "I don't have to have that damned farm to finish the park."

Burr sat back in his chair. It started to fold up on him. Burr grabbed the seat and held on for dear life.

Sleeper grinned at him. "You got the chair that folds when you least suspect it to."

Burr ignored the grand poohbah of the Park Service. "Oh, but you do need the farm, Dale. Your master plan calls for all the land on both sides of Port Oneida Road from M-22 to Pyramid Point and the old dock at the end of Point Oneida Road. And it's not worth a tinker's damn without the farm." Burr paused. "Is it?"

Sleeper swiveled around in his chair and looked out the window, his back to Burr. "I don't have to talk to you. I shouldn't be talking to you and you shouldn't be here. I'm going to call Powers and have you cited for contempt. Judge Cooper will throw you off the case." Sleeper stood and looked out the window at the hole where the headquarters building was supposed to be.

Burr studied the back of Sleeper's head. The ranger had all his hair. Burr felt around the back of his own head for the thin spot. "Damn it all."

"What's that?" Sleeper said.

"Nothing," Burr said. "Dale, I'm here about the murder case. That's the only reason I'm here."

"What about the farm?"

"We'll deal with that later. No promises."

Sleeper turned back to Burr. "What do you want?"

"All I want are a few suspects."

"Suspects?"

"Who do you think might have wanted you to get the farm so badly that they might have murdered Helen?"

"Other than Tommy?"

Burr walked over and stood beside Sleeper. "Imagine what the new headquarters building will look like. And where your office will be."

"All you have to do is look at the other land acquisition files."

"Dale, I want to know what you think."

Sleeper sat back down. He put his hands behind his head and rocked back and forth. Finally, "You know what, Lafayette? You are one clever son-of-a-bitch."

\* \* \*

Burr poured the last of the Sauvignon Blanc into Maggie's glass and stuck the dead soldier upside down in the ice bucket. She drank some of the wine and set her glass down. Burr saw a smudge of rose-colored lipstick on her glass. She pushed her chair back and stood.

"Shall we?"

"Shall we?" Burr said.

"The salad bar."

Burr shook his head.

"Come on."

Burr shook his head again.

Maggie sat. "You must."

"We're at a fine restaurant, a lovely place. The Bluebird is known all over this part of the state, and the whitefish is spectacular. But I am not going to a salad bar. I hate salad bars. I didn't come here to make my own salad."

"You are impossible." She finished her wine, got up and walked to the salad bar by herself.

Burr looked at the lipstick on her wine glass again, then at Maggie at the salad bar. She looked back at him and stuck her tongue out.

The winsome Maggie Winston, late thirties, tall, willowy, blond and glasses with big black frames and lenses that were a little too thick to suit her. Actually, Margaret Winston, PhD, professor of ornithology at the University of Michigan, fly fisher and grouse hunter. Burr was quite taken with her. She was easy on the eye, but he'd met his match, and he knew it. She knew it, too.

She came back with two plates and set one in front of him. She sat before he could get up and pull her chair out. She put her napkin on her lap. "Eat your salad. It's just what you like."

"I don't like salad bars."

"This isn't a salad bar. This is a salad I made you."

He started to say something but thought better of it. He ate his salad.

Their waitress, a college-age woman, brought over a second bottle of Kim Crawford, Burr's favorite summer white wine, from New Zeeland but not expensive. Crisp and grapefruity. The silhouette on the bottle reminded him of Maggie. She poured them each a glass, then, "Are you ready to order?"

"We'll each have the sautéed whitefish," Burr said.

The waitress nodded. "I see you've helped yourself to the salad bar."

Burr didn't say anything.

"May I get you anything else?"

"Could we please have more of your sticky buns," Maggie said.

"I'm sorry but we only serve one order per table."

Maggie reached into her purse and handed the waitress a twenty.

"Of course."

The Bluebird, on the north side of the Leland River, just upstream from M-22, looked out on the lazy, green river drifting to the dam, then Fishtown and Lake Michigan. Burr had the best table in the house, next to the windows, a garden overflowing with daisies, black-eyed Susans just beyond the windows. Michigan lilies, their orange flowers drooping, grew next to the river.

The waitress delivered the sticky buns. Maggie smeared hers in butter. "Burr, this is spectacular. Thank you so much."

"I wanted to make it special."

This was their anniversary, of sorts. The anniversary of a wild night that had begun at Tapawingo, near Charlevoix, Northern Michigan's finest and most expensive restaurant. They had been an item ever since, and Maggie, who had no earthly business falling in love with Burr or anyone like him, had, and she was ready for the next step, which Burr wasn't. It wasn't that he didn't love her, but he'd already ruined one marriage that he still hadn't finished paying for.

\* \* \*

After dinner, they walked hand-in-hand toward the big lake. They stopped on the M-22 bridge at the three-foot dam below them, which kept the water level in Lake Leelanau just so and kept the cottagers' cottages and their beaches just so and oh, so pricy. Burr looked down the river at Fishtown and Lake Michigan, the sun just above the horizon casting an orange glow on the blue water. What was left of the dying wind brushed against their faces.

*How could there possibly have been a murder here?*

They crossed the bridge, walked into the hotel and took the stairs to their second-floor room at Falling Waters, Leland's tony hotel. Burr preferred the Riverside Inn, but bathrooms down the hall would never do tonight.

Burr joined Maggie on the balcony of their room. She leaned over the railing and looked at the river, not quite so lazy as it poured over the dam. She had on a short, sleeveless sapphire dress, tucked at the waist, strappy wedge sandals and dangly silver earrings. Burr put his hands around her waist. She turned and looked at him with her sky-blue eyes. Eyes the same color as his. She kissed him full on the lips, then turned back to the river and leaned over the balcony again.

"This is so lovely."

*It is as long as the Lafayette and Wertheim credit card holds out.*

"I love the sound of the water."

"I do, too." Burr thought it sounded like a ringing in his ears.

Maggie leaned farther over the railing. "Burr…"

"Yes."

"Let's do it here."

"Do what?"

"Make love."

He took her by the hand.

"No. Here."

"Here? Someone will see us."

"I hope so."

"I can't do it here."

She turned around and put her hand on him. She unzipped his pants and got down on her knees.

"Maggie."

"It's almost dark," she said, mumbling. Burr put his hands on her shoulders, doing his best to give them as much privacy as he could, which wasn't much. She stood and bent over the railing again. She lifted up the back of her dress and pulled her black satin panties to the side. "Now. Right now." She backed up against him.

* * *

Burr rode shotgun in Maggie's black Ford Explorer. He had the window down, and the wind in his face, just like Zeke does, but Zeke was in the care of the dock boy at the marina along with Finn, Maggie's English Setter.

After breakfast at the Early Bird, an omelet with toast from homemade bread sliced as thick as a filet mignon, she drove south on M-22, what other road would she take, then left on M-109 toward the lake. He had no idea where they were going.

She turned on a freshly paved blacktop, stopped at a booth next to a toll gate and paid the ranger on duty. He opened the gate and in they went.

"Do you know where we are?"

"No."

"My point exactly."

Burr cocked his head, just like Zeke.

Maggie drove through a hardwood forest, the woods so thick the canopy covered the road. They drove through a covered bridge.

"Beautiful, isn't it."

Burr nodded.

"Do you know where we are now?" She looked at him with her sky-blue eyes, full of daggers.

Burr had a sinking feeling.

"You're fighting to keep Helen's farm out of the park, but you don't even know what the park is."

"That's not true."

She drove up a steep hill and pulled off the road where it overlooked Glen Lake, woods on one side of them, scrub and sand plains below them. She drove on, muttering. They stopped at another turnout. Maggie walked out on a wooden platform built on twenty-foot pilings hanging over the dunes, Lake Michigan hundreds of feet below them. The wind blew from the southwest, a soft summer breeze that made catspaws on the lake. Burr followed her.

"There's the Manitous," she said, pointing to the two low-slung islands rising out of the lake off to the north. That's Sleeping Bear Bay and there's Pyramid Point, where Port Oneida Trail ends." She looked at Burr. "Now do you know where we are?"

Burr nodded.

"This is probably the most beautiful place in the whole state."

She started back to the Explorer. Burr watched her ponytail swing back and forth in time with her hips. He admired her long, lanky legs disappearing into her thigh-length blue jean skirt. He followed her back, dutifully.

Off they went, slowly, through the maple and beech trees, the meadows, marsh and dunes. She looked over at him. "It's so beautiful here, and you're fighting over it."

"I'm not fighting this."

"It's all part of the park." She drove a little further, pulled over again and walked out on another dune platform, this one almost five hundred feet above Lake Michigan. Burr followed again, like a puppy. He stood behind Maggie. She leaned over the railing.

"Don't even think about it," she said.

*At least we're not having the "our relationship" talk.*

Maggie pointed off to the north. "There's Sleeping Bear dune. Where the mother bear is sleeping. The wind and water have eroded her away, but if you use your imagination, you can still see her." She looked at Burr. "I'm sure you knew that."

"This is beautiful."

"Then why are you fighting so hard?"

"Because the government is heavy-handed."

"Is that it?"

"Every client deserves representation."

"It's the money, isn't it?"

*There is that.*

"And you like to fight."

*That, too.*

"This is Pierce Stocking Trail. You must know that by now. It was named after the logger who built the road. He thought it was so beautiful, it needed to be protected."

Burr put his hands in his pockets. "Actually, he charged his own toll and fought with the government over buying it."

"You're hopeless." She marched back to her Explorer, her tennis shoes slapping on the wood.

# CHAPTER ELEVEN

Maggie dropped Burr off at his floating headquarters, picked up Finn and left in a bit of a huff. Burr had done his best to make things right, but he thought he was doing the right thing. And he needed the money.

Burr started south on M-22, along Grand Traverse Bay to Traverse City, where the fabled road ended. An hour later, he walked up the sidewalk to what had to be the ugliest building he had ever seen. A four-story, perfectly square, dirty red block building. It had room-size windows that looked like so many peering eyes and an oversized cupola that looked like the head of the beast. Burr thought it an archetype of a building from the Grotesque Revival period. It was the Grand Traverse County Courthouse, which also served as the circuit courts for Leelanau and Antrim counties, which were too small to have their own circuit courts.

Burr found the stairs and climbed to the third floor. The receptionist ushered him into the judge's chambers. There was an oriental area rug on the hardwood floor, floor-to-ceiling curtains, and overstuffed furniture. Floor and table lamps instead of the fluorescent overhead lights, which were turned off. A single rose in a bud vase perched on the corner of the judge's desk.

Peter Brooks was sitting across from Judge Mary Fisher, laughing at something she said. The judge looked down at her watch, then up at Burr. "So nice to see you."

Burr sat down next to Brooks.

Judge Mary Fisher, daughter of Jack Fisher, the namesake at Burr's former law firm, had been a circuit judge for Grand Traverse, Leelanau, and Antrim counties for fifteen years. She was three years younger than Burr and had never quite forgiven him for not marrying her. Neither had her father.

*She'd never have let me name a son after my dog, and she'd have killed me over Suzanne, if her father didn't kill me first.*

"Burr, are you with us?" the judge said.

"Quite," Burr said, who wasn't.

Judge Fisher opened the file in front of her. She brushed a stray blond hair out of her eyes and tucked it behind her ear. She had a long, thin face, a tan from the Grand Traverse Bay summer, hair pulled back with a clip, and pearl earrings against a black A-line dress and crimson jacket. A pretty woman. Judge-like enough, but barely.

Judge Fisher studied the file. "I see you've decided to waive the preliminary exam."

"That's right, Mary."

She looked up at him.

"Judge," he said. Burr shifted in his chair.

"Why would you do that?"

"I can't possibly see how my client won't be formally charged with murder."

"That's right, Your Honor," Brooks said. He ran his hands through his slicked back hair.

"I'd like to hear it from Burr," the judge said.

"Your Honor, the prosecutor says he has the murder weapon, which he says belongs to my client. He says he has witnesses who saw him board the ferry on the day Helen went missing. And he says my client killed his wife because he wanted to sell Port Oneida Orchards and she didn't. Respectfully, Your Honor, would you dismiss the charges based on all that?"

"Lafayette really isn't a criminal lawyer," Brooks said. "The prosecution will allow him to withdraw his motion."

Burr ran his thumb and forefinger along the crease in his slacks, just like Jacob – except it was a bit difficult to find the crease in his slacks after they had been in a duffel bag on a boat. "My motion stands."

Judge Fisher put her lips together like she was smoothing out her lipstick. Burr couldn't take his eyes off her. She looked at him and smiled. "Suit yourself." She closed the folder.

"There is one other thing, Your Honor," Brooks said.

"Yes?"

"There is a criminal complaint sworn out against Mr. Lafayette. I hardly think it appropriate that he serve as an officer of this court with that pending."

"Really?" Judge Fisher said.

"Nonsense, " Burr said.

"The prosecution asks that counsel for the defense be disqualified pending resolution of the criminal proceeding."

Burr put his hands on his knees and turned to Brooks. "Alimony isn't a criminal matter," Burr said.

"It's child support," Brooks said.

Burr stood and looked down at Brooks. "I've never been a day late on child support."

Brooks stood, eye to eye with Burr. "That's not what your wife's lawyer says."

"He's just stirring things up."

"Have you posted bond?" Brooks said.

"Boys," the judge said, "that's quite enough testosterone. Peter, please leave us. Burr and I are going to have a little talk."

"Yes, Your Honor," Brooks said. "Lafayette, I'll file a motion to get you thrown out if I have to."

"You do that," Burr said.

"Stop it, both of you. Mr. Brooks, you are excused." Brooks nodded and left.

"Burr, please sit down."

Burr sat. He looked at his slacks and searched for a crease on the other leg.

"I think you had that suit when you were at Fisher and Allen."

"I don't remember," Burr said, who did.

*This suit is just about as worn out as I am.*

"What have you gotten yourself into this time?"

Burr looked up at her. "Which time?"

She laughed. "With Grace."

"Maury is trying to get more money out of me."

"Maury Litzenburger." She nodded. "Are you behind?"

"Not on my child support."

"Alimony."

"That's a civil matter."

"How far behind?"

Burr counted on the fingers of his left hand. Then he started on his right.

"Never mind," the judge said. "Please take care of it so I don't have to deal with Petey."

Burr nodded at her. He stood to go. She pointed at his chair. Burr sat back down.

"I hope you know what you're doing. Peter Brooks is a smart man."

"Judge?"

"Mary." She pushed the same stray hair behind her ear again. "It's possible that Petey won't be able to get all his witnesses here for the trial, especially if it's in the winter. Then you might just have him."

"That's not it."

"Of course that's it. And he knows it."

"There's nothing to be gained by having a preliminary exam, and I don't want bad press to spoil the jury pool."

"Peter's right, you know. You've won a few, but you're really not a criminal lawyer."

"I'll take my chances."

Mary Fisher shook her head. "Burr, Burr, Burr. Things could have been so different."

Burr didn't say anything.

"But really ... things wouldn't have been any different. You're still who you are."

\* \* \*

Back at the Jeep, Zeke was not happy to see Burr, for about ten seconds. Then all was forgiven. Burr thought better of changing out of his suit and tie in the parking lot of the courthouse and headed around the bay to the state park. He changed his clothes in the community bathhouse and took Zeke to the beach. The aging lab found a stick right away. Burr threw it in the lake for him so many times he thought his arm was going to fall off. "Zeke, if only the affairs of man, including my own, could be so straightforward."

Zeke sprawled in the back seat all the way back to Northport, snoring softly. Burr rolled down the window and smelled the crisp lake breeze, sand, and wet dog all the way there.

\* \* \*

Burr dodged potholes on the gravel driveway, past picked cherry trees on each side, and two more orchards toward the lake from Port Oneida Orchards. About halfway up the driveway, an old red tractor came at him full tilt. Burr slammed on the brakes. Zeke flew off the seat beside him and landed on the floor. The tractor skidded to a stop just before it crashed into him. The driver waved his arms from side to side at Burr. He had on a baseball hat that might have once been orange. Burr thought he was in his seventies and hadn't shaved in at least a week.

"Zeke, it looks like there really is an Old MacDonald, and I don't think he's too happy that we're at his farm." Zeke climbed back on the seat and barked at the farmer with the flailing arms. Burr got out of the Jeep and walked up to the tractor.

"You get out of here. This is private property."

"Of course it is, Mr. MacDonald. I'm sorry to trouble you, but I wonder if I might ask you a few questions."

"No. Get out."

*If this is what all of the people on Dale Sleeper's list are like, I'm really in for it.*

Burr kicked at the dirt with his shoe. "Mr. MacDonald, my name is Burr Lafayette. I represent…"

MacDonald cut him off. "I know who you are and what you're doing."

"Mr. MacDonald…"

The cherry farmer climbed down from the trailer and stood eye-to-eye with Burr. He put his hands on his hips or, rather, his left hand and his right wrist. His right hand was missing.

"Sliced clean off by the belt drive on the shaker."

"I'm sorry, Mr. MacDonald."

"Don't matter. I got another one." He pointed back down the driveway with his good hand.

"I'm trying to find out who might have wanted Helen Lockwood dead."

MacDonald took off his hat and wiped his forehead with his stub wrist. "Me and just about everybody else on the border of this damned park."

"Where were you when Helen was killed?"

"You think I did it? I would've but I hate boats."

"Were you with anyone when she was killed?"

"Three barn cats and …" a German shepherd came running, full speed. "…and Jerry here." The dog ran right at Burr. Zeke barked from the Jeep.

"Jerry, no." The dog stopped about a foot from Burr and sat. Old MacDonald looked at Burr. "You're OK. He don't bite." MacDonald smiled at Burr. "Unless I tell him to."

"That's comforting."

"I like a dog that minds," MacDonald said. "Tommy Lockwood farms circles around me. So did Helen's father and her grandfather. Their dirt's better. My best chance is to sell out to the government. Just like everybody else, except some of them damn cottagers have more money than brains. I might have killed her if I had the chance, but not on a boat. I'd a used a rifle in deer season."

"Was anyone here with you?"

"Nope." MacDonald looked down at Jerry. "Jerry's a good dog, but I'm not sure how much longer he can sit still." MacDonald scratched the German shepherd behind his ear.

"It would be easier if you had an alibi," Burr said.

"It would be a helluva lot easier if you got the hell out of here, but I'll tell you who to look at." He pointed toward Port Oneida Orchards. "Tommy's the one. You need to look at that."

"Mr. MacDonald…"

"That's it."

"Why would…"

"I said that's it." MacDonald climbed back on his tractor. Burr reached up to stop him.

"Jerry, go."

The dog jumped to his feet and charged Burr. The dog was up to him before he could get away. He put his snout on Burr's hand – and licked it. MacDonald started up the tractor, turned around and headed back up the driveway.

"That dog never bit no one. Come on, Jerry, let's go." The dog trotted after the tractor.

Burr had no sooner gotten into the Jeep when a blue Impala about the same vintage as the tractor bounced and bumped up the driveway, skidding to a stop a foot from his trailer hitch. An older woman hustled out and trotted up to the Jeep. Burr rolled down his window.

"You must be Mrs. MacDonald."

"None other," said an equally seventyish woman. "Did that old goat get you with Jerry about to bite your head off?"

Burr nodded.

"That's going to backfire on him one of these days."

"No harm done. Mrs. MacDonald…"

"Call me, Ruth."

*Ruth it is.*

Burr told her who he was and why he was there.

Mrs. MacDonald leaned on the Jeep. "Tommy loved Helen like, like I don't know what. He loved her. He followed her around like a puppy dog. He'd no sooner kill her than he'd chop his hand off, which is what that old coot of mine did. Hasn't been the same since."

*I can believe that.*

"Now let me tell you about them Sisters of Outrage."

"Sisters of Outrage?"

"Helen and her sisters."

*Ruth may be loonier that her husband.*

"Them three girls are as different as night and day, but they all got one thing in common."

Burr stuck his elbow out of the window to rest his arm on the door.

"They all want what they want, and they all go about gettin' it in their own way."

"Mrs. MacDonald…"

"Ruth." She patted Burr's elbow. "Don't let that Karen fool you with her quiet ways. She's got an iron will, that one. They kick and they scream, and they just stay at it. You oughta hear Lauren lay into the cable company."

*Sisters of Outrage. That's a new one.*

Burr smiled at Old MacDonald's wife. "Ruth, do you have any idea who might have killed Helen?"

"And one more thing. They might act all lovey-dovey about each other, but they're sisters just the same."

"I beg your pardon."

"It's called pecking order. And not all of the hens like it." She turned to go, then turned back to Burr. "Me and Hal had all the reason in the world to get rid of Helen. This farm wasn't worth much before the government wanted to make a park out of it. Then it was. Now it's not. We can't do a thing with it until this mess with Helen and Tommy is settled. Who'd buy it?" She clapped her hands together. Burr jumped. "Sorry. We had all the reason in the world to kill her."

"Where were you when Helen went to South Manitou?" Burr said, hoping against hope.

"With Hal."

"He said…"

"He said three barn cats and Jerry."

* * *

Burr got back on M-22 and turned south. Ten miles down the road, M-22 ran downhill to Lake Michigan. He turned toward the lake and into Glen Haven. He passed five or six buildings, then the road ended at the lake. "Zeke, I could have driven right in." He turned around and pulled into Land's End Cabins. Six peeling white cabins with a fresh coat of blue trim. A matching house with a sign that said *Office* stood at the east end of the cabins. "They look like a hen and her chicks." Zeke looked longingly out at the lake, hoping that another game of fetch was next. Burr climbed out of the Jeep and walked into the office.

A woman with henna colored hair and glasses that hung on a chain around her neck stood behind the check-in counter. She picked up a nearly finished cigarette from an ashtray and took a long drag. Her lips puckered around the cigarette. She blew the smoke out of her nose and stubbed out the cigarette in the ashtray. A haze hung over the office like fog hanging over a lake.

*If this place had a smoke detector, it would have gone off by now.*

"Need a room?" the woman said, hopefully. "Only one left."

"Just a few questions."

"Questions are for Al." She lit another cigarette.

"Al?"

"I told him not to buy this place. He quit a great job in Warren for this dump. Tool and die. Sold our house, took our savings and bought this place. Said it would be a goldmine as soon as he fixed it up. It's OK in the summer, but in February … well, February … the only one ever shows up is the snowplow. Al don't get around like he used to, but he drives in to Traverse and works at a hardware. Me, I'm a cashier at the Frankfort IGA. Some retirement."

"I suppose you want to sell to the Park Service."

"Are you kidding? I begged that stuffed shirt Dale Sleeper." She took another long drag, then blew it out.

"Why haven't they bought it?"

"Says he's not ready. They're going to make this a historical place, fishing village and lifesaving station, like it used to be." She tapped her ash. "A lifesaving station, can you believe it? Course the damn road ends right down there." She nodded with her head. "You could drive right in the damn lake. In the winter, you could drive the ice all the way to Milwaukee. As far as I'm concerned, this is the end of the world." Then she jerked a thumb toward Point Oneida Road. "He says they got to finish up the road."

"Why is that?"

"They got to buy that big orchard first. Just why do you want to know?"

"I represent Tommy Lockwood."

"You just tell Mr. Tommy Lockwood and his beautiful wife to come down here and see Barb and Al Wyzinski. They can buy this place and I'll be on my way back to Warren."

"Helen Lockwood is dead."

"Oh." Barb Wyzinski stubbed out her cigarette and lit another one.

*I may be ill.*

The reluctant cabin keeper turned around and opened a door behind her. Burr heard Ernie Harwell say something to George Kell. "Al, come on out here a minute."

"Trammel's batting."

"Damn him and those Tigers. Can't win a game this year."

A half cigarette later, Al Wyzinski shuffled out with his cane.

\* \* \*

Burr retreated to Zeke and the Jeep. He drove to the end of the road, which really did end at the lake, and let Zeke out. Burr took off his shoes and walked to the beach. Zeke showed up with a piece of driftwood the size of a baseball bat. "Zeke, old pal, go find something smaller." Burr took the stick and sent Zeke off. He took Sleeper's list out of his pocket and studied it. "I wonder if Sleeper made up this list out of thin air. He must think I'm a fool. Maybe I am."

Zeke came back, this time with a baton-size stick. Burr threw it in the water and looked out at the lake, waves running onto the shore, cheerful little waves, one after the other, all in a row. He looked down the beach to the south, to miles and miles of beach, dunes, woods. The same to the north. Lake Michigan, as far as he could see, the lighthouse at Manitou Shoals, South Manitou and North Manitou. He threw the stick for Zeke again. And again. And again. "It's all out there. Whatever happened, it happened out there." Burr threw the stick one last time. "It's so beautiful, but was it worth killing for?" Burr scrunched his toes in the sand. "Somebody thought it was."

\* \* \*

Burr retrieved Zeke from retrieving, and the two pals set off, back the way they came. A mile past Port Oneida Orchards, Burr turned toward the lake again. They passed fruit trees, row after row, then vines wrapped around wire fences. Burr turned in at the sign marked *Sleeping Bear Vineyards*.

"Zeke, I may at least get a glass of wine out of this."

Burr parked in front of a low-slung, planked building that said "*Tasting Room*." He got out of the car. "Here goes nothing."

Burr walked into the Sleeping Bear Winery tasting room, a long bar at the back of the room. Half a dozen high-top tables. Windows, opened up to the day, all around. Burr sat at the bar and a sunburned forty-something man with thinning blond hair appeared from the back. "A tasting?" Burr bit his cheek.

"Of course."

The sunburned man reached down below the bar, then raised his arms with two bottles of wine in each hand. He put four wine glasses in front of Burr and poured two fingers of white wine in one of them.

"Try this."

Burr stuck his hand out. "Burr Lafayette."

The man grabbed Burr's hand. "Joey Maguire. It's a medium Riesling. Try it."

Burr swirled his glass, then sipped. It was sweet. Sickeningly so.

*This is quite possibly the worst wine I've ever had.*

Burr swirled his glass again and took another sip. "Very nice. Hints of apricot."

"Try this." Joey poured another white. "It's a Sauvignon Blanc."

Burr tipped his glass.

*This tastes like a wet tennis shoe.*

Another swirl. Another sip. "Grapefruit."

"You have a sophisticated palate."

"Joey…"

"This is my estate Chardonnay." He poured three fingers in Burr's glass.

"That's a generous pour."

"Wednesdays are slow, even in August."

Burr took as big a swallow as he dared.

*This is the best one so far. Wet grass clippings.*

"Look, Joey, I don't want to take advantage of your hospitality, but I'm really here on a most urgent matter."

Maguire reached under the bar. Burr looked at his shiny, red, bald pate. He popped up with a bottle of red and another glass. He uncorked the bottle and poured Burr a much too generous pour. "What could possibly be so urgent?"

"I'm here about Helen Lockwood's murder."

"Terrible business." The winemaker pushed Burr's glass closer to him. "Drink up."

Burr took a swallow.

*This is the worst yet. Sour grape juice with hints of rancid cranberry.*

Burr set his glass down. "Traditional hints of cherry and vanilla with a hint of coffee."

"You're too kind." Maguire filled Burr's glass.

"Joey, my dog is outside in my Jeep, and it's getting hot. Would you mind if I brought him in?"

"Bring him in."

Burr quite liked the balding winemaker's style but not his wine. Zeke, delighted to be invited anywhere, curled up under Burr's bar stool.

"Where were we?" Maguire said.

"Helen Lockwood's murder."

"And?"

"Well." Burr said, "I was wondering if you killed her."

Joey rubbed an eyebrow. "Actually, yes. I did kill her. Again and again. A gun was too good for her. I stabbed her with a stiletto. Then I strangled her with a garotte. Just to make sure she was really dead, I caved her head in with a hammer. Just to make sure."

Burr looked down at Zeke, who was looking at Joey, then he looked back at Joey. "I beg your pardon?"

Maguire poured the rest of Burr's wine down the sink "We both know this is possibly the most awful wine anyone ever made." He smiled a forlorn smile at Burr. "This is the 45th parallel, and the temperature is right, but the soil is too fertile and there's too much rain. It's just damn hard to make a decent red wine here." Maguire reached under the bar and brought up two more glasses and another bottle of red, which he uncorked. "Let's let this breathe for a minute or two."

*I can't possibly drink any more of his wine.*

"I'm a dentist. Was a dentist. From Grand Rapids. My only chance is to sell this disaster of a winery to another sucker or have the Park Service buy it." Joey walked over to the west side of the building and looked out the window. "What a view." He came back and poured them two big glasses of a garnet-colored wine.

Burr gritted his teeth.

"Don't worry. This is a Russian River Cab. From Sonoma."

Burr drank up. It wasn't open yet, but it actually tasted like wine.

Joey swirled the wine in his glass and took a sip. "Not quite open but so much better than the grass clippings I make." The frank winemaker swirled and drank. "This place does OK when I get people in here who don't know anything about wine. Which is most of them."

Burr knew that whatever questioning skills he had, had fallen by the wayside three fingers ago. "So, you didn't murder Helen Lockwood."

"I don't have the nerve."

Maguire wouldn't let him leave until they walked his vineyard, twenty acres under vine and forty acres of hardwood. Burr then bid his host adieu, fairly certain Maguire wasn't a murderer and absolutely convinced he was a terrible winemaker.

\* \* \*

Burr and Zeke drove back to the marina in Northport. Once aboard *Spindrift*, Burr pried up one of the floorboards and took out a bottle of Oregon Pinot

Noir. While it aired, he lit the midships alcohol stove and dumped in a can of Bush's Original Baked Beans. He sliced two Koegel's Frankfurters into the beans, and sliced two more into Zeke's dry food. He poured himself a glass of the Pinot and dished himself a generous helping of beans and franks. "Zeke, anyone who says he doesn't like baked beans is lying." He drank the Pinot. "As far as that goes, they're all lying around here. Every single one of them."

# CHAPTER TWELVE

Burr sat across from Tommy at the kitchen table at Morningside. He unfolded the list Sleeper had given him and handed it to Tommy. The cherry farmer looked at it, crumpled it up and threw it in the wastebasket.

"And?" Burr said.

"There's no one on that list that would've killed Helen."

"How do you know?"

"I know everyone on that list, and none of them are capable of murder."

"You might be surprised what people will do for money." Burr fished Sleeper's list out of the trash. I saw the MacDonalds, the Wyszinskis and Joey Maguire yesterday.

"Did he make you taste his wine?"

Burr nodded.

"He should have left that ground in cherries."

Burr nodded again.

Tommy stood up and walked over to the window, still framed by Helen's string of Christmas lights. "If there's anyone around here that could have killed Helen, it's Sleeper."

"Sleeper?"

"That damned park is all he cares about."

"He's a civil servant."

Burr walked over to the window and stood next to Tommy. The orchardist pointed to a cherry tree at the edge of the orchard. "Look over there. Those are palm warblers. They're down from Canada already. They're here for the bugs. The farm will be full of all kinds of warblers in a month. Then they'll head south. All the way to South America." Tommy looked at Burr. "Helen loved it when the warblers came through."

*If he did kill her, he's putting on a good show.*

Burr walked back to the kitchen table and looked at his list from the trash. *This list might not be any good, but it's all I've got.*

"How could it have gotten this far?" Tommy said, still looking out the window.

"It happened because Helen was shot with your pistol. You were seen on the ferry, and you talked to Sleeper about selling him the farm. Brooks is alleging that you wanted her declared dead so you could sell the farm."

Tommy looked at Burr. "That's not how it was."

"Do you want to sell the farm?"

"It's not the same without Helen."

"I know it's not. I'm sorry, but it looks bad. Calling Sleeper. It would have been better if you'd called me instead. I could have handled it."

Tommy turned around and looked at Burr with his big brown eyes. "I probably should have. I didn't think about it at the time. I just wanted out."

"And there's no one who can say they saw you fishing."

Tommy shook his head. His black hair flopped back and forth. "Please help me. I didn't kill Helen. I loved her."

"I'm trying to help, but you have to tell me the truth."

"I am. I swear I am."

*That's what they all say.*

* * *

The next morning Burr and Zeke drove back to Leland. He thought he'd try to find out how much Brooks' witnesses really remembered about seeing Tommy on the ferry. They parked next to where the ferry docked. Except the ferry wasn't there. *Maybe I should get a schedule.* They waited and waited. And waited. Zeke napped. "This is a fine mess." Zeke looked up from his nap. "If I can bill Tommy by the hour, we can sit here all day. Of course, it doesn't matter how much I bill him if he doesn't pay me. And if I get fired again, none of this matters." Zeke put his head back down and resumed his nap. Burr waited.

At last, the ferry cruised up the river. Burr got out of the Jeep and walked over to the dock. He looked down at the water, drifting slowly to the big lake, in no hurry to get anywhere. He smelled the diesel from the ferry mixed in with the smell of the fish house. He waited until the passengers disembarked and their gear was offloaded. Then he walked up to the captain.

"Captain Sutherland, Burr Lafayette. We met on the island about a month ago." Burr stuck his hand out, but the ferry captain didn't shake it.

"I remember you."

Burr took a picture of Tommy out of his pocket and showed it to Sutherland. "Is this him?"

"I know who Tommy Lockwood is."

"Captain, do you remember Tommy Lockwood riding over on the ferry a little over a year ago?"

"Yep."

"Do you remember about when last year?"

The ferry captain took off his hat and rubbed his forehead. "Nope."

"Why is that?"

"I make two runs a day, seven days a week. Except for time off. There's no way I could remember when."

*That's something. Not much, but something.*

"Captain Sutherland, may I ask where you live in the winter?"

"Not here. It's too damn cold. I run a dive boat in Key West."

"That's a long way from here."

"You can't hardly get there from here." The captain put his hat back on and climbed back aboard.

Burr found the two deckhands standing next to a pile of backpacks, tents and coolers. It turned out they were boyfriend and girlfriend and were here for summer jobs. They said they went to the University of Alabama, and they both remembered Tommy.

*They'll never come back for the trial.*

Burr walked over to the ticket office. He showed the picture of Tommy to the woman behind the counter, a very short woman with a very long braid wound around the back of her head. He asked if she remembered selling Tommy a ferry ticket.

She looked at the picture. She said her name was Connie Gardener and, yes, she did remember selling him a ticket.

"How do you know?"

She looked up at Burr. "I see 'em all day, but I just don't forget. I just don't forget a face. The detective showed me a picture, too. Just like you. I seen you before, too. You bought a ticket. About a month ago. On the fifteenth, right?"

Burr nodded at her. "How do you know when it was?"

"Who are you anyway?"

"I represent Thomas Lockwood."

"I'd say you got your work cut out for you."

"How can you possibly remember the day?"

"I remember you asking me why I was smiling. It was my birthday. That's why." She smiled at him.

"Would you mind if I asked you where you live?"

She pointed toward Leland. "Right up there behind the Bluebird."

"Thank you. I do have my work cut out for me."

\* \* \*

Burr put the Jeep in park and turned off the engine. It was three o'clock exactly. Punctuality wasn't his strong suit, but when it came to court and Zeke-the-Boy, he did his best to be on time. He had had enough of both Tommy and Helen Lockwood at least until Monday. It was Friday afternoon and the weekend was for the two Zekes.

At 3:15 he was still waiting. "Zeke, this isn't like Grace." She wouldn't let him in the house he still made payments on, not that he blamed her, but she always came right out with Zeke. Except for today. He thought he'd call her on his car phone, but after what happened with Eve, he thought better of it.

At 3:30, a black Benz pulled up beside him in the driveway.

"Nuts," he said.

Out popped Maury Litzenburger, the nastiest, sleaziest but not the smartest divorce lawyer in all of Detroit. Burr rolled down his window but didn't say anything.

Litzenburger was stocky and all of five-six. He had a broad nose and big black glasses that were too big for him. What really set him apart, though, were his shirts. Every time Burr saw him, Maury had on a white pinpoint oxford that was so white it hurt Burr's eyes.

Litzenburger stuck his hand through the open window.

"Just a minute, Maury." Burr reached into the glovebox for his sunglasses. He shook Litzenburger's hand.

"Very funny."

"Where's Zeke?"

"Zeke is inside with Grace."

"Go get him."

"Your visitation has been suspended pending the outcome of the criminal case."

Burr threw the door open and knocked Litzenburger down.

Litzenburger sat in the driveway. "I am going to add assault to the complaint."

"Go get Zeke."

Litzenburger straightened his tie, stood up and brushed off the seat of his pants. "I will do nothing of the sort."

"Maury, we all know you're a slimeball. Go get Zeke before I throw you through the garage door." Burr got out of the Jeep. Litzenburger took refuge on the far side of his Benz. He shook his head no.

"Maury, we both know your criminal complaint is a sham. Being late on alimony isn't a crime."

"The line between child support and alimony can be a blurry one."

When Burr started around the Benz, Litzenburger retreated to the other side. "Maybe I have been a little overzealous."

Burr stopped.

"But look here, Burr, you're six months behind on your alimony and Grace has bills to pay."

Burr stuck his hands in his pockets. "I'm making all the child support payments and I'm still making the payments on this house."

"But not your alimony."

"I made that deal when I was still at Fisher and Allen."

"You never should have left."

"I don't have that kind of money right now and Grace knows it."

"She wants the deal you made."

"We need a new deal."

Maury moved a bit closer, now eye-to-eye with Burr. "You need to get a real job."

Burr thought that if he moved quickly, he could grab Litzenburger around the neck and strangle him. He started toward the divorce lawyer, who ran back to the other side of his car.

"Here's what I can do," Maury said. "Five months alimony and I drop the criminal complaint. We'll see about the custody when you're all caught up."

Burr was in a bad way and Litzenburger knew it. Even though the criminal complaint was a sham, Burr had to get it dismissed if he wanted to stay in the good graces of all the judges he was up in front of, most especially Mary Fisher. But he couldn't just give up. Not with Maury.

"Can't do it, Maury."

Litzenburger didn't miss a beat. "Three months and the criminal complaint. The rest later. Maybe."

"Done."

They shook hands. Maury turned to go. "If you think I'm leaving here without that check, you're crazy." He disappeared into the house and came right out with Zeke-the-Boy and a boy's-size canvas suitcase. Burr handed Maury a check.

\* \* \*

In spite of the debacle with Maury Litzenburger, Burr and the two Zekes had a grand weekend in East Lansing. Cheese pizza, hide and seek – the two Zekes' favorite game – more cheese pizza, fetch, and more cheese pizza. By Sunday night, all three of them were exhausted. Burr was sure he would never be able to look another cheese pizza in the eye.

\* \* \*

First thing Monday morning, Eve ambushed Burr with a stack of bills. He thought about leaving, but she was guarding the door, so he stayed in his chair behind the relative safety of his desk. Jacob came in and stood next to Eve.

Jacob and Eve left their posts and sat down in front of him. Burr shuffled through the bills three times. "These are okay to pay." Burr handed her all of the bills except one. "As soon as we have some money."

"What about that one?"

"Which one?"

Eve reached over and picked up the lone bill. "Your mortgage payment."

"That one can wait."

"They're all waiting," Eve said.

"That one can wait longer."

"You're already two months behind. The bank is going to take this building away from you."

"If only they would."

"Alimony?"

"I had to write Maury a check."

"I knew it," Eve said.

"Didn't you get a check from Tommy? " Jacob said.

"Not yet."

"I knew it. I knew something would go wrong." Jacob twirled a curl.

"You can't keep living like this," Eve said.

"Like what?"

"Hand-to-mouth, which also means hand-to-mouth for me. And for Jacob."

Burr turned to the window, his back to Eve and Jacob. It was raining cats and dogs, but he thought it was a much nicer day outside than in his office. "I've always made sure you were paid on time."

"Mostly on time."

"I'll worry about the mortgage when the bank sends us a certified letter."

There was a pause. Burr was sure Eve was tugging at her earring. He turned back around.

*I knew it.*

Zeke, napping on the couch, woke up and was about to jump down.

"No, Zeke," Burr said.

*The last thing I need right now is you licking Jacob.*

"If you would just pay attention to business and stop all this fooling around," Jacob said.

"What fooling around?"

"Your boat for one thing. You can't conduct a murder investigation from a boat."

Burr ran both hands through his hair.

"Would you please stop that," Jacob said, still twirling.

"He's thinking," Eve said, tugging at her earring. "All right. Let's all stop our tics. I'll count to three and we'll all stop."

"The boat," Burr said, still doing his tic.

"One, two, three." Eve stopped tugging. Jacob stopped creasing. Burr snapped his pencil in two.

"It's the boat. Helen's boat. *Achilles*. Don't you see?" Burr said.

"See what?" Jacob said.

"We haven't looked for Helen's boat. It's probably the last place she was alive. There's got to be something in the boat that will help us find the killer."

"My dear Burr, she was missing for over a year. A dog found what was left of her in a shallow grave. Whatever happened on that boat, if anything did happen, happened so long ago it won't be of any use," Jacob said.

"Where is that boat?" Burr said, hands through his hair one more time.

# CHAPTER THIRTEEN

Burr and Zeke, followed by Jacob in his Peugeot, drove out of the rain at Clare. By the time they reached Traverse City, the sun was out.

Back at Tommy's kitchen table, Burr and Tommy each had a cup of coffee in front of them. Jacob nursed a tea.

"The boat," Burr said.

"Here we go again," Jacob said under his breath.

"What?" Tommy said.

Jacob twirled a curl on the side of his head. Burr kicked Jacob under the table. Jacob stopped twirling.

"Tommy, where is *Achilles*?" Burr said.

"I have no idea."

"Did the sheriff seize her?"

"No. Not that I know of." Tommy looked out the window, then back at Burr. "Why?"

"Where is *Achilles*?"

"I haven't seen that damn boat since Helen disappeared."

"What happened?"

"We've been through this," Tommy said. He got up and poured himself another cup of coffee. He held the pot up and looked at Burr.

"None for me."

*I might not get a check today, but it doesn't look like I'm going to get fired.*

Tommy sat back down at the table. He sipped his coffee. "The sheriff towed the boat into Leland and put her in a slip. They had me go down there and look at it."

"What was it like. Was there anything missing?"

"Missing? Helen was missing. That's what was missing."

"I'm sorry, Tommy." Burr sipped his coffee. It was watery to begin with. Now it was cold and watery. "What was it like on the boat?"

"I told you. Everything was there. As far as I know."

"What did the sheriff do?"

"They searched the boat. They didn't find anything that I know of. They told me I could have the boat back. That was over a year ago."

Burr nodded. He reached for his coffee but thought better of it. "Did Brooks or the sheriff look at the boat again? After Helen's body was found?"

"Not that I know of."

"Where is she now?"

"*Achilles*?" Tommy looked out the window again, then back at Burr. "At the boatyard. Next to the marina in Northport."

\* \* \*

Somehow Burr managed to leave Morningside with a check. Half an hour later he found *Achilles* tucked up against a corner in the shed at Craker's. She was sitting on a wooden cradle, her deck about eight feet above him. Craker's had three steel sheds. Burr thought *shed* wasn't really the right word for these buildings. They were each about half the size of a football field with concrete floors, twenty-foot ceilings and steel walls with windows two-thirds of the way up. There were naked lightbulbs that lit the buildings like it was half an hour before dawn. The sheds were hot and stuffy and smelled like gasoline, sawdust and mildew. The boats were packed right up against each other, no more than a foot apart.

Burr had found *Achilles* in the second shed. Now he had to find a ladder to board her. Jacob clung to his side.

"Burr, you have to get me out of here."

"We just found *Achilles*."

"I can't stay in here with my claustrophobia. And there are bats in here."

"Those are sparrows," Burr said, lying. He found a ladder tucked behind a sailboat, carried it back to *Achilles* and set it against her transom. "Jacob, climb up. You can see all the way across the shed. You won't be claustrophobic."

"I'm afraid of heights."

Burr climbed the ladder.

"Don't leave me down here by myself."

Burr ignored him. Neither the lightbulbs nor the windows did much to light up *Achilles,* but the light seemed to slow down the bats. There was more light up here than down on the concrete, but it was still dim as sunrise, Burr thought. Fortunately, he did bring a flashlight. Burr played the beam over the cockpit, not that there was much to see. *Achilles* hadn't been covered, so bat droppings were splattered on the teak.

"What a shame."

A table and four chairs in the cockpit. Two lockers. He opened the first and found life jackets and a flare gun. The second one had a small grill. The lazarette was empty. He walked down the companionway into the main salon and galley. It had a musty smell. He opened the drawers. Dishes and silverware. In the aft stateroom, he found a drawer with women's clothes. *Helen's*. And one with men's.

*They must be Tommy's.*

There was nothing of interest in the forward stateroom.

Burr heard a thud from the cockpit.

*That must be Jacob.*

Burr walked back to the companionway. There lay Jacob in a heap, motionless.

Burr stepped over him and made his way to the bridge and steering station. Port and starboard throttles were next to the steering wheel. The instruments just below the wheel.

"Aren't you going to help me up?" Jacob said.

"I thought you were unconscious."

Jacob sat up. "It is better up here, but I'll never get down. And those are bats."

Burr ignored his partner, who wasn't nearly as fragile as he acted. To Burr's left, the nav station, a small built-in table with a hinged top and drawers. He lifted the top. Charts, binoculars, flashlight, flare gun, pencil, and paper.

*So far, this is a colossal waste of time.*

He opened the top drawer and found a transistor radio, a deck of cards, a backgammon board. The second drawer had more charting tools, more pencils, paper, a checkbook and a notebook the size of a thin paperback.

Burr took out the checkbook. It was from Empire State Bank. It was in her name only, not joint with Tommy. Burr flipped to the check register. The last check she wrote was to Rexall Drugs, on the day before she disappeared.

*Probably for booze.*

The one before that was written on the same day to Dame's Market, the grocery store in Northport.

Burr put the checkbook in the drawer and took out the notebook.

*This is her ship's log.*

There were dates with weather next to them, wind speed and direction, temperature and conditions. Clear, cloudy, rain. The entries were spaced apart. "Yes, her logbook," Burr said out loud. He skipped to the last entry, June 9th, the day she disappeared. Wind SE at 10. Seventy degrees and clear. The last entry. "Did she make it to South Manitou? Or did she just not update the log when she got there?" Burr ran his finger along the entries. "Jacob, please come up here. I may have found something."

"I can't possibly."

"Why not?"

"I'll be seasick."

Burr put the logbook back in the drawer and made his way back to the cockpit. Jacob was still sitting where he had landed. "Jacob, please."

"I'll be seasick."

"We're on dry land."

"This is a boat. If I go inside, I'll surely be ill. I never should have climbed that blasted ladder." Jacob put his head in his hands.

"Let me help you, " Burr said. He hoisted Jacob to his feet and pulled him up to the bridge. He opened the drawer and took out the checkbook and the logbook. "Take a look."

"Stop. Stop where you are and put your hands up," said a voice from behind him.

Burr turned around.

"Hands up."

A sheriff's deputy, standing on the ladder, pointed his service revolver at Burr.

Burr smiled. "Deputy Holcomb. How nice to see you."

"Hands up, I said."

Jacob raised his hands. Burr put his hands in his pockets. "What are you doing here?"

"You're under arrest."

"For what?"

"Interfering with a crime scene. Hands up, I said."

"This is Tommy Lockwood's boat. He gave us permission."

"Helen Lockwood was murdered on this boat."

"Maybe she was. Maybe she wasn't. But we have permission to be here."

Deputy Holcomb climbed on board, his gun still pointed at Burr. "Don Craker called and said somebody was up here nosing around. I called the prosecutor's office and they told me to get right up here." He waved his gun at Burr. "Come with me."

Burr went out to the cockpit. "Deputy Holcomb, if this is a crime scene, why isn't it marked? There's no tape around the boat. There's no signs and the boat wasn't locked."

"You're under arrest."

"You go tell Petey Brooks that if he wants to make this a crime scene, mark it like one. And then tell him that I want access to it."

The teenage deputy smacked his lips, then put down his gun.

Burr walked by him and started down the ladder. When Burr was off the ladder, Jacob looked down at him. "What about me?"

"Deputy, go ahead and arrest him."

Burr stormed out of the shed and into the sun. He shielded his eyes with his hand and squinted. Burr found his Jeep and climbed in. He was furious with Brooks. *I'm going to get back on that boat and get another look at that logbook. No matter what.*

He drummed his fingers on the steering wheel.

*I need to calm down and figure something out.*

Jacob staggered out the door and leaned up against the shed. Deputy Holcomb came out next. He said something to Jacob and then walked over to the Jeep. "This is a crime scene. You may not enter that shed. Understood?" He stomped off before Burr could answer. Jacob, apparently recovered from his ordeal, got into the backseat.

"Get in the front seat," Burr said. "Zeke can sit in the back."

"I give up," Jacob said.

"What exactly are you giving up?"

Jacob leaned against the door, "Everything. All of it. In its entirety."

"As in?"

"I give up on boats. I give up on ladders. I give up on the front seat. You win. Zeke wins."

Burr pointed to the backseat. "Zeke," he said.

"No, no. Please don't. I can't possibly sit where your miserable dog has been. There's dog hair everywhere. And I don't have it in me to get out of this accursed Jeep and get back in." Jacob looked out the window. "I never should have ridden here with you. I want to be in my own car."

"That Corvair you drive is a foolish piece of machinery that hardly ever works right."

"It's a Peugeot and you know it."

*Maybe I should have helped him down the ladder.*

Burr put the Jeep in gear and started off. "Jacob, what you need is lunch."

"No, no. Not another one of your hole-in-the-wall eateries posing as restaurants."

"Jacob, I'm sorry I didn't help you off the boat." Burr pulled out of the boatyard and onto the road. "We've got to get back in there."

"Holcomb told us to stay out."

"I don't care what he said."

"You'll get yourself arrested again."

"I've got to get another look at that logbook."

Jacob reached into his pocket and passed the logbook to Burr.

"I take back everything I've ever said about you. And your car." Burr beamed. "How did you manage it?"

"I slipped it into my pocket when Holcomb wasn't looking."

"I'll buy you lunch."

\* \* \*

Buying Jacob lunch had seemed like a good idea, but The Little Finger couldn't come close to his exacting standards. Jacob had insisted that water was all he wanted, but then he didn't like the plastic glass with a chip on the rim. Burr had finally ordered his partner a grilled cheese on white. Jacob cut off the crusts and nibbled on it. Burr had the special, a Reuben with split pea soup, which he would recommend.

After lunch, Burr dropped Jacob off back at the boatyard to watch *Achilles* and make sure nothing came off or on until he got back. Then he drove out of Northport south on M-22. Grand Traverse Bay rose and fell in lazy swells coming in from the northwest, a shiny blue in the brilliant sunshine.

"Zeke, if I spend any more time on this damn road, they're going to start calling it the Burr Lafayette Memorial Highway."

He drove through Omena, a hamlet not quite big enough to be a village.

Twenty minutes later he sat across from Peter Brooks in his Suttons Bay office. The prosecutor ran a hand through his slicked-back hair. Burr thought he looked a little too dapper for a government employee, but then his family did own hundreds of acres of orchards, so he didn't have to live on what the county paid him.

"Helen Lockwood's boat is a crime scene."

"It wasn't until I climbed aboard."

"You're lucky you weren't arrested."

"Deputy Holcomb and I are friends," Burr said. "Tommy had *Achilles* pulled over a year ago. She's been in that shed for over a year. No one has set foot on her since the inquest. Whatever evidence that might be on that boat has long been corrupted."

Brooks looked up at Burr. "Corrupted?"

"You know exactly what I mean. That boat has been sitting in that shed for all the world to tamper with. It wasn't a secure site. Anybody with a step-ladder could have taken evidence off that boat. Or put evidence on the boat." Burr looked out Brooks' window at the sunshine.

"It's a crime scene and you are to stay off," Brooks said.

"You botched this, Petey." Burr looked back at Brooks. "And all the king's men can't put Humpty back together again."

Brooks pointed at Burr with a long, manicured finger. "You will not talk to me that way."

"Just in case there is anything worth looking at, I want back on *Achilles*."

"Over my dead body." Brooks put his hands flat on his desk. "For all I know, you've already taken evidence off that boat."

Burr tapped the logbook in his pocket.

*If you only knew.*

"What's that in your pocket?"

Burr put his hands in his lap. "That," he paused, searching for an answer, "is my appointment book."

"Let me see it."

"Are you kidding?"

Brooks picked up his desk phone. "Send a deputy in here."

"You need a warrant and probable cause." Burr stood. "You're preventing me from representing my client. Get me back on that boat." Burr walked out the door.

\* \* \*

By the time Burr made it back to the boatyard, Brooks had the shed where *Achilles* was stored cordoned off and yellow crime scene tape wrapped around the boat. Burr picked up Jacob and dropped him off at his silly Peugeot with instructions to go through the crumpled-up list of suspects.

Burr drove to Woody's in Northport, a white two-story building that had once been a hotel and could use a little paint. He parked himself at the bar. Woody's, so named because all of the interior had old fashioned pine paneling, made the best Bombay martini in Leelanau County. After two martinis and an eye on a third, Burr ordered the cherry chicken, Woody's specialty, partly ruined because he couldn't get back on *Achilles*. He took the logbook out of his pocket and flipped through it. "Sunny, sunny, sunny. Cloudy, sunny, cloudy, cloudy, cloudy." Burr chewed on a piece of his ribeye. "Rain, rain, rain." He closed the book. "I've got to get back on that damn boat."

He spent a restless night on *Spindrift*. After taking Zeke for his morning walk, they set off in the Jeep. After filing his motion in circuit court, he stopped at Munson Hospital on the chance he could see Lauren. Burr waited for her in the maternity lounge. He felt decidedly out of place. He wasn't married and there was no one remotely close to him giving birth, and certainly not in Traverse City. Burr sat in an overstuffed beige chair in the corner. The fathers-to-be were glued to the TV, the Tigers and White Sox playing an afternoon game.

And there she was. Lauren, her hair pulled back, in forest-green scrubs and white tennis shoes, looking every bit like the nurse she was.

"Is something wrong?" she said.

Burr stood. "I just filed a motion at the courthouse and thought I'd stop by."

"I may only have a few minutes." Lauren sat in a chair next to him.

Burr told her what had happened on *Achilles* and showed her the logbook. She thumbed through it, raised her eyebrows once or twice, then handed it back to Burr.

"Did you see anything that stood out?"

She shook her head. "No, I knew she used the boat, but I had no idea she used it that much." Lauren brushed a strand of her brown hair out of her face. "Who do you think killed her? I know you probably can't say, but do you think it was Tommy?"

Burr sat back in his chair. *I hope not.* He ran his hands through his hair. "No. No, I don't."

Lauren's pager beeped. "It's time. Finally."

* * *

Burr and Maggie woke up at the same time, cuddling in *Spindrift's* starboard berth, barely big enough for one. Zeke slept at one end of the port berth, Finn at the other. Maggie kissed Burr, then struggled to get out of their sleeping bag. She moved over to the other bunk, quite naked. She put on Burr's shirt and squeezed in between the two dogs.

"Burr," she said.

"Yes?"

"I'm leaving you."

Burr sat up. "What?"

"It's clear to me that you like things just the way they are."

He thought it was much too early for this.

"I love you. I think you love me, but this isn't enough."

"Maggie…"

"Call me if you change your mind." She threw her things in her suitcase and boosted Finn into the cockpit. She jumped onto the dock, wearing Burr's shirt and not much else.

# CHAPTER FOURTEEN

A week later, Burr pulled down the cuffs of his baby blue pinpoint oxford that didn't need pulling down and straightened his red silk tie with the tiny black diamonds, which, of course, didn't need straightening.

Here he stood in the windowless courtroom of Judge Mary Fisher, ivory walls with the pictures of her predecessors, illustrious and otherwise, a church pew gallery, varnished oak turning black. Matching jury box, witness stand, and the judge's rostrum with a single rose in a bud vase perched on the corner.

*Just like in her office.*

Judge Fisher looked down her nose at him but didn't say anything.

"Your Honor, we are here today because the prosecution has refused to allow the defense access to what might be vital evidence located on the late Helen Lockwood's boat, *Achilles*."

Peter Brooks stood. "Your Honor, that is not true. Mr. Lafayette was corrupting evidence at a crime scene."

"That is patently false," Burr said. He turned to the judge. "Your Honor, that boat sat abandoned in a shed in Northport for over a year. The prosecutor had absolutely no interest in that boat until the defense looked it over."

"You didn't look it over," Brooks said. "You tore it apart."

"I did nothing of the sort."

Judge Fisher slammed her gavel. "Stop it. Both of you. We're all Michigan grads here, and we're going to have a civil discourse."

*I doubt it.*

She looked at the prosecutor. "Mr. Brooks, do not say another word until Mr. Lafayette is finished. Then you can have your turn." She looked at Burr. "And then you will be quiet. Is that clear?"

"Yes, Your Honor," both lawyers said.

"We're going to do it just like we learned in kindergarten. It's called taking turns." She put her gavel down and folded her hands. "Mr. Lafayette, it's your turn."

"Thank you, Your Honor," Burr paused. "As I was saying, the defense was conducting an examination of the deceased's boat in the shed at Craker's Boatyard in Northport. Over a year earlier, the sheriff's department searched the boat in connection with the disappearance of Helen Lockwood. After their investigation, they released the boat to the deceased's husband, Thomas Lockwood, who had the boat stored at Craker's. Approximately two weeks ago, my partner and I were examining the boat in connection with our defense of Thomas Lockwood when we were summarily removed from the boat and threatened with arrest. Since that date, the prosecutor has denied all access to the boat. Your Honor, we believe there may be important evidence on board that will be vital to the defense of my client. Mr. Brooks' continued refusal to allow me access to the boat under the ruse that it is a crime scene is not only prejudicing my client, it is a clear violation of the evidentiary rules laid down in case after case, namely…"

"Stop right there, Mr. Lafayette," the judge said. "I have read the able brief of your associate, who I believe is sitting next to you."

Jacob nodded.

"Is there anything you'd like to add, Mr. Wertheim?"

Burr looked back at Jacob, who was turning a whiter shade of pale. Jacob was terrified of speaking in court.

*If he opens his mouth, I am lost.*

Jacob shook his head "no."

*Thank God.* Burr turned back to the judge.

"Somehow I didn't think you would." She smiled at Burr's quaking partner. "Your reputation precedes you." Then to Burr, "Do you have anything further?"

"No, Your Honor." Burr walked back to his table and sat next to Jacob, whose color was slowly returning.

"Mr. Brooks," Judge Fisher said.

Brooks stood. He slicked his hair, then approached the bench. "Your Honor, as you well know, the sheriff discovered Helen Lockwood's body on South Manitou Island earlier this summer. There was a bullet hole in her forehead. The bullet came from a gun owned by Thomas Lockwood. The gun was found in the harbor on South Manitou where Mrs. Lockwood anchored her boat on or about the time she was killed. Numerous witnesses saw Mr. Lockwood on the ferry to South Manitou during the same time period."

"This isn't an opening statement," Burr said, *sotto voce.*

Brooks looked back at Burr. Judge Fisher scowled at him. Burr smiled.

Brooks turned back to the judge. "As I was saying, based on the evidence, the State charged Thomas Lockwood with murdering his wife. Since that time, we have treated Mrs. Lockwood's boat as a crime scene. Mr. Lafayette has flagrantly disregarded that designation."

Burr jumped up. "Your Honor, that is absolutely false. The prosecution totally forgot about the boat until…"

"Sit down, Mr. Lafayette. It's not your turn."

Burr sputtered but sat.

Brooks continued. "Not only did Mr. Lafayette disregard the crime tape, we believe he may have removed evidence from the crime scene."

Burr jumped to his feet again. "It wasn't marked as a crime scene when we boarded the boat."

Judge Fisher slammed her gavel. "Mr. Lafayette, sit down and don't say another word. It appears that you never learned turn-taking in kindergarten. "She looked at the prosecutor. "Mr. Brooks?"

"Your Honor, the State has two requests." Brooks raised his forefinger. "Enjoin Mr. Lafayette from entering the crime scene and…" Brooks raised another finger. "Compel Mr. Lafayette to return all evidence, particularly the log book kept by the deceased, which he stole from the boat."

Burr couldn't help himself. Up again. "Your Honor, this is an outrage."

Judge Fisher pointed at Burr and motioned him to sit back down. Burr sat for the third time.

"The lady doth protest too much, methinks," she said to Burr.

"Double, double, toil and trouble," Burr said, mostly to himself.

Judge Fisher nodded at him but put a finger over her lips and shushed him. To Brooks, "Anything further?"

"No, Your Honor." Brooks walked back to his table and sat.

The judge cleared her throat. "Counsel," she said to both of them, "if today's performance is a sample of what I have to look forward to at the trial, I shall certainly need to equip myself with a large bottle of aspirin." She paused. "As to the merits of your arguments, you are both right." She paused again. "And you are both wrong. Mr. Brooks, you may rightly treat

Mrs. Lockwood's boat as a crime scene. As such, you have every right to ask Mr. Lafayette to return anything he may have…" She paused again and looked at Burr. "Pilfered."

"It wasn't a crime scene when I took it," he mumbled.

"What's that?" she said.

"I said, 'of course' Your Honor."

"Of course you did."

Burr, careful not to open his mouth again, thought, *so far, I'm the big loser here.*

She looked over at Brooks and said, "Mr. Lafayette, as counsel for the defense, has every right to examine the crime scene and all evidence found there."

"Yes, Your Honor."

"You say that, but you haven't allowed it, have you, " the judge said, not asking.

Brooks squirmed in his chair.

"Mr. Brooks, you have one week to finish examining the boat. During that time, you will catalog everything on the boat and everything you remove from the boat. One week from today, you will grant Mr. Lafayette access to *Achilles*. You will present him your list of cataloged items and make them available for inspection. Is that clear?"

"Yes, Your Honor," Brooks said.

"As for you, Mr. Lafayette, you will stay away from *Achilles* for one week. You have forty-eight hours to turn over anything you may have taken from the crime scene to Mr. Brooks. Is that clear?"

"Yes, Your Honor, however…"

She cut him off. "Don't say another word."

* * *

Burr sat at his desk, hunched over his new car phone. Zeke lounged on the couch. He had the bag that held the phone and the battery on his desk. He'd run the cord that connected the phone to the antenna on the window behind him, where he'd taped the antenna to the glass.

"Zeke, the moment of truth." Burr dialed his office number. He held the receiver to his ear. It rang and rang and rang and rang. Finally, "Lafayette and Wertheim."

"By God, it works," although he could still hear the phone ringing.

*That's just a little problem.*

"I beg your pardon?"

"Eve, it's me. Burr."

"Of course, it is."

"It works, Eve. It works." Burr jumped to his feet and did a little jig.

"What do you want?"

"Watson, I need you."

"I'm right here."

"Of course, you are."

"Burr, look up from your jig."

Burr, still jigging, looked at the door to his office. There stood Eve at the door to his office, hands on her hips.

Burr stopped jigging. "You're not on the phone."

"And neither are you."

"I called you and you answered."

"I heard you from my desk."

"So, it didn't really work."

"No, Alexander Graham Bell, it didn't."

Burr looked at the receiver, then put it back to his ear. He heard the phone still ringing. "That explains that." Burr slammed the receiver down.

Eve sat down across from him. "Now what?"

"Please ask Jacob to come in."

"Why don't you call him on your car phone?"

Jacob, whose hearing was almost as good as Eve's, came in with a yellow legal pad. "Did I hear my name?"

"Jacob, old friend, we need a little research."

Jacob ran a finger along the knife-like crease in his linen slacks. "I am not going on another of your wild goose chases masquerading as legal research. The research I do is in a law library."

"It's about our suspects."

"Do we have any suspects?" Eve said.

Burr ignored her. "Jacob, this is very simple. I want you to see if anyone on Sleeper's list or anyone else associated with this case has a criminal record."

"Somehow I knew I would be roped into another frivolous research project," Jacob said, groaning. "This is grasping at straws."

Burr turned around. "Grasping at straws is all we have right now.

\* \* \*

Burr woke at first light, Zeke licking his cheek. "All right, old friend." He got out of his bunk, dressed and took Zeke ashore. His first night on *Spindrift* since Maggie had broken up with him had been uneventful, disappointingly so. "I miss her, Zeke. I surely do." The aging lab wagged his tail. "Maybe we could get engaged." They started off to the Jeep. "No, that won't work." Burr opened the door for Zeke. "How about dating with a view toward marriage. That's it." He let Zeke in the passenger door. "She'd never agree to that."

They drove to the Little Finger. Burr had the breakfast special of eggs, toast and bacon. He thought so highly of it, he took a takeout order to Zeke.

Five minutes later he parked behind the sheds at Craker's. "I've already proved I don't do marriage very well," he said to his now napping dog.

Burr ducked under the yellow tape and climbed the ladder ever so quietly. Once on board, he turned on his flashlight and made his way to the nav station. He slipped the logbook in between two of the charts.

"As long as I'm here, I might as well have a look. I'll just make it quick." He looked where he'd looked before, the nav station, the lockers, under the bunks, in the galley, in the head. He searched the engine compartment. The silver-colored valve covers gleamed in the beam of his flashlight. "I could eat off those." He got back on the ladder and looked at *Achilles* one last time. "There's something else here. I just don't know what it is."

\* \* \*

A week later, Burr stood in front of Judge Fisher, Brooks at the prosecutor's table. "Your Honor, I'm here to request a mistrial."

Judge Fisher's jaw dropped. "I beg your pardon?"

"Your Honor, you gave the prosecutor one week to complete his investigation of the so-called crime scene after which he was supposed to grant me access to *Achilles*." Burr paused. "Which he has not done."

Brooks jumped to his feet. "Mr. Lafayette failed to return the logbook within the forty-eight hours you gave him."

"The logbook is not in my possession."

"That's because you snuck on the boat and put it back."

Burr looked back at Brooks. "You found the logbook? Where was it?" Burr winked at him.

"In the chart table. Right where you put it."

Burr ignored Brooks and turned back to the judge. "Your Honor, this proves my point. The prosecutor ignored your seven-day order. And the defense has not been able to inspect the evidence." Burr started in on his tie.

"Stop that," Judge Fisher said.

"I beg your pardon?"

"Your theatrical preening."

Burr cleared his throat. "Your Honor, it is impossible for Mr. Lockwood to get a fair trial because the evidence has been corrupted and because of Mr. Brooks' unethical and felonious conduct."

"Are you kidding?" Brooks said. "That is the most outrageous thing I've ever heard. Lafayette has thumbed his nose at everything this court has ordered and every evidentiary law known to man. He's flagrantly violated every ethical canon I can think of, not to mention his smart-ass attitude."

"Watch your language, Mr. Brooks." She turned to Burr. "Counsel, you are nothing if not bold, but boldness does not carry the day. It's still not clear if the deceased's boat is a crime scene. You said so yourself."

Burr shifted his weight from one foot to the other, then back to both.

"Further, I can't see how you've been prejudiced. Mr. Brooks is to allow you immediate access to the defendant's boat. And the logbook."

"Thank you, Your Honor," Burr said.

"Mr. Lafayette, your motion for a mistrial is denied. We are adjourned." She slammed down her gavel before Burr could object. She stood and walked out.

*Maybe I should have married her.*

Burr walked back to his table. Brooks walked up to him and offered his hand to Burr, who shook it, reluctantly. "Nice try," Brooks said.

Burr turned his back to Brooks and picked up his papers.

"Let me know when you want on board. And when you want to see the logbook."

"I've seen it," Burr said, his back to Brooks.

# CHAPTER FIFTEEN

Burr and Zeke drove back up the Leelanau Peninsula through Cedar and up the north side of Glen Lake to M-22. The clouds had drifted off to the east. By the time he knocked on the door at Morningside, there wasn't a cloud in the sky, but the late summer sun wasn't nearly as brilliant as it had been in June. Consuela answered the door and led him out into the backyard to Tommy, sitting in the shade of a sugar maple with what looked very much like a martini. He had on a white polo shirt, khaki shorts and sandals.

*He looks more like a cottager on Glen Lake than a cherry farmer accused of murder. But his face is lined, maybe from the sun, probably from the murder charge.*

Tommy stood and shook Burr's hand. "Will you join me?"

Burr nodded.

*If I see one more maple tree, I'm going to buy a chain saw.*

Tommy pulled up a chair for Burr. "Please sit down. I'll be right back."

Burr sat. Zeke sniffed the tree trunk lifted his leg on it, then lay at Burr's feet. Burr looked past the yard to the cherry trees standing in rows like soldiers. They looked different somehow. They were all green. Of course. The red of the cherries was gone, and the branches weren't drooping with the weight of the fruit. Burr thought they looked naked.

Tommy appeared and handed Burr a rocks glass.

"Thank you, Tommy."

Tommy sat. Burr sipped his drink. *Thank God it's a martini.* "This is superb."

"I remembered you like a very dry, very dirty Bombay."

"This is perfect." Burr took more than a sip. "Tommy…"

"Helen and I sat here late in the day. Just like now. She loved it here, looking out at her orchards. All that was hers."

"So why do you want to sell?"

"I told you. It's not the same without Helen."

Burr took another swallow of his drink.

"It makes me look guilty, doesn't it?"

Burr fished an olive out and chewed it slowly. "It doesn't help, but if you don't want to farm anymore, who could blame you."

"It would be different if we had kids, but we never got around to it. I'm not really sure why."

"Lauren doesn't want to sell," Burr said.

She also doesn't want to grow cherries, and her kids aren't old enough. Karen's kids don't want to grow cherries. That's why she wants to sell."

Burr licked the gin off his finger. *This martini is heaven.*

He reached into his pocket, took out the once crumpled, now folded suspect list. He handed it to Tommy. "Please look at this again and see if there's anyone who could have possibly killed Helen."

Tommy looked over the names. He shook his head 'no' and handed it back to Burr.

*At least he didn't crumple it up.*

Burr studied his drink. He looked longingly at the olives, then, "Tommy, as of right now, we don't have much of a defense. Brooks has witnesses who are going to testify they saw you board the ferry. Your gun killed Helen, and Sleeper is going to testify that, after Helen's body was found, you talked to him about selling the farm."

Burr looked at the list for the umpteenth time. He folded it, put it back in his pocket and took a big swallow of his martini. "We could use a few suspects."

"What are you going to do?"

"As of right now, I think our best defense is reasonable doubt," Burr said, who had his own reasonable doubts.

\* \* \*

Jacob paced back and forth in front of Burr's desk. "I won't do it."

Burr sat behind his desk. He looked at the formerly crumpled list. "Jacob, old friend, you must."

"It will take forever."

"Not quite forever."

Burr looked at Jacob. "We don't have any suspects. I need to know who in Leelanau County has been accused or convicted of a violent crime and isn't in prison." Burr drummed his fingers. "In the last five years."

"That will take forever."

"Jacob, we really do need more than a list of accused and convicted felons, but right now this is all we have."

Jacob twirled a curl in his steel wool hair.

"There's something else going on here. Something that we don't know. I'm not sure if Tommy knows, but I'm also not sure he's telling us everything."

"I don't see how this helps," Jacob said.

"As I've said, *ad nauseum,* the police lie. Witnesses lie. Most of all, clients lie."

Eve came in with a letter and handed it to Burr.

Burr read it, then frowned.

"What is it?" Jacob said.

"It's the scheduling order from Judge Fisher," Eve said. "She wants to meet with Burr and Brooks in her chambers."

* * *

Burr sat in Judge Fisher's chambers next to Peter Brooks and across from the judge herself.

*I've gone from sitting in my own office with two people who were annoyed with me to another office where two more people are annoyed with me.*

He smiled at the judge, then, "Your Honor, I do understand that you want to start the trial on September 15th, but I simply haven't had enough time to prepare."

The always attractive Judge Fisher smiled back at Burr, but he thought her smile was a tad on the icy side. "Mr. Lafayette, you've had all summer."

"Yes, Your Honor, but it's difficult to get to South Manitou. The witnesses are hard to track down, and the prosecutor has been unwilling to give me access to all of the evidence…"

Brooks interrupted. "Your Honor, Mr. Lafayette declined to go on board the boat."

"Your Honor…"

Judge Fisher interrupted him. "After all this, you haven't even been on the boat?"

Burr smiled at the judge again.

"Don't be cute with me," she said.

"I would never do that, Your Honor," Burr said, who, of course, would. "I just need a little more time."

Judge Fisher glared at him. "How much?"

Burr thought she was even prettier when she was mad at him, but he knew enough to not say so. "Your Honor, I'd like to start the trial December 1st."

"I object, Your Honor. That is far too long."

Burr turned away, as if he was thinking about a reply, which he wasn't.

*If I can get to November 1st, I'll be just fine. By that time the ferries will have stopped running and the charter boats will be out of the water.*

"Your Honor," Brooks said. "Mr. Lafayette is toying with the court."

Burr turned back to the judge. "Your Honor, I don't see how I can be ready before December 1st."

The judge drummed her fingers on her desk. "Mr. Lafayette, I will extend the trial date."

Burr smiled again.

"The trial is postponed to October 1st."

Burr cringed.

Brooks stood. He whispered in Burr's ear. "The ferry runs until Halloween and the steelhead fishing is good through October."

* * *

Burr sat in his office. This time there was only one annoyed person, Jacob, sitting in front of him. Eve was in her garden, something about deadheading and roses. He didn't know what any of that meant, and he didn't care. He was just glad she wasn't here. He had his hands full with Jacob.

His partner creased his slacks again. One leg, then the other. And back again. "You bounce back and forth between here and that judge's courtroom like a ping-pong ball. I think she has her eye on you, by the way." Jacob re-creased.

"Would you please stop that," Burr said. "Yes, there is a lot of back and forth, but I find a personal touch is much more effective."

Jacob looked up from his slacks. "It's so effective that your grand plan of skipping the preliminary exam and having the trial after all the witnesses left has backfired."

"Touché, my dear friend. So, this is what we must do."

"We?"

"The royal we. As in you."

"Whatever it is, I won't do it."

"Money problems always play into these things. So, Jacob, take all the suspects and see who might have money problems."

* * *

Today, a week before the trial, Burr sat at his desk, Zeke napping on the couch again. He'd spent the past three weeks getting ready for the trial. He'd pored over Brooks' witness list. There were no surprises. Brooks' list laid out his case just the way Burr thought it would. The witnesses would tell the story Brooks wanted told, and they'd all still be in Leelanau County. Burr's strategy had failed. More than failed, it had backfired. He hadn't had the benefit of hearing what they were going to say because he'd waived the preliminary exam and there wasn't time to notice them for depositions, even if Judge Fisher would have allowed it, pre-trial discovery not being favored in criminal cases.

So far, Jacob hadn't turned up much of anything. He had a few suspects but no one he could pin Helen's murder on. He did have a few suspects who could have, might have actually murdered Helen. The ones with criminal records, and the ones who had money troubles that a check from Sleeping Bear Dunes National Lakeshore would fix.

It wasn't much but it was all he had, and it just might be enough. No one had seen Tommy with Helen on South Manitou or on *Achilles*, and certainly no one had seen Tommy kill his wife.

Still, it would have been much better if someone, anyone, could vouch for Tommy when Helen was killed. Burr didn't believe Tommy had been fly fishing by himself on the Betsie and hadn't seen a soul who would say so. He didn't think Helen's sisters believed Tommy either. Someone or someones weren't telling him everything.

His defense was going to be reasonable doubt, but he was damned if he was going to give up on his plan to delay the trial, so he'd tried again, unbeknownst to both Jacob and Eve.

And here was the *denouement* right in front of him. He turned the envelope over and over, the envelope from Judge Fisher and the circuit court for the counties of Grand Traverse, Antrim and, most importantly, Leelanau.

"Zeke, old friend, this will fix Brooks." Burr ripped open the envelope. He read it. Once, twice, three times. "Damn it all. The worst has happened." Burr crumpled the letter into a ball and threw it across the room. Zeke, ever vigilant, opened one eye. He hopped off the couch and retrieved the balled-up letter. He dropped it in Burr's hand. "Thank you, Zeke," Burr said.

Eve, who Burr was sure could hear what went on even from a bomb shelter, walked in, Jacob in tow. They both sat down.

"Yes?" Burr said.

"You sent for us," Eve said.

"I did no such thing."

"When you say, 'Damn it all. The worst has happened,' it means we're supposed to come in." Eve tugged at her earring.

"Not this time," Burr said. He reached for the letter-crumpled-into-a-ball but Eve snatched it. She uncrumpled it and read it. Then she looked up at Burr.

"Now you've done it."

"Done what?" Jacob said.

Burr leaned over his desk and reached for the letter, but Eve pulled it away.

"Done what?" Jacob said again.

"It's nothing. Just a little procedural hoo-hah that didn't quite go as planned," Burr said.

"I should say so," Eve said. "Burr, what are you going to do? Or should I say, Jacob, what are you going to do?"

"Me?" Jacob twirled a curl in his hair.

"Genius, Burr. Absolute genius," Eve said.

"Thank you, Eve." Burr ran his hands through his hair, front to back.

"Brooks does that, too," Jacob said.

Burr put his hands on his desk. "I don't care what Brooks does."

"It's hard to fool a Michigan lawyer," Eve said.

"What is going on and why does it affect me?"

"It's a minor thing," Burr said.

Eve cleared her throat. "It seems that Burr has a highly infectious and highly contagious disease that will require postponing the trial for at least thirty days."

"That will get us the delay you want. It's genius," Jacob said. "I didn't know you were ill."

"He's not," Eve said. "This is what the judge said, and I quote, 'Mr. Lafayette, I am sorry to learn of your unfortunate and untimely illness. I note that it is your firm, Lafayette and Wertheim, that is representing Mr. Lockwood. With such an able partner in Mr. Wertheim, I am confident that he can carry on the defense until such time as you have sufficiently recovered to resume your duties.'"

"Burr, how could you? You'll just have to tell her you're completely recovered. Ahead of schedule."

Eve cleared her throat again. "Further, because of the contagious nature of your disease, you are forbidden to enter the courtroom for at least thirty days. Please direct Mr. Wertheim to be in my courtroom at nine a.m. on the morning of October 1st for jury selection." Eve paused, then, "Wishing you a speedy recovery. Sincerely, Mary Fisher, Judge for the Circuit Court of Antrim, Grand Traverse and Leelanau Counties."

"Burr, how could you?" Jacob sank in his chair.

Burr swiveled in his chair and looked out the window.

*A perfectly beautiful day. Not a cloud in the sky, but it's stormy in here.*

He stood and paced in front of the window.

*This seemed like such a good idea at the time. I never thought she'd do this. She's outsmarted me. Jacob is a disaster in a courtroom. An absolute nightmare.*

He turned to Jacob. "Jury selection is very easy. I'll help you do that."

"From your hospital bed?" Eve said.

Jacob lost all the color in his face and his hands started to shake.

"Jacob, you're very convincing," Eve said. "Maybe you should be the one who is ill."

# CHAPTER SIXTEEN

The next morning, Eve came into Burr's office and took her side chair. She smiled at Burr. "Come sit beside me." She patted Jacob's chair.

*This can't be good.*

Burr did as he was told.

"Burr…"

"Eve, I'm sorry that we don't ever quite seem to have enough money."

"That's not it."

Burr tried again. "I'm sorry I keep asking you out. I'm just teasing."

"You're hopeful."

"Eve, you're leaving. Quitting."

"Burr, Burr, Burr. You're such a fool."

*At least she's not quitting.*

"It's Maggie."

"Maggie?"

"She loves you. You love her." Eve paused. "You should marry her."

"We hardly know each other."

"How long has it been?"

"And there's Zeke-the-Boy. And Grace."

"You're divorced."

*If I had a pencil, I'd break it.*

He fidgeted in his chair.

"You're stuck, and you can't live your life like this."

"Like what?"

"You're just marking time. Your life is a mess. And you know it."

Burr looked down at his feet. His tennis shoes didn't need polishing.

*I'll think about this later. Maybe after the trial.*

\* \* \*

Burr sat in his Jeep in the courthouse parking lot. A soft, patient rain fell, soft enough that it fell soundlessly on the Jeep. Burr had the windows part way down so the windows wouldn't fog up. Zeke sat in the backseat, his head in the rain. Jacob sat in the passenger seat, his head buried in his hands.

"It can't be all that bad," Burr had said, who was sure it was every bit as bad as Jacob said it was. Burr was afraid it was probably worse.

It was 10 in the morning on Monday, October 1st, the first day of the trial. Jury selection had started at 9. Try as he might, the wily judge refused to allow Burr in the courtroom as long as he was contagious, which, of course, he wasn't. He'd done his best to prep his shy partner.

"Jacob," he'd said, "jury selection is very simple," although it wasn't. Burr knew it wasn't and so did Jacob. "You don't have to fight or confound Brooks, unless of course you want to, which of course is what I'd do. What we're looking for is a jury full of divorced men or unhappily married men. We don't want anyone who'd be sympathetic to Helen, which would be women, especially divorced women or unhappily married women, which is probably most women. If you have to pick a woman, try to pick one who's unhappily married. Or maybe single and doesn't want to be married."

Jacob had looked over at Burr. "How am I ever going to do that?"

*At least he looks the part.*

Jacob had on a charcoal suit with a chalk stripe, a white shirt and a red tie with black diamonds. He certainly looked the part. But Jacob didn't act the part. He was flat out terrified. Jacob was a brilliant researcher and writer of appellate briefs, but he was deathly afraid of public speaking, not to mention arguing in a courtroom. The two of them were a grand team as long as they each played their own parts, which they weren't doing today.

"How could you do this to me?" Jacob said. "I simply can't do this. I can't."

"Of course, you can."

Jacob wrung his hands. "No, I can't."

"Jacob, all you have to do is object to whatever Brooks says."

"This will never work."

"Of course it will," Burr said, who had grave doubts. "Object to whatever Brooks says. Use your challenges wisely. Find out about the jurors' personalities. What they're like. We'll probably be better off with more educated, well-to-do jurors." Burr patted Jacob on the shoulder. "Break a leg. It's showtime."

Burr watched Jacob's hands shake as he tried to open the door.

*I think I may have said the wrong thing.*

Burr got out of the Jeep and opened the passenger door. Jacob, standing in the rain, didn't budge. Burr was starting to get wet.

"Jacob, it's time to go."

"It's raining."

Burr got Jacob's umbrella from the back seat. He opened it and pulled Jacob out of the Jeep like a boy might pull a stubborn nightcrawler out of its hole. With one hand on Jacob's elbow, and the other on the umbrella, Burr led Jacob up the courthouse steps. Eve met them at the door.

"This will never work," she mouthed at Burr.

"Of course it will."

But, of course, it didn't. An hour later, Jacob sat next to Burr in the Jeep, his head still buried in his hands. Burr patted Jacob on his shoulder. His partner's suit jacket was wet. He had fled without his umbrella.

"Why aren't you in court?" Burr said.

"I had to have a recess," Jacob said.

"It can't be as bad as all that."

"Worse."

"Who did you pick?"

"No one."

"How about Brooks?"

"Three. No, four. Four so far."

"Men?"

"All women."

*This is bad.*

Jacob buried his head in his hands again. Zeke stretched over the back seat and licked Jacob's ear. Jacob didn't say a word. Zeke licked his ear again. Jacob didn't shoo him away.

*This is really bad.*

Jacob looked up at Burr. "How could you do this to me? How could you? You knew I'm deathly afraid of things like this."

"It can't be all that bad," Burr said.

"You never should have insisted I come with you when you left Fisher and Allen. Never."

Burr had begged Jacob – and Eve – not to leave Fisher and Allen when he so unceremoniously beat the broom out the door, but this wasn't the time to argue with Jacob about his revisionist history.

*This is bad, very bad.*

The right jury wasn't everything, but it was critical, especially in a case like this where so much turned on circumstantial evidence. It was critical to have an empathetic and sympathetic jury. With Jacob at the helm, Burr was afraid he wasn't going to get either.

*I'm doomed from the start. If only I hadn't been too clever by half. Again.*

Just then, a rap on his window. It was Eve with the umbrella. Burr rolled his window down.

"Time to go," she said.

Jacob shook his head *no.*

"How's it going?" Burr said.

Eve shook her head.

"Jacob did get a recess, though, to collect himself."

"I got the recess," Eve said. "Jacob turned white and started choking. It was medical."

Burr cringed.

"Judge Fisher is looking for you. If you don't come back right now, she said she was going to let Brooks pick all the jurors."

"Let him," Jacob said.

* * *

Burr sat in the Jeep, Zeke now in the front seat. The rain was falling harder now. Big drops splitting on the windshield. Burr started to count them. He got to eighty-seven when he heard the passenger door open.

"Have we lost already?" he said to the windshield.

Burr looked to his right, and there in her long, black robe was Judge Fisher. He shooed Zeke to the backseat. The judge sat next to him. This close to her, he could see that she had a touch of eye shadow, a hint of blush, and a pale lipstick.

Speechless, for perhaps the first time in his life, Burr looked over at her but didn't say a word.

"Have you had enough of this silliness yet?" she said.

"I beg your pardon?"

"You know exactly what I mean."

"I'm afraid I don't."

"You look quite healthy to me. And not a bit contagious."

"I beg your pardon?"

"If your partner says one more thing, you're going to lose before you start. Peter Brooks is eating him alive."

Words failed Burr.

"Mr. Lafayette, I want a fair fight. The only way to have one is with you in the courtroom. I know full well you haven't been ill. I'm disappointed that a lawyer of your caliber would stoop so low." She licked her lips. "And more disappointed that you thought you might fool me."

"Your Honor, I would never…"

"Be quiet. Mr. Wertheim became so nervous it looked like he was choking to death. I was afraid he was going to faint. I adjourned us for the day." She opened the door and got out. "I expect you to be in my courtroom tomorrow at 9 a.m. sharp." She slammed the door.

\* \* \*

Two days later, Burr sat in the courtroom of Judge Mary Fisher. Tommy Lockwood to his left, in a sincere, not-too-expensive blue suit with a white shirt and striped tie, dressed just as Burr had told him. Jacob sat next to Tommy. Eve, Karen and Lauren sat in the gallery immediately behind them. The gallery overflowed.

*A juicy murder will do that.*

The ever-so-suave Peter Brooks sat across the aisle from Burr.

Yesterday had gone better than Burr expected. They'd started the day with the four jurors picked on Jacob's watch. Four women, two of whom were divorced. Jacob was 0 for 4 but by the end of the day, the jury had seven women, five men, and one alternate, a woman. Burr had pressed Brooks, over and over, with his preemptory challenges, *voire dire* and plain old cussedness. He did his best to obfuscate the kind of juror he was looking for. He wasn't sure if Brooks ever figured it out, but he was damned if he'd under-estimate the prosecutor.

"All rise," the bailiff said. "The court of the Honorable Mary Fisher is now in session."

In walked Judge Fisher, gliding in her black robe, her hair pulled back neatly, her ever-present pink lipstick and pearl earrings. She sat, then looked around the courtroom and all that were in her domain. She nodded at Brooks, then Burr. Did he see a sparkle in her eyes?

"Be seated. The court of the Honorable Mary Fisher is now in session," said the bailiff.

Here they all were, in a courtroom, Burr's favorite place in the entire world. He tap, tap, tapped his just-sharpened Number 2 yellow pencil. All was as it should be.

Judge Fisher cleared her throat. "We are here today in the case of the People versus Thomas J. Lockwood. Mr. Lockwood is accused of murdering Helen Erickson Lockwood, his wife, on or about June 9th of last year." She looked at the prosecutor. "Mr. Brooks, you may begin."

Brooks stood. He walked toward the jury.

*He cuts a dashing figure*, Burr thought. *Sophisticated in his tailored black suit and starched white shirt. He didn't buy that on a government salary, but we all know there's money in cherries. Maybe too much money.*

Brooks stopped in front of the jury. "Ladies and gentlemen, we're here today because this man," Brooks pointed a long, manicured finger at Tommy, "murdered his wife."

*Brooks doesn't call Tommy by his name. Just 'this man.' It's a nice touch.*

"We're here because he murdered his wife. He shot her between the eyes with his pistol. Then he buried her on South Manitou in a shallow grave."

Brooks paused for effect. "And he almost got away with it. With the help of this man." Brooks pointed at Burr. "His lawyer."

Burr jumped to his feet. "Objection, Your Honor. The prosecutor is fabricating his own version of the truth. Not only is my client innocent, I have never been accused of such a thing and would never do such a thing."

Judge Fisher puckered her pink lips, then looked down her nose at the prosecutor.

"I will show it in my proofs." Brooks smoothed his shiny black hair in place.

Judge Fisher looked back at Burr. "Mr. Lafayette, this is an opening statement. Some theatrics are allowed."

Burr sat.

*It's a nice touch when he doesn't use Tommy's name. It's not a nice touch when he doesn't use mine.*

"Thank you, Your Honor," Brooks said. He turned back to the jury and put his hands in his pockets.

*How folksy. Brooks is a man of the people.*

"Ladies and gentlemen," Brooks said. "The defendant is accused of first-degree murder. First-degree murder means that the defendant killed his wife intentionally. He did it on purpose, and he planned to do it. It wasn't an accident and it wasn't done on the spur of the moment, in a fit of rage or passion. The defendant didn't lose his temper and kill his wife. He planned to kill her and that's exactly what he did. That is what first-degree murder is."

Brooks took his hands out of his pockets and put them on the railing of the jury box. "The legal term is 'malice aforethought' but for our purposes, it just means planning to kill someone and actually killing them. It's a crime so hateful that conviction requires life imprisonment without parole. That's how bad it is, and that's exactly what *he* did." Brooks pointed at Tommy again.

*It's time for another objection.*

Burr stood. He didn't jump to his feet this time. He pushed his chair out and stood.

"Your Honor, I object. It isn't the prosecutor's job to sentence Mr. Lockwood before this proceeding has even begun. Further, it is the sole responsibility of the court, not the prosecutor, to determine the sentence, if any."

Judge Fisher puckered her lips again. She looked at the jury. "Ladies and gentlemen, disregard Mr. Brooks' comment about sentencing." Then, to Brooks, "You may continue."

"Thank you, Your Honor."

Burr thought she could have been a little sterner with Mr. Smooth.

The prosecutor smiled knowingly at the jury. "The defendant's crime was a long time in the making. Let me tell you how it all began. You may well know or have heard parts of this before, but I'll tie it all together for you.

*Please do.*

"Helen Lockwood and her two sisters, Karen Hansen and Lauren Little-field, owned Port Oneida Orchards, a cherry orchard on Port Oneida Road." Brooks pointed at them. Burr had them sit right behind Tommy as a show of support. Brooks, of course, made a point of not bringing that up. "The Park Service needs that land for the Sleeping Bear Dunes National Lakeshore. The family, led by Helen, has fought the Park Service for years. They didn't want to sell their land at a more than fair price so the people of Leelanau County can benefit from the tourists that would bring much-needed commerce to our county.

"And they hired this man to stop the government." Brooks pointed at Burr again. "The defendant did the farming. He worked and worked until he was tired of working. Then he wanted to sell the orchards to the Park Service so he could enjoy the money and not have to work anymore. But his wife, the murdered Helen Lockwood, refused to sell. So, the defendant..."

*I wonder if the defendant has a name.*

"So, the defendant made a plan. He would kill his wife, then he could sell the orchards and get his share of the money."

Brooks stopped. He paced in front of the jury, letting all this sink in. He stopped, looked over at Burr and Tommy, then back at the jury, hands on the railing once more. "And this is what he did. When Helen took her boat to South Manitou, the defendant followed her there on the ferry. He got on board her boat and shot her in the face with his with his own pistol. He buried her in a shallow grave on South Manitou. Then he set her boat adrift on Lake Michigan to make it look like she had fallen overboard and drowned." Brooks walked back to his table and shuffled his papers.

*He's letting this sink in. Another nice touch.*

Brooks turned back to the jury.

"And do you know what he did then?" They didn't but they wanted to.

"This is what he did. Nothing. He did nothing. He played the grief-stricken husband. He waited. Then, after she'd been missing for a year..." Brooks pointed at Burr again, "he had this man go to court to have Helen Lockwood declared legally dead. Had he been successful, the farm would have been sold and the defendant would have had his share of the money."

Brooks paced in front of the jury, back and forth, back and forth.

"And it would have worked, except the sheriff found Helen Lockwood's body in a shallow grave on South Manitou Island. She had been shot between the eyes with Mr. Lockwood's pistol." Brooks clapped his hands. All of the jurors and everyone else in the courtroom jumped in their seats, including Burr.

*Well done.*

Burr wanted to object, but he couldn't think of anything to object to, and for one of the few times in his life, he couldn't think of anything to say.

Brooks stood with his hands in his pockets while the courtroom buzzed. At last, Judge Fisher had enough. She slammed down her gavel and the courtroom quieted without her saying a word. She looked at the prosecutor. "Do you have anything further, Mr. Brooks?"

"Yes, Your Honor." Brooks turned his back to the jury. "The people of the State of Michigan ask you to find the defendant, Thomas Lockwood, guilty of first-degree murder."

*Finally, a name.*

Brooks walked back his table and sat down. Judge Fisher looked over her glasses at Burr.

"Mr. Lafayette."

# CHAPTER SEVENTEEN

"Thank you, Your Honor." Burr stood. As was his ritual, he pulled down his cuffs and straightened his tie.

He walked up to the jury. He didn't have much to say, but what he had to say was important. "Ladies and gentlemen, the fact that you have been chosen to serve on this jury shows in itself that Judge Fisher, Mr. Brooks and I have the highest regard for your judgment. Because it will be your judgment that determines Thomas Lockwood's – Tommy's – fate. As citizens, it is perhaps the greatest responsibility you will ever have."

Burr paused and looked at each juror.

Then, "And to find Tommy guilty, you must find him guilty beyond a reasonable doubt." Burr paused again. "Beyond a reasonable doubt. Mr. Brooks didn't mention that, did he?" They shook their heads a collective *no*. "No, he didn't." Burr had them now. "Because to convict Tommy of killing his wife of twenty-three years, you can't *think* he did it. You can't *think* he *probably* did it. Or even that it's *likely* he did it." Burr looked down at his shoes, the tasseled oxblood loafers with tassels perennially in need of polishing, then back up at the jury. "You have to be sure beyond a reasonable doubt, which means you're convinced. *Absolutely positive.*"

Brooks bolted out of his chair. "Objection, Your Honor. That is not the definition of beyond a reasonable doubt."

"Sustained," Judge Fisher said. "Mr. Lafayette, you know better than that."

Burr nodded at her.

*Of course, I do. I'm surprised Brooks let me get this far.*

"Ladies and gentlemen, you must be convinced beyond a reasonable doubt. And that means you must be sure Tommy is guilty. You must be convinced."

"Objection, Your Honor," Brooks said.

Burr turned to the judge. "Your Honor, that is the definition of reasonable doubt. As has been said over and over again. In court after court. Trial after trial."

"Ladies and gentlemen of the jury, Mr. Lafayette is correct. Beyond a reasonable doubt means you are sure of the defendant's guilt. You must be convinced."

"Thank you, Your Honor." Burr turned back to the jury. "When this trial is over, when it's all said and done, you won't be convinced beyond a reasonable doubt."

Burr walked back to his table. He picked up a file he didn't need and pretended to look at it. He wanted to give the jury a little time to think about reasonable doubt. He finished pretending, closed the file, walked back to the jury.

"The prosecutor has a twisted and convoluted case. It's held together with Scotch tape and paper clips. It's held together this way because it doesn't make any sense. He's trying to push square facts into round holes. And it just doesn't hold together."

Burr looked down at his shoes again. He didn't want to overdo it, but his opening statement was going well so far. He looked up at them. "Helen Lockwood was murdered. Yes, she was." Burr looked over at Tommy, who looked at the jury with a sad, sincere look on his face, just like they had practiced.

*Well done.*

"No one saw Tommy kill Helen. No one even saw Tommy on the boat the day she went missing. No one. There were no witnesses. Not a soul." Burr paused again.

*This is going swimmingly.*

"It is true that Mrs. Lockwood was shot with a gun registered to Mr. Lockwood, but Helen often took the gun with her on her boat. In fact, Tommy insisted that she take it for her own protection. It's also true that Tommy, the widower, decided to sell the orchards. But who wouldn't? The orchards were their life, and it just wasn't the same without Helen.

"What could have happened? No one knows. None of us were there. My guess, though, is that Helen fought back. She was that kind of woman. She got her gun. They fought. The murderer took it from her and somehow she was shot."

Burr clapped his hands together. Everyone, every single soul in the courtroom, including Brooks, jumped. The courtroom erupted.

*Two can play that game.*

As before, Judge Fisher slammed down her gavel, louder than before. The courtroom quieted.

Burr pointed at Brooks. "His case is all speculation and conjecture. It's held together with Scotch tape and paper clips," he said again.

Brooks jumped to his feet. "Your Honor, defense counsel is lying. He's making things up."

Judge Fisher looked down her nose at the prosecutor. "This is an opening statement, Mr. Brooks. As I told Mr. Lafayette, there is room for some theatrics. Let's let the proofs tell the story."

*That went nicely.*

Burr looked up and down the jury. "As I was saying, it's really very simple. Helen Lockwood was murdered. But not by Tommy."

Except it wasn't plain and simple. Burr knew it and he knew Brooks knew it. If the trial could end here, right here and now, he'd win. But it wasn't that simple, and Brooks was too good a lawyer to let him win this easily.

Burr rapped his knuckles on Brooks' table as he walked back to the defense table.

*My opening statement was better than yours.*

He sat down next to Tommy and waited for the firestorm.

Judge Fisher looked down at the prosecutor. "Mr. Brooks, you may call your first witness."

Brooks stood. "Thank you, Your Honor. The State calls Emily Shaw."

Burr watched a tan, blond, twentyish woman walk past him to the witness stand. She had on a black dress, knee-length, long sleeves, crew neck, tucked at the waist. Modest but it couldn't hide her supple figure with all the curves in just the right places. Definitely not a little black dress, but certainly attractive. She wore no makeup but didn't need any. Burr thought her mouth was a little crooked, but no matter.

*I'd start with her, too.*

The conventional thinking would have been to start with the coroner, to get the body introduced. Everything Brooks needed would flow from the body, but Emily Shaw and what she knew was too good to pass up.

The bailiff, a thick, jowly man in his fifties, swore in Miss Shaw and lingered too long near her. Judge Fisher, well aware what was going on, shooed him away. Brooks walked up to his witness.

"Miss Shaw, would you please tell us where you were on June 23rd of this year."

She sat up straight and put her hands on her lap. "I was on South Manitou Island."

"Thank you, Miss Shaw. And what were you doing there?"

"I was camping."

"Miss Shaw, who, may I ask, were you with?"

"My boyfriend and my dog."

"Thank you, Miss Shaw. And what were you doing there?"

"We were camping out past the lighthouse, just off the beach. Riley, my dog, disappeared, which was unusual because he hardly ever lets me out of his sight. I went down to the beach because he loves the water, but he wasn't there. I went back to our campsite and he wasn't back yet. My boyfriend and I looked and looked but we couldn't find him. I was really worried."

She pulled at the hem of her dress which, like Burr's cuffs, didn't need pulling. "Finally, he came back. I was so happy to see him and so mad. He had a bone in his mouth. Then…"

"What kind of bone?"

"I didn't know. Not then, anyway. It was about, you know, this long." She held her hands about eighteen inches apart.

"Then what happened?"

"I took the bone away from him, which he didn't like. Then he took off."

"Thank you, Miss Shaw. Where did he go?"

Judge Fisher curled her finger at Brooks, who came over to the far side of the judge's rostrum. She spoke softly. "Mr. Brooks, far be it from me to tell you how to examine your witness, but perhaps you could ask Miss Shaw to just tell her story."

"I beg your pardon?"

"If you keep going like this, we'll be here until Christmas."

"Of course, Your Honor."

Brooks walked back to Emily Shaw. "Miss Shaw, would you please tell us in your own words what happened."

"Riley took off up the beach and came back with another bone. He took off again. This time I followed him. He ran about a quarter mile or so up the beach, then up into the weeds. I followed him. When I got there, he was digging, so I went to the hole he'd made. And... and...." Emily Shaw bit her lip. A tear ran down her cheek.

*Bravo. Just the way they practiced it.*

"What was it, Miss Shaw? What did you find?"

"It was a body. A skeleton mostly, with some clothes and...it was awful." She put her head in her hands.

Brooks walked back to his table and came back with an eight-by-eleven envelope. He took out four or five glossy photographs. "Your Honor, the State would like to introduce these photographs of the late Mrs. Lockwood as People's Exhibit One." He passed them to Judge Fisher. The unflappable judge looked like she might be ill.

Burr leapt to his feet. "I object, Your Honor. The witness has already testified that she found the body. There is no need for these pictures. All they will do is upset and prejudice the jury."

"Would you like to look at them, Mr. Lafayette?" Judge Fisher said.

"No, and I don't want anyone else to look at them, either."

The judge turned the pictures face down. "Objection denied. Mark these as People's Exhibit One."

*I knew that would happen.*

The bailiff marked the photographs and handed them back to Brooks. "Ms. Shaw, I have in my hand photographs taken by the sheriff's office of Mrs. Lockwood's body. As found on South Manitou."

"You told me I wouldn't ever have to look at them again."

Brooks ignored her. "Please tell us if these pictures are of the body you discovered on South Manitou." He showed her the pictures.

She shut her eyes, then looked away.

"Ms. Shaw, this is important."

"I can't look at them."

"I'm sorry, but you must."

She looked at Brooks, then glanced down at the pictures. "Yes, that's what I found. It was so terrible." She put her head back in her hands.

*Damn it all. Why does she have to cry like that?*

Brooks walked over to the jury. "Ladies and gentlemen, I'm afraid I have to ask you to look at these photographs of the late Helen Lockwood. They are extremely graphic, but it's necessary."

Burr stood. "I object, Your Honor. This is not only unnecessary, it is inflammatory. There is no reason to pass these pictures around. The witness identified that she found Mrs. Lockwood's body. That is all that is necessary. Showing the jury these horrible photographs will prejudice my client, perhaps irrevocably."

"I'm going to allow it," the judge said.

*The worst is going to happen.*

Brooks passed the photographs, one by one, around the jury. They shuddered, all of them. Burr thought two or three of them were going to be ill.

Brooks collected the photographs and walked back to Emily Shaw. He leaned over the witness box and put his hand on her shoulder. "I'm so sorry, Miss Shaw. Thank you for your testimony. I have no further questions, Your Honor." Brooks returned to his table and sat.

Burr tapped his pencil.

*If the trial ended now, Brooks would win.*

There was nothing Burr could do without making things worse. It was a stroke of genius on Brooks' part to call Emily Shaw as a witness. She was beautiful, sympathetic and showed the horror of finding a dead body. The photographs were genius. They were also totally unnecessary. The sheriff and the coroner were all that was needed, but it was genius. Burr didn't have any questions worth asking, but it would look worse if he didn't do something.

*I must be very careful.*

Burr stood and walked up to the still sobbing Emily Shaw. Burr handed her his handkerchief. She wiped her eyes and handed it back "Miss Shaw, I'm so sorry about what you found. I only have a few questions."

She nodded at him.

"Where are you from?"

"Atlanta."

"Atlanta. That's a long way from here. I must say you don't have a trace of a Southern accent."

She smiled at him, a weak little smile. "I grew up in Grosse Pointe. My family moved to Atlanta.

"Are you in school?"

"I go to the University of Georgia."

"I see. And who paid your way here?"

"Mr. Brooks."

Brooks jumped to his feet. "Objection, Your Honor. Irrelevant."

"Your Honor, it is most relevant if Mr. Brooks is paying to fly witnesses hither and yon."

"The county paid, not me," Brooks said.

"A poor county like Leelanau County, which does not have its own circuit court, is paying for witnesses to fly hither and yon." Burr liked the ring of it.

"I object, Your Honor." Brooks turned red under his tan.

"You said that. And this poor girl isn't even necessary to whatever your case might be."

"Stop it, Mr. Lafayette," Judge Fisher said. "You are out of line."

"I'm sorry, Your Honor. I don't like to see witnesses mistreated. I have no further questions." Burr walked back to his table. He hadn't hurt Brooks much, and if the prosecutor was going to pay to fly in all of his witnesses, it wouldn't matter if the trial was in the dead of winter.

Brooks called Fred Harris, the Leelanau County Sheriff, a big man who hadn't missed many meals. The prosecutor went through Sheriff Harris' qualifications, then got to the point.

"Sheriff, how and when did you learn that there was a body on South Manitou?"

The sheriff pulled up his belt. No mean feat since he was sitting down and his belly hung over his belt buckle.

"The Park Service called our office. Miss Shaw told the ferry captain, who called Park Service headquarters. They called us."

"And what did you do then?"

"I took a detail to the island right away. The girl led us to the body. We secured the crime scene. I left a deputy to guard the site. Then the crime scene boys came over."

"What did they find?"

"Not much."

"Could they identify the body?"

"No. It was badly decomposed and there was no identification." The sheriff pulled on his belt again. "I had a pretty good idea who it was, though."

"And why would that be?"

"She was the only missing person we had."

"Then what did you do?"

"I brought him over to look at the body." He pointed at Tommy.

Brooks turned to the court reporter. "For the record, the sheriff is pointing at the defendant, Thomas Lockwood." Brooks turned back to the sheriff. "And did the defendant identify the body?"

"He said he recognized her clothes, her coat and her shoes."

"Was he upset?"

"No, not really."

Burr popped up. "Objection, Your Honor. Counsel is leading the witness."

"Sustained. Mr. Brooks, you know better than that."

Brooks looked over at Burr, who smiled at him, then sat back down.

"Sheriff," Brooks said, "how did the defendant seem?"

Harris looked at Tommy, then, "He didn't seem too much of anything. Matter of fact, I'd say."

"What did you do after the defendant identified the body?"

"We sent it over to Dr. Murray for the autopsy." The sheriff hitched up his belt again.

"And what about the crime scene?"

"We took all the evidence back to my office."

"Thank you, sheriff. No further questions."

Burr walked up to the sheriff, who hitched up his belt for the third time.

"Must you?" Burr said under his breath.

"What's that?"

Burr hitched up his own belt. "It's annoying."

The sheriff turned red.

"Speak up, Mr. Lafayette," Judge Fisher said.

"Yes, Your Honor. I just wanted to make sure Sheriff Harris and I understood each other." Burr hitched up his belt again, just to make sure.

"Sheriff, was anyone at the crime scene when you got there?"

"I beg your pardon?"

"When you arrived at the crime scene, who was there?"

"No one."

"I see. So, between the time the body was discovered by Miss Shaw and the time you reached the crime scene, no one was guarding the site, preventing tampering with evidence and, of course, the body."

"No one knew about it."

"Sheriff, as soon as Miss Shaw told the ferry captain everyone within earshot knew, and as soon as the ferry captain radioed in, many more people knew."

"There was no one there when I got there."

"I wasn't asking you a question just now." Burr glared at the witness. "Just because no one was there when you got there doesn't mean someone hadn't been there." Burr paused. "Does it?"

"No one had been there."

"Please answer the question."

Brooks stood. "Objection. This is irrelevant."

Burr was going to keep going until Brooks objected, but he didn't think Brooks would object so soon.

"Sheriff Harris, please answer the question," Judge Fisher said.

"I suppose someone could have been there."

"Sheriff, how long was it from the time you learned about the body until you reached the crime scene?"

"Not very long."

"That is not an answer."

"I don't remember."

"Let me help you. You would have to get your equipment. You would have to get your deputies. You would have to launch your boat and take it out to the island. Once you got to the island, you'd have to walk to the crime scene. Since you don't remember, I'd say that would take the better part of a day."

"Four hours, no more." The sheriff started to hitch his belt. He looked up at Burr, then stopped.

"So, there was a known crime scene left unguarded for at least four hours."

"No."

"Was anyone from the sheriff's department guarding it?"

"No."

"Did you ask the Park Service to watch over it?"

"It wasn't necessary."

Brooks jumped up again.

"Sit down, Mr. Brooks," Judge Fisher said.

Brooks sat.

"Are you quite through, Mr. Lafayette?" she said.

Burr wasn't about to let the tubby sheriff off the hook.

"Not quite, Your Honor."

Burr looked at the sheriff. "You didn't ask anyone from the Park Service to watch the body until you got there and, in fact, when you got there, there was no one guarding the body. Is that right?"

The sheriff looked past Burr to Brooks. Then, "It really…"

Burr raised his hand. "Yes or no. That's all."

The sheriff turned redder than Brooks had. "Yes."

"Yes, you didn't ask anyone from the Park Service to guard the site and, yes, no one was guarding the site when you got there."

"Objection, Your Honor," Brooks said. "Asked and answered."

"Your Honor, I am just asking for a yes or no."

"Answer the question, sheriff."

"Yes."

"Thank you, sheriff." Burr started back to the defense table. The sheriff hauled himself to his feet. Burr turned around. "One more thing…."

Sheriff Harris, clearly flummoxed, plopped back down in his chair.

"Did the coroner come out to South Manitou to examine the body?"

"No."

"No? Isn't it customary for the coroner to come to the crime scene before performing an autopsy?"

"Sometimes."

"Sometimes? Why not this time?"

"We didn't think it was necessary."

"Why is that?"

"We'd done all that was necessary at the crime scene."

"Was anyone at the crime scene a doctor?"

"No."

"So, you didn't think it was necessary. Was it because Dr. Murray is too old?"

"Objection," Brooks said. "Sheriff Harris has been in office for over twenty years. His judgment is beyond reproach."

Burr walked up to Judge Fisher. He was just above eye level with her rostrum and her gavel.

*It could be dangerous standing so close to that gavel of hers.*

He pressed on. "Your Honor, the reason this is all so important is that it is impossible for my client to receive a fair trial with all of the evidence so corrupted."

"It's not corrupted," Brooks said.

Burr looked over at Brooks. "Oh, but it is." Then, to Judge Fisher. "Your Honor, I move for a mistrial."

Judge Fisher looked down her nose at Burr. "Counsel, you are everything I feared and more. Motion denied."

Burr made a point of looking outraged, but he knew he didn't have a chance at a mistrial. Not yet, anyway.

*It's good to plant a seed. And I've made Brooks pay for not starting with the coroner.*

"I have no further questions, Your Honor."

# CHAPTER EIGHTEEN

Brooks called Claude Murray, M.D., the coroner.

*I wish Brooks had started with Murray.*

Burr watched the ancient man shuffle to the witness stand. The bailiff swore him in.

Brooks led the doctor through his qualifications and his service, neither of which Burr intended to question.

"Dr. Murray," Brooks said, "were you able to identify the body?"

"Yes."

"And who was it?"

"Helen Lockwood."

"How did you identify it?"

"The body was badly decomposed. I used dental records."

"Thank you, Dr. Murray. And what was the cause of death?"

"Death by gunshot. There was a bullet hole in her forehead."

"Where in the forehead?"

"Right in the middle."

Burr watched the jury cringe.

Brooks continued, "Can you tell how far the gun was from her head when it was fired?"

"Not more than ten feet. More like four, I'd say."

"Did the bullet come out the back of the deceased's head?"

"No, the bullet lodged in her skull. There was no exit wound."

"Is that unusual?"

"No. It was a 380 Auto, so it wasn't terribly powerful."

"Were there any other wounds or signs of a struggle?"

"No."

"Would you say that it is likely that Mrs. Lockwood knew her killer?"

"She certainly could have."

"I have no further questions."

Burr let his breath out.

*This good doctor is remarkably coherent for a man his age. For any age. I must tread lightly.*

He walked up to the coroner.

"Dr. Murray, you testified that the body was badly decomposed. Is it possible that there could have been other wounds, bruises or scratches that would have been gone by the time the body was discovered?"

"Yes."

"So, it's possible that Mrs. Lockwood fought with her attacker. She could have been beaten, even tied up. Then shot, then carried to a grave, untied and buried."

"That is possible."

"I have no further questions, Your Honor."

Judge Fisher recessed for lunch. Lauren led them all – Burr, Jacob, Eve, Tommy and Karen – to Stacy's, a diner in a storefront on East Front Street. The only waitress was an older woman named Julie who called everyone either *Fatso* or *Slim* in a thick Greek accent. Burr was delighted that she called him Slim.

No one was particularly hungry except Burr, who always had a ferocious appetite when he was in trial. He ordered a cheeseburger and fries. Julie brought him the *de rigueur* Traverse City cherry pie.

"On the house," she said.

Burr asked for the check. She handed it to him and told him to take his money to the cash register and make his own change.

"Don't you get shortchanged?"

"If I get shortchanged, my customers will have to answer to God," she said.

*If only my life could be like that.*

* * *

After lunch, Judge Fisher called them to order. Burr wasn't surprised when Brooks called Deputy Glen Holcomb, the gangly deputy with the underage mustache and clear blue eyes who'd done his best to keep Burr from the body on the beach.

"Deputy Holcomb, you do the diving for the Leelanau County Sheriff's Department. Is that right?"

Holcomb sat up, ramrod straight. "Yes, sir."

*Deputy Glen's a one-man band. The sheriff's department really must be broke.*

"And you're a certified scuba diver."

"Yes, sir."

"Thank you, deputy." Brooks walked back to his table and picked up a sealed plastic bag. He returned to the witness stand, opened it, and took out a small pistol with a short barrel and a black handle.

*Here it comes.*

"Deputy Holcomb, do you recognize this pistol?"

"Yes, it's the one I found in the harbor at South Manitou."

"You're sure?"

"I can tell from the splotches of rust on the barrel."

Brooks handed the pistol to Holcomb. "Please examine it. Just to be sure."

"Stop right there," Judge Fisher said. "How do we know that the gun is unloaded."

"I checked it myself," Brooks said.

"Bailiff, take the gun and make sure it's unloaded. And don't point it at anyone."

The bailiff waddled over to Holcomb and took the gun. Then he pointed it at the floor and made sure there was no clip in the pistol. He checked the chamber, also empty. When he snapped the action back into place, everyone in the courtroom, jury included, jumped in their seats.

*That didn't help.*

The bailiff handed the gun back to Brooks, who passed it back to Holcomb.

"Deputy," Brooks said, delighted with what had just occurred, "is this the gun you found in the harbor at South Manitou?"

"Yes."

"Please tell us how and when you found it."

Holcomb sat up even straighter, if that was possible. "After Mrs. Lockwood's body was found, the chief had us look all over for the murder weapon. We couldn't find it anywhere, so he told me to get my gear and dive in the harbor. The ferry captain gave me an idea of where *Achilles* had been anchored, so I got a helper and went to looking."

"And what did you find?"

*The gun. Obviously.*

"Nothing. Couldn't find a thing. The water is clear as a bell there, but anything like a gun or anything like it would have settled in the sand, especially after a year."

"What did you do?"

"I kept on looking. It wasn't deep. No more than ten feet. I tried raking. That didn't produce nothing. So, I got the bright idea to get a metal detector which takes some doin' on account of it had to be the kind that worked underwater."

Brooks nodded.

Deputy Holcomb continued. "Well, I finally got her rigged up and then, *whammo*, I found this thing right away."

"What is it?"

"A 380 Auto. The one used to kill Mrs. Lockwood."

"Objection," Burr said. "That has not been established."

"It's about to be," Holcomb said.

Judge Fisher looked down at Holcomb. "Deputy, Mr. Lafayette's objection was not for you to reply to."

Holcomb lost his ramrod posture and looked like a puppy who'd just been caught with his mistress' shoe. "Yes, ma'am. Sorry."

"Counsel, you are quite right, if only for the next few minutes." Then to the jury, "Ladies and gentlemen, disregard Deputy Holcomb's statement that the pistol was used to kill the deceased." The jury gave the judge a collective nod.

Brooks cleared his throat. "Deputy Holcomb, was this the pistol you found in the harbor at South Manitou near the area where the ferry captain told you that the deceased's boat had been anchored on or about the time she disappeared?"

"Yes," Deputy Holcomb said. Ramrod straight again.

"Thank you." Brooks took the pistol back and pivoted to the judge. "Your Honor, the prosecution would like to introduce this pistol as People's Exhibit Two."

"Mr. Lafayette?" Judge Fisher said.

Burr had examined the pistol prior to the trial and didn't want to make any more of it than he needed to. "I have no objection, Your Honor."

Judge Fisher smiled at him. "Bailiff, mark this pistol as People's Exhibit Two."

"Thank you, Your Honor. I have no further questions."

Burr didn't really have any questions, but he thought he should try to muddy the waters a bit, so to speak.

Standing in front of Deputy Holcomb, Burr said, "Deputy, you testified that you found the pistol in the harbor at South Manitou earlier this summer. Is that correct?"

"Yes, sir."

"But you have no way of knowing when or how it got there, do you," Burr said, not asking.

"It got thrown over the side after she was killed."

"How can you know that?"

"That's what I'd a done."

"Deputy, you testified that you found the pistol at the bottom of Lake Michigan. For all you know, it could have been there for five years or dropped in the day before you got there."

"There was rust on it."

"It could have had rust on it when it was dropped in the lake."

Deputy Holcomb squirmed in his chair and lost his good posture. "That doesn't seem likely."

"The point is, you found the pistol, but you have no way of knowing how long it had been there or who put it there. Do you?" Burr said, the furthest thing from a question.

"No, no. I guess not."

"No further questions."

Burr sat down at his table. Tommy whispered to him. "Aren't they going to show that it was the murder weapon?"

"That's next."

"Does it matter what you just did?"

"Of course, it does. I'm going to make Brooks fight for every inch. When he gets tired or sloppy, that's how we win."

"I'm not sure I can take all this."

"Neither can Brooks."

The prosecutor called Boyd Wilcox, a sergeant with the Michigan State Police Crime Lab in East Lansing. Burr knew him all too well. The sergeant was short and thick and had a flat top you could land an airplane on. His wire-rimmed glasses pressed so tightly against his face, Burr thought it would take pliers to peel them off. Wilcox had testified in another of Burr's criminal cases. His evidence had almost gotten Burr's client convicted.

But what really confounded Burr was the sergeant's voice. He squeaked like a chipmunk.

Brooks read through the litany of Wilcox's credentials.

"Yes, those are my credentials," Wilcox squeaked.

"Thank you, sergeant." Brooks walked back to his table and picked up a sandwich-size plastic bag. He handed it to Wilcox. "Sergeant, are you familiar with the contents of this bag?"

Wilcox held it up to the light, turned it over in his hand, and passed it back to Brooks. "This is the bullet delivered to me by the sheriff's office. It was the bullet that killed the deceased."

"And how do you know that?"

"According to the autopsy, the coroner removed a bullet from the skull of the deceased. He delivered the bullet to the sheriff's office, who then delivered it to me."

*So much for arguing about the evidentiary chain.*

"Thank you, sergeant." Brooks looked up at Judge Fisher. "Your Honor, the people would like to introduce this bullet into evidence as People's Exhibit Number Three."

"Mr. Lafayette?"

"No objection, Your Honor." Burr thought it smart of Brooks to introduce the gun first, then the bullet, even though he could have had the bullet admitted when the coroner testified. Guns are always more impressive.

The judge admitted the bullet.

"Sergeant Wilcox, when you examined the bullet along with the handgun, what did you find?"

The sergeant cleared his throat, then squeaked, "I found that the bullet had been fired from the handgun."

Brooks paused and walked over to the evidence table. He picked up the bag with the bullet and the pistol. "Sergeant, you found that the bullet that killed Mrs. Lockwood was fired from this gun?"

"That's right."

"So, this gun is the murder weapon."

"Yes."

"You're sure."

"Without a doubt."

"Thank you, sergeant." Brooks walked back to his table.

Burr stood and walked up to Wilcox. The two of them had sparred before. Burr didn't like Wilcox, and the feeling was mutual. Wilcox pushed his glasses back into his face.

*If he pushes them back any further, they'll have to be surgically removed.*

Burr did his best to look at Wilcox, but it was painful. "Sergeant Wilcox, you testified that the pistol introduced into evidence is, in fact, the murder weapon. Is that right?"

"Yes," said the sergeant, knowingly.

"You're sure of that?"

"Absolutely."

Burr walked over to the evidence table and picked up the pistol. He showed it to Wilcox. "This is the murder weapon?"

Brooks stood. "Objection, Your Honor. Asked and answered."

Judge Fisher sighed. "I'm so tired of all of these theatrics." Another sigh. "I'll allow the question. But Mr. Lafayette, please get to the point."

He nodded at the judge. "Yes, Your Honor." Burr was getting there, but he had a point to make and wanted it set up for a big payoff. He took the pistol up to Wilcox, making sure the jury could see it, too. "As I was saying…" Burr looked back at Brooks, then at Wilcox, "Sergeant, this is the murder weapon, is that correct?"

"Yes."

"Thank you, sergeant. So, it's true that you know what killed Helen Lockwood. It was this pistol." Burr paused. "But you don't know who fired the pistol."

The gruff state policeman with the chipmunk voice sat there. He didn't say a word. Not a word.

"Do you?" Burr said. "Do you know who shot Helen Lockwood?"

"The pistol was registered to the defendant."

Burr raised his hand. "Stop right there. That wasn't my question. I'll ask you again. Do you know who shot Helen Lockwood?"

Wilcox mumbled.

"What did you say? Yes or no."

"I object, Your Honor," Brooks said. "Counsel is berating the witness."

"Your Honor, I am trying to get a simple answer. Yes or no."

The judge looked down at Wilcox. "Sergeant, please answer the question so that we can all hear you."

"No," Wilcox squeaked.

"No," Burr said. "You don't know who fired the pistol that killed Helen Lockwood."

"No."

"So, it could have been fired by someone who robbed her and then shot her."

Wilcox squirmed in his seat. "I suppose so."

"Yes or no, sergeant," Burr said.

"Yes."

"It could have been fired by the charter captain who found the boat?"

"Yes."

"Or the commercial fisherman who towed her boat in?"

Wilcox looked down at his hands. "Yes."

Burr looked at the jury. "It could have been fired by anyone. And there is no way for you to know." Burr looked back at Wilcox. "Is there?"

Wilcox looked up at Burr. The sergeant had turned blood red. "No, there isn't."

"I have no further questions," Burr said, in triumph. He walked back to the defense table.

Jacob reached in front of Tommy and shook Burr's hand. "Brilliant."

"Call your next witness, Mr. Brooks," Judge Fisher said.

Brooks stood. "Redirect, Your Honor." The judge nodded. Brooks stood at his table. "Sergeant, could the defendant, Mr. Lockwood, have fired the murder weapon? After all, it was his gun."

Wilcox brightened. "Why, yes, the defendant could certainly have fired the murder weapon." He beamed. The blood red complexion faded, and a glow came to his face.

*Damn it all.*

Burr stood. "Objection, Your Honor. Counsel is leading the witness."

"Isn't that what you were doing, Mr. Lafayette?" She slammed down her gavel. "Overruled."

Burr sat.

*Of course, that's what I was doing, but that doesn't mean Brooks can.*

"I have no further questions." Brooks sat.

"Call your next witness."

Brooks turned to the jury. "Ladies and gentlemen, we showed you where Mrs. Lockwood's body was found, how she was killed, and the murder weapon. Now we're going to show you how the defendant got to the scene of the murder."

Brooks faced the gallery. "The State calls Constance Gardener."

Burr watched the woman who sold the ferry tickets walk past him. She was short, barely five feet. She was thin, with a thin face. She wore a long skirt and had her hair in a braid that hung down past her waist. An aging hippie, Burr thought. After the bailiff swore her in, she pulled the braid over her shoulder so that it coiled up in her lap like a pet snake. Burr cringed. So did Brooks, and more importantly, so did the jury.

Brooks did his best to block the jury's view of the coiled hair snake while still letting them see her face. Burr thought the prosecutor had twisted himself so that he looked like a pretzel.

"Mrs. Gardener."

"Ms."

Brooks nodded. "Ms. Gardener, you sell tickets for the Park Service ferry to South Manitou. Is that right?"

"Yes."

"In Leland."

"That's right." The witness wrapped her braid around one hand, like a snake. Brooks flinched and moved closer to her.

"Thank you, Ms. Gardener. On or about June 9th of last year, did you sell a ticket to the defendant, Thomas Lockwood?"

"Yes." She coiled the braid tighter. Brooks moved in closer.

"Is there something wrong?" she said.

"No, of course not."

"You're standing awfully close to me."

Brooks took a step back and one step sideways, so the jury couldn't see her at all.

"After you sold him the ticket, did you see him board the ferry?"

"Yes."

"No further questions."

Burr walked up to the diminutive witness.

*The Park Service must not let her wear her hair down when she's at work.*

He made sure the jury could see her every move. "Ms. Gardener, I must say you have long hair."

She smiled and rewrapped the braid around her hand. The jury recoiled. *Perfect.*

Burr put his hands in his pockets. "Ms. Gardener, you testified that you sold Mr. Lockwood a ferry ticket on or about June 9th. Is that right?"

"Yes."

"Do you know the exact date?"

"No."

"Could it have been before June 9th?"

"Yes."

"Or after?"

"Yes."

"Ms. Gardener, Mrs. Lockwood's boat was found drifting off Sleeping Bear on June 11th, two days after she disappeared. Could you have sold Mr. Lockwood a ticket after that?"

"Well…" She started wringing her hands with her braid tangled between her fingers.

*This is perfect.*

"Answer the question, please."

"No…well…I don't know."

"Ms. Gardener, does the Park Service record who buys tickets?"

"No."

"So, you have no way of knowing when or even if Mr. Lockwood bought a ticket?"

"We'd know if he wrote a check or paid with a credit card."

"Do you know how Mr. Lockwood paid, assuming he even bought a ticket?"

"No."

"Do you keep records of those who pay you in cash?"

"No." The former hippie kept wringing her hands and now had her hair so tight, her braid was pulling her head down.

*That has to hurt.*

Burr smiled at her. "So, you have no way of knowing when, or even if, Mr. Lockwood bought a ticket."

She unwound her hair from her hands and sat up straight. "I know I sold him a ticket."

Burr ignored her. "Ms. Gardener, may I ask how tall you are?"

"Objection," Brooks said. "Irrelevant."

Burr looked up at the judge. "I am about to show the relevance, Your Honor."

"Please do," she said.

"Thank you, Your Honor." Burr turned back to the diminutive witness. "How tall are you Ms. Gardener?"

"Five foot."

"Ms. Gardener."

"Almost five foot. Four eleven."

"You're four-foot-eleven inches tall. Is that right?"

"Yes," she said, proudly.

"And how far is it from your ticket booth to the ferry?"

The witness looked away, then back at Burr. "I don't know. Fifty feet. Maybe more."

"And are there people standing and walking between your booth and the ferry?"

"Sure."

Burr had her now. "So, at four-eleven, how could you possibly know if Mr. Lockwood boarded the ferry? There are people in the way and you can barely see over the counter," Burr said, triumphant. "Isn't that right?"

"Sometimes I stand on a stool."

"Of course, you do. I have no further questions." Burr sat.

"Call your next witness."

"The State calls Frank Sutherland."

Burr watched the ferry captain, a short, thin man with short, gray hair, walk up the aisle. He had traded his captain's uniform for a navy-blue, summer-weight suit. Burr thought it surprisingly well cut, but then, the captain did live in Key West half the year.

The bailiff swore in the witness.

"Mr. Sutherland," Brooks said. "Actually, Captain Sutherland. You are a captain on the *Northern Lights*, the ferry that runs between Leland and South Manitou. Is that right?"

"Yes."

"And were you aboard the *Northern Lights* on or about June 9th of last year?"

"I was."

"And did you see Mr. Lockwood board the ferry?"

"I did."

"How, may I ask, did you know it was him?"

"I know who he is. From living here."

"You're sure it was him?" Brooks said.

"Absolutely."

"Thank you, Captain Sutherland," Brooks said. "You live in Key West in the winter. Is that right?"

"Yes."

"And when do you usually leave for Key West?"

"About the middle of October, give or take."

"That would be in about two weeks?"

"That's right."

Brooks turned to Burr and grinned. "I have no further questions."

*I didn't miss it by much.*

Burr pushed his chair back and stood. "Captain, do you remember the day, the exact day, you saw Mr. Lockwood board the ferry?"

"The exact day?" Sutherland straightened his tie, which didn't need straightening.

*That is annoying.*

Burr took a step back toward the witness. "Yes, the exact day."

"No."

"So, it's possible that Mr. Lockwood could have taken the ferry to South Manitou after Mrs. Lockwood went missing?"

"I suppose so."

"Thank you, Captain." Sutherland started to stand.

"One more question. Did you see Mr. Lockwood take the ferry back to Leland?"

Sutherland sat there. Not a word.

"Captain Sutherland?"

"I don't know."

"You're sure you saw him board the ferry, but you didn't see him get back on at South Manitou. Is that right? Perhaps he never got back on at South Manitou because he never got on in Leland. Is that possible?"

Brooks jumped to his feet. "I object, Your Honor. This is sheer speculation. Captain Sutherland already testified that he saw the defendant board the ferry in Leland."

"Sustained," Judge Fisher said. "Mr. Lafayette, no more speculation. Is that clear?"

"Yes, Your Honor, but I wasn't speculating. I merely asked a question and then connected the dots."

"That is the very essence of speculation."

"Yes, Your Honor." Burr turned back to Sutherland. "Captain Sutherland, is it true that you have been convicted of drunk driving?"

Sutherland sat bolt upright. "No."

"Should I get the court records? I have them right over there." Burr pointed to the defense table.

"It was a long time ago."

"So, you were convicted of drunk driving," Burr said, not asking.

"It was a long time ago."

"Yes or no."

"Yes."

"So, you were lying just now." Sutherland started to say something. Burr cut him off and turned to the jury. "Ladies and gentlemen, how can we know when Mr. Sutherland is telling the truth and when he isn't. Or what he has seen and what he hasn't." He looked back at Judge Fisher. "I have no further questions." Burr walked back to the defense table and sat.

Jacob leaned over. "That was exquisite."

"Your research was exquisite."

Brooks popped up. "Redirect, Your Honor."

The judge waved him on.

"Captain Sutherland, are you the only captain on the *Northern Lights*?"

"No."

"So, Mr. Lockwood could have taken the ferry back when another captain was in command?"

"Yes."

Burr popped up. "Objection, Your Honor. Calls for speculation. Captain

Sutherland has no way of knowing how Mr. Lockwood returned from South Manitou." He paused. "If he went over there in the first place, which I doubt."

"Enough, Mr. Lafayette." Judge Fisher looked at the jury. "Ladies and gentlemen, you will disregard Mr. Brooks' question, Captain Sutherland's answer, and..." she paused, "...Mr. Lafayette's comments."

"Your Honor, I'll rephrase the question." The judge nodded. "Captain Sutherland, is it possible that the defendant could have returned from South Manitou when you were not on board?"

"Yes."

"Thank you. I have no further questions." Brooks sneered at Burr on his way back to the prosecutor's table.

*We're splitting hairs, but I made my point.*

Brooks called two more witnesses, the his and her deckhands on the *Northern Lights*. They both testified they had seen Tommy board the ferry, but they weren't sure what day it was, and they hadn't seen Tommy on a return trip.

Burr was convinced Tommy was lying about fly fishing on the Betsie, but he thought he was in fine shape if this was all Brooks had.

Except it wasn't.

# CHAPTER NINETEEN

Burr looked at his watch. It was 3:30. Would Judge Fisher adjourn for the day? There was probably time for one more witness, but it had been a long day. Burr hoped she would adjourn them, but she didn't.

"Call your next witness."

"The State calls Lynne Flannery."

The bailiff swore in a twenty-something woman with freckles and a turned-up nose, all dolled up in a Park Service uniform. Or as dolled up as she could be in her Park Service uniform of gray shirt, green slacks, a badge and her name tag.

"Ms. Flannery, please tell us where you were on June 9th of last year and what you were doing."

"I was near the harbor on South Manitou. I'm a park ranger on the island."

"Did you see Mr. Lockwood?"

"Yes."

"What did you see?"

"I saw him get off the ferry."

"Anything else?"

"I was in the interior of the island after that, but later that day, I came back to the harbor. I saw a dinghy, a rubber raft, leave the powerboat anchored in the harbor. It came ashore. Mr. Lockwood got in and they went back to the powerboat."

"Do you know who was in the dinghy with Mr. Lockwood?"

"It was a woman."

"Do you know the name of the boat?"

"It was *Achilles*."

"Thank you, Ms. Flannery. And do you know what day this was?"

"It was June 9th."

"And how do you know that?"

"I remember because it was supposed to be my day off." She smiled at Brooks. "But somebody was sick so I got called in."

Brooks put his hands in his pockets. He turned to the jury and rocked back and forth on his feet. "Ladies and gentlemen, Ms. Flannery has not only placed the defendant on South Manitou on the last day the defendant's wife was seen alive, she also saw him go by dinghy to Mrs. Lockwood's boat." He stopped rocking. "And that confirms the testimony of the four witnesses who said they saw Mr. Lockwood board the ferry on that day." Brooks pointed at Tommy, then turned to the jury. "Ladies and gentlemen, just to be clear, Mrs. Lockwood was murdered with the defendant's gun. The ticket seller, the ferry captain and two deckhands have all testified that they saw the defendant board the ferry the day Mrs. Lockwood was killed." Brooks paused. "And Ms. Flannery has just now testified that she saw Mrs. Lockwood pick up the defendant in her dinghy and take him back to her boat. Where he murdered her."

Brooks looked at the judge. "I have no further questions, Your Honor."

On the way to his table, Brooks stopped in front of Burr. "I saved the best for last."

*This is terrible. It's worse than terrible.*

Burr tapped his pencil, then snapped it in two.

*This is just ducky.*

He looked over to Tommy. "Is this true?" Burr said, under his breath. Tommy didn't say anything. Burr grabbed Tommy's shoulder. "Is this true?"

Tommy nodded.

"Mr. Lafayette," Judge Fisher said.

Burr ignored her. To Tommy, "You've been lying to me all along."

"No."

"What would you call it?"

"Mr. Lafayette, if you would rather speak with your client than cross-examine the witness, I'm going to excuse her."

Burr pushed his chair out and walked slowly to the park ranger. Waiving the preliminary exam had just blown up in his face. The best he could do was try to muddy the waters again.

"Ms. Flannery, about how far away were you from the person you saw get in the rubber raft?"

"Oh," she said, surprised by Burr's question. "Well, I'm not sure. A hundred feet. Maybe a little more."

"That's a long way." Burr looked at the back of the courtroom, then back at the ranger. "Ms. Flannery, I think the back of this courtroom is probably about thirty feet. So, it was at least three times as far as that."

She scrunched her turned-up nose but didn't say anything.

"Let me help." Before Brooks could object, Burr hurried to the back of the courtroom. He turned back to the park ranger with the scrunched-up nose. "Can you see me back here?"

"Yes," she said, weakly.

"So maybe three times as far as this?"

"Maybe."

Burr raised three fingers and held them at his waist. "Ms. Flannery, how many fingers am I holding up?"

The ranger squinted.

Brooks erupted. "Your Honor, this is outrageous. Lafayette's eye exam has no relevance to what Ms. Flannery saw on South Manitou."

*I've made it to a last name basis with Brooks.*

Brooks wasn't done. "Ms. Flannery testified that the defendant got into the raft. That's all we need to know."

"For the record, I was holding up three fingers," Burr said.

"Mr. Lafayette, stop what you're doing and join us up here." Judge Fisher wasn't screaming at him, but she certainly wasn't using her indoor voice.

Burr strolled up the aisle and stopped in front of the jury. "Ladies and gentlemen, I don't doubt that the witness saw someone get in the raft, but I have grave doubts whether, at that distance, she could be sure it was Mr. Lockwood." Burr leaned on the railing of the jury box. "Ms. Flannery, did you ever speak with either Captain Sutherland or the deckhands about seeing Mr. Lockwood get into the dinghy?"

"No."

"I see. So, while you saw someone get into the dinghy, you didn't corroborate that with anyone else?"

"No."

Burr looked back at Brooks, who was seething. "For all you know, if they had seen Mr. Lockwood, they could have seen him on an entirely different day."

"I suppose so."

"And, isn't it possible that when Mrs. Lockwood picked up whoever it was she picked up, that she had dropped him off on the beach earlier?"

She squirmed. "I don't know. I suppose so."

"And isn't it possible that whoever was on the boat came over to the island with her?"

"I don't know."

Burr walked over to her. "Of course you don't know." Burr put his hands on the railing. "This is all speculation. I have no further questions." Burr returned to his chair, the waters duly muddied.

Brooks wasn't done. "Redirect, Your Honor."

The judge raised her eyebrows but nodded at him. Brooks stood and pointed at Tommy.

"Ms. Flannery, in your opinion, was it the defendant, Mr. Lockwood, who got in the dinghy with his wife?"

"Yes."

Brooks sat, the waters a little less muddy.

The learned Judge Mary Fisher had finally had enough for the day, but before adjourning, she called Burr and Brooks to the bench. "Gentlemen," she said, "this is a trial, not a two-man play."

"Your Honor?" Brooks said.

"Enough of the theatrics. Especially you, Mr. Lafayette. Do I make myself clear?"

The lawyers nodded.

*This is nothing if not theater.*

Burr walked out of the now empty courtroom, his entourage a few steps ahead. When they reached the hallway, he took Tommy by the arm and pulled him into the coat room. He spun Tommy so they were face-to-face, Tommy's back to a coatrack on wheels.

"I knew you were lying to me. You never went fly fishing. You took the ferry over to South Manitou and you killed your wife."

Tommy took a step back. "I didn't. I swear I didn't."

"Five people just testified they saw you. You bought a ticket, rode the ferry and climbed in the dinghy. It was all I could do to stop you from being convicted on the spot."

"I didn't kill her."

Burr moved right into Tommy's face. "You lied to me."

Tommy stumbled backed into the coatrack. It crashed to the floor. Tommy tripped over it and fell, too. Eve rushed in. "Don't shout. Everyone can hear you." She bent over Tommy. "Let me help you."

Tommy scrambled to his feet. "I did go fishing on the Betsie."

"After you murdered your wife."

"I didn't kill her."

Burr closed in on Tommy again. Eve stepped between them. "Burr, please."

Burr glared at Tommy over Eve's shoulder. "All you had to do was tell me the truth. I can work with the truth. Now, no one will believe me."

"People always believe you," Eve said. "Especially women."

"Not now, Eve." Burr backed up and leaned against the wall. "Tell me what happened, Tommy. What really happened."

Tommy stood the coatrack back up, then pushed it away from him. The wheels squeaked when it rolled across the floor. He looked straight at Burr.

"I'd planned to go fishing after Helen left that morning. I got up and packed, but I decided that Helen and I needed to talk about selling the orchards. I wanted to talk to her right then. So I drove to Leland and bought a ticket for the ferry."

"Why didn't you wait until she got back?" Burr said.

"I was ready to sell. I knew she wouldn't listen to me, especially when we were at home. Around the orchards. I thought if we could talk about it away from the farm, it might make a difference."

*He's still lying.*

Burr bit his lip. "Go on."

"I took the ferry over. I got her attention and she came and picked me up. I told her what I wanted to do, but she wouldn't hear of it."

Burr looked Tommy in the eyes. "You lost your temper and killed her."

Tommy shook his head. "No. No. It wasn't like that. We argued about the orchards. I told her the feds were going to win anyway so we might as well get on with life. She said she'd never give up. I finally gave up, just like

I always do with her. She took me ashore, I took the ferry back and I went fishing."

*He's still lying, but I'm not sure what he's lying about.*

Burr paced back and forth in the cramped coatroom.

Burr stopped and stared at Tommy again "Why didn't you tell me? It would have made things much easier."

"I don't know. I should have. I guess I didn't think you'd believe me."

"I don't believe you now."

"I didn't think anyone would notice me. I didn't think they'd find out."

Burr nodded.

*This sounds a little more like the truth. Not much, but a little.*

"I'm sorry," Tommy said.

"No one would have noticed if Helen hadn't been killed. It wouldn't have mattered, but Brooks has it that you went over on the ferry in plain sight, killed Helen, then took the ferry back. If that's what you did, it was genius. It would have worked if the dog hadn't dug her up." He started toward Tommy.

Eve stepped in front of him. "Burr, please."

"Now what do we do?" Tommy said.

"Now we have dinner." Burr walked away.

\* \* \*

Back at the Northport marina, Burr picked up Zeke, who had been watched over by a generously tipped dock boy.

Burr met the rest of them – Jacob, Eve, Tommy, Lauren, her husband, Curt, Karen, and her husband, Glenn – at the Happy Hour, which was the only 'happy' anywhere in sight.

Karen asked how Burr thought it had gone today.

Jacob, who refused to eat "dead cow," pushed away the macaroni and cheese he had ordered from the children's menu. "Burr did a magnificent job of confusing things. He's always been a master of confusion."

Eve picked at her chicken Caesar salad.

"Tommy, there was nothing confusing about you taking the ferry to South Manitou," Karen said. She picked at her hamburger patty, sans bun, but with onion.

"Why didn't you tell us?" Lauren said.

Tommy studied his french fries. "I should have. I'm sorry," he said without looking up.

"Right now, it looks like you killed her," Curt said.

"Stop it, Curt," Lauren said.

Tommy looked up from his fries. "She was alive when I left. She dropped me off at the beach. The last time I saw her, she was taking the dinghy back to *Achilles*."

"The dinghy," Burr said through a mouthful of burger. "Where is the dinghy?"

"What difference does it make?" Karen said. "We need to find out who got on *Achilles* after Tommy."

"Unless it was Tommy," Lauren said.

# CHAPTER TWENTY

Burr and company waited for Judge Mary Fisher to make her grand entrance. The single rose in the bud vase, fresh each day, waited for her on the corner of her rostrum. At last, she appeared, wearing her signature pearl earrings, gliding into the courtroom, her black robe billowing around her.

The bailiff called them to order.

Brooks stood and looked at the jury. "Ladies and gentlemen, as you will recall, we have already established that poor Mrs. Lockwood was murdered with her husband's pistol. Then we established the fact that the defendant took the ferry to South Manitou Island, where his wife picked him up in their dinghy and took him back to her boat. That was the last time she was seen alive. Alone with her husband on the way back to her boat. Where he murdered her with his pistol." Brooks looked over at Tommy. "I am now going to show you why he murdered his wife."

*Brooks is already in rare form.*

Burr thought the prosecutor had done a good job so far. Too good. So good that the sisters were beginning to believe Brooks. It was all Burr could do to keep them from running Tommy over in the parking lot of the Happy Hour.

Brooks looked at the gallery. "The State calls Dale Sleeper."

Burr watched the overfed park ranger, in charge of taking private property from unsuspecting landowners, lumber up to the witness stand. He collapsed into the witness chair and the bailiff swore him in.

Burr thought Sleeper's eyes, separated by his broad, flat nose, were still too far apart.

*If I could push them closer together, he'd be easier to look at.*

Brooks walked Sleeper through his job, what he did, how long he'd done it, and what he'd gotten done.

*Brooks certainly brought out the best in Sleeper. After all he's done for the Park Service, he should be up for sainthood.*

Brooks got to the meat in the sandwich. "Mr. Sleeper, do you know the defendant, Thomas Lockwood?"

"I do."

"And how do you know him?"

"The Park Service has been trying to acquire his late wife's and her sisters' orchards for the past seven years."

"Seven years." Brooks wagged his finger. "That's a long time."

"It sure is. Cost the taxpayers a fortune in lawyers."

"And, Mr. Sleeper, Mr. Lockwood's wife was the late Helen Lockwood, who he is accused of murdering. Is that right?"

Burr, on his feet. "Objection, Your Honor. The witness may identify Mrs. Lockwood but the second part of his question is inappropriate." Burr knew it wasn't much of an objection, but it was all he had, and he was damned if he'd let Brooks put words in Sleeper's mouth.

Brooks looked back at Burr. "I withdraw the question," Brooks said, the damage done to Burr and his client. Back to the witness, "Mr. Sleeper, you knew the defendant and his late wife."

"That's right."

"And you were trying to purchase their farm for the new National Lake-shore. Is that right?"

"Yes."

"And how would you describe your relationship?"

"She fought me tooth and nail." Sleeper pulled up his slacks by the belt buckle, no mean feat for a big man sitting down. "Every step of the way."

Brooks smiled at Sleeper.

*This is going swimmingly for both of them.*

"In your opinion, what was Mr. Lockwood's position about selling the farm?"

"I'd say he sided with her right along. But after she died, he came to see me. Said he was ready to sell."

"Did that surprise you?"

"You could have knocked me over with a feather."

*That would take a very big feather.*

"So, Mr. Sleeper, Mr. Lockwood didn't want to sell the farm while his wife was living, but after she died, he suddenly changed his mind. Is that right?"

"Yes."

"In your opinion, do you think Mr. Lockwood murdered his wife so he could sell the farm and get the money?"

"Seemed that way to me."

Burr, on his feet. "Your Honor, I object. The witness is purely speculating. This is outrageous." Burr looked down at his feet as if he was thinking something over, which he wasn't. He looked up at the judge. "Your Honor, I move for a mistrial."

"Your Honor, I withdraw the question," Brooks said again, more damage done.

Judge Fisher sat up straight in her chair. She looked at the jury. "Ladies and gentlemen, you are to disregard Mr. Brooks' question and Mr. Sleeper's answer." She took off her glasses and looked down her nose at the prosecutor. "Mr. Brooks, you will stop asking questions that you know are not allowed. Is that clear?"

"Yes, Your Honor," Brooks said.

*He doesn't care at all.*

"Let me make myself perfectly clear. If this continues, I will grant Mr. Lafayette's request for a mistrial." She leaned toward him. "Do you understand me?"

"Yes, Your Honor," Brooks said, insufficiently chastened. "I have no further questions."

Brooks sat. Burr stood. He walked up to Sleeper.

"Mr. Sleeper, you testified that you were in charge of condemning and taking all of the property from local property owners for the park. Is that right?"

"I am in charge of land acquisitions."

"About how many pieces of real estate have you acquired to date?"

"Maybe two hundred."

"You've taken the property of two hundred people. Is that right?"

"Objection, Your Honor," Brooks said.

"Your Honor, the witness's job is critical to my questions."

"I'll allow it."

"Thank you, Your Honor." Burr didn't think it was particularly relevant, but he knew the locals didn't like the government to begin with, and they all knew someone who had lost their property to the new park.

"Mr. Sleeper, how long have you worked for the Park Service?"

"Twenty-nine years."

"And how long have you worked on condemning, excuse me, acquiring property for the Sleeping Bear Dunes National Lakeshore?"

"Ten years."

"And would you say putting this together is the crowning achievement of your career?"

"I suppose so."

"And would you say you had a hostile relationship with Mrs. Lockwood?"

Sleeper wiggled in his chair. "I suppose so."

"Would you say you were enemies?"

"I don't know."

"Mr. Sleeper, isn't it true that the Lockwoods' family orchard, one of the biggest and most productive orchards in Leelanau County, is the largest piece of property you have yet to acquire?"

"Yes."

"And isn't it true that the Lockwoods' orchards are almost two miles from the beach?"

"It's the gateway to the park."

"What does a cherry orchard possibly have to do with a beach?"

"Objection, Your Honor. Irrelevant."

"I am about to show the relevance, Your Honor," Burr said.

"Do so quickly," the judge said.

"Mr. Sleeper, isn't it true that you hated Mrs. Lockwood? Isn't it true that you fought publicly?"

"We were adversaries."

"You were adversaries." Burr paced back and forth in front of Sleeper. "You hated Mrs. Lockwood. You wanted that farm so much it became personal. Didn't it?"

"No."

"Do you ever go to South Manitou?"

"Yes."

"Did you go the day Mrs. Lockwood was killed? Did you hate her so much you killed her?"

"No."

"I have no further questions," Burr said, his own damage done. Burr sat down.

*I can't believe I got that in.*

"Redirect, Your Honor."

"Go ahead."

Brooks stood at his table. "Mr. Sleeper, did you go to South Manitou on the day Mrs. Lockwood was killed?"

"No."

"I have no further questions," Brooks said.

Judge Fisher looked at Burr. "Counsel?" Burr shook his head.

Brooks stood back up. "The State calls Consuela Rodriquez." The longtime housekeeper walked slowly toward the witness stand. She looked this way and that, as if she were about to be eaten alive, which, of course, she was.

After the bailiff swore her in, she sat primly, hands clasped together on her lap. Burr thought she was trying to keep them from shaking, which she almost succeeded at doing.

Brooks picked up on how she was feeling and started out slowly.

*He's no fool.*

"Ms. Rodriquez, you were the housekeeper for the Lockwoods. Is that right?"

She nodded.

Brooks smiled and put a hand on the rail to the witness box. "Would you please answer so the court reporter can get it on the transcript?"

Consuela nodded again.

"With your words, Ms. Rodriguez. Yes or no."

"Yes," she said softly.

"For the record, that's a 'yes'," Brooks said. "Ms. Rodriguez, you are still the housekeeper for Mr. Lockwood."

"Yes," she said, softly.

"Another 'yes'," Brooks said. "Ms. Rodriguez how long have you worked for the Lockwoods up through today?"

"I don't know. A long time."

"More than twenty years?"

"Sure," she said, a little louder and with a smile.

"Did you ever overhear Mr. and Mrs. Lockwood talk about selling the orchard?"

"Yes."

"And what did they say?"

Burr stood. "Objection, Your Honor. Hearsay."

Consuela looked at Burr.

Brooks lost his avuncular style. "Your Honor, Mrs. Lockwood has been murdered and obviously can't testify. I assume the defendant will choose not to testify, as is his Fifth Amendment right. This is an exception to the hearsay rule."

The housekeeper looked at Brooks.

"This is inadmissible hearsay," Burr said.

She looked at Burr.

"Your Honor, as I'm sure you know, the purpose of the hearsay rule is to make sure that witnesses who actually said something, testify. So that we know what the person actually said and not get it second-hand. Because Mrs. Lockwood has been murdered, she can't testify. The law allows hearsay in these situations."

Consuela looked at Brooks.

*She's going to get a stiff neck if she keeps twisting her head like that.*

Judge Fisher pounded her gavel. "Stop it, both of you. Because of Mrs. Lockwood's unfortunate demise, I'm going to allow the question."

"Please reserve my objection for appeal," Burr said.

*At least poor Consuela won't have to keep turning her head.*

Uncle Pete was back. "Let's start over, Ms. Rodriquez. Did you ever hear Mr. and Mrs. Lockwood talk about selling the farm?"

"Yes."

"And did Mrs. Lockwood want to sell the farm?"

"No."

"She never wanted to sell the farm?"

"No. Never."

"Not even just before she disappeared?"

"No."

"Thank you, Ms. Rodriguez." Brooks leaned on the railing.

*Aren't they just the best of friends.*

"What about Mr. Lockwood?"

Consuela bit her cheek. "No. He didn't either. Not at first."

"Did he change his mind?"

"At the end, he said he did want to sell."

"Did they argue about it?"

"Yes."

Brooks took a step back, acting incredulous. "Would you say they fought about it?"

"Oh, yes."

"Did Mr. Lockwood threaten Mrs. Lockwood?"

"Yes."

Brooks leaned in. "What did he say?"

"Something like, we need to sell the orchards. Now. You'll be sorry if you don't."

"Did he say anything else?"

"Oh, yes."

*He's really got her going now.*

"What did he say?"

"Oh, I don't know. Something like, you better do it. You'll be sorry. Things like that."

"Was he ever angry?"

"Yes."

"Did you think Mr. Lockwood might kill his wife?"

"Objection, Your Honor. What Ms. Rodriguez may have thought about Mr. Lockwood's state of mind is pure speculation and totally irrelevant."

"Sustained." Judge Fisher took off her glasses and waved at the prosecutor. "Mr. Brooks, I allowed the hearsay. I will not allow speculation."

"Yes, Your Honor." Brooks, the avuncular uncle, went back to work. "Were you personally afraid for Mrs. Lockwood that Mr. Lockwood might harm her?"

"Yes."

"I have no further questions."

It was Burr's turn. He thought he'd be the kindly uncle from the other side of the family. He leaned on the other side of the railing.

"Ms. Rodriquez, how long did you say you worked for Mr. and Mrs. Lockwood?"

"Twenty-three years."

"Twenty-three years. That's a long time."

Consuela nodded.

"And you cooked and kept house?"

"Except Sundays." She smiled.

"Of course."

"I went to the store, too."

Burr nodded. "So, you were very involved in the domestic life of the Lockwoods."

She nodded again.

"You were in their home. Every day." Burr paused. "Except Sunday."

"Yes."

"And who did the farming? Worked and ran the orchards?"

"Mister. He did."

"What about Mrs. Lockwood?"

"No."

"What did she do?"

"The money."

"I see." Burr put his hands in his pockets. "Did Mrs. Lockwood get involved in the farming?"

"She told Mister what to do."

"I see. And did Mr. Lockwood work hard in the orchards?"

"Oh, yes. Very hard." She smiled again.

"Was he tired at night?"

Brooks stood. "I object, Your Honor. This is irrelevant."

Burr looked at Brooks. He took his hands out of his pockets and put them on his hips. Then he looked at Judge Fisher. "I am about to show the relevance."

"Please get on with it."

"Thank you, Your Honor."

He put his hands back in his pockets. "Ms. Rodriguez, was Mr. Lockwood tired at night?"

"Oh, yes. He worked very hard."

"And was he ever discouraged after work?"

She cocked her head again.

"Did he ever say that running the farm was hard?"

"Yes."

"Did he ever say he'd like to sell it?"

Brooks stood again. "Objection. Leading the witness."

"Your Honor, this is a simple yes or no question. It is not leading the witness."

"You may continue."

"Thank you, Your Honor. Did Mr. Lockwood ever say he'd like to sell the farm?" Burr said. He purposely left out *when he was tired.*

"Yes. Once in a while."

"Did anyone else in the family want to sell the farm?"

"Miss Karen. She did. Not Miss Lauren."

"Thank you, Ms. Rodriguez." Burr turned to the jury, hands still in his pockets. "Ladies and gentlemen, it seems that, sometimes over the years, Mr. Lockwood did want to sell the farm. And so did Mrs. Lockwood's sister Karen. This wasn't new, and there certainly was no reason to believe Mr. Lockwood killed his wife over it." Burr looked at Brooks. "I have no further questions."

"Redirect, Your Honor."

Judge Fisher looked up at the prosecutor. "Mr. Brooks, is it possible for you to ask all your questions at once?"

Brooks stood. "I could, Your Honor, if Mr. Lafayette would stop twisting the truth."

She scowled at Brooks but didn't say anything.

"Ms. Rodriguez, would you say that Mr. Lockwood was more interested in selling the farm just before Mrs. Lockwood disappeared?"

Consuela put her hands on the railing. "Yes."

"And did Mr. Lockwood raise his voice?"

"Yes."

"Did he threaten her?"

It was Burr's turn. "Asked and answered."

Consuela put her hands back in her lap and wrung them.

"You need not answer the question, Ms. Rodriguez," the judge said.

She looked down at her hands.

"I have no further questions, Your Honor," Brooks said.

"Thank you, Ms. Rodriquez," Judge Fisher said. "You are excused.

After Consuela had taken her seat, Brooks turned to the jury. "Ladies and gentlemen, you have just heard the witness testify she heard the defendant threaten his wife." He walked over to the jury box. "We have shown that Mrs. Lockwood was killed with her husband's pistol. The pistol was found in the harbor at South Manitou, where she anchored her boat on the day she was murdered. Four witnesses have testified that they saw the defendant on the ferry. Another witness has testified that she saw Mrs. Lockwood pick up the defendant on the island in her dinghy and take him back to her boat." He paused. "And now Mr. Sleeper and Ms. Rodriguez have testified that the defendant wanted to sell the orchards, but Mrs. Lockwood did not."

Brooks looked at Tommy, then back at the jury.

"And we've just heard that the defendant threatened his wife." Brooks pointed at Tommy. "That man murdered his wife. You have all the proof you need to convict him of first-degree murder."

Tommy looked away, which Burr had told him never to do.

"Your Honor, the prosecution rests."

*Damn it all. I can't let it end here.*

Burr stood. "Your Honor, I have a few more questions for the witness."

Judge Fisher sighed, clearly exasperated. "Mr. Lafayette, I have already excused the witness, and Mr. Brooks just finished presenting his case."

"Your Honor…."

She cut him off. "If you have more questions for Ms. Rodriguez, you may call her during your defense, which will begin in the morning. We are adjourned." She slammed her gavel and left the courtroom.

# CHAPTER TWENTY-ONE

It was raining when Burr walked outside. A cold, fall rain. The sky was the gray of fall and the gray of winter to come. He brushed the rain off his suit, climbed into the Jeep and made his way to M-22 and up the shoreline. The wind blew about twenty from the northwest and waves were crashing on the beach.

"It's almost duck season," Burr said to Zeke, who wasn't with him. He kept heading north on M-22, the rain beating on the windshield and the windshield wipers not really keeping up. He looked in his rearview mirror. The rain streamed down the back window with the broken windshield wiper. It was like looking through a glass of water. "I don't need to know what's behind me," he said, out loud again. "It's a good way to live. Mostly."

It was dark and still raining by the time he reached Northport. "I have to do *something*," he said out loud again. "Brooks has me. I'm euchred if I can't come up with something." He drove past the marina, turned into Craker's and parked at the shed where *Achilles* lay on the hard. He tried the door. Locked. "Damn it all." He took a credit card out of his wallet and made for the door. He slipped it between the casing and the door.

*This might be the only thing this is good for.*

He fiddled with the card, getting wetter by the second. Finally, the latch clicked, and he was inside.

He fumbled around in the dark until his hand swiped across the light switch. The shed lit up but not much. He threaded his way between the boats, packed together like commuters in the subway. Maybe a foot between them. He found *Achilles*, still in the corner, and then a ladder. He climbed the ladder and stood in the cockpit, careful not to slip with his leather soles. "Where would I keep an inflatable dinghy?"

Helen could have launched the dinghy, then towed it, but towing a dinghy in any kind of sea was difficult. Maybe she stowed it. Burr searched the boat, all the likely places, the lockers in the cockpit, the engine compartment, down below. Nothing. He couldn't find it anywhere. Then he remembered. He raced back to the cockpit. He opened the lockers again, one by one. Then he opened the lazarette. Empty. It was empty.

*This must be where she stowed the dinghy, but it's sure not here now.*

He sat in the main salon.

*Maybe the dinghy doesn't matter. Maybe it sunk while Achilles was adrift. Filled up and sank. That's probably what happened.*

*But what if the killer anchored Achilles around the other side of the island and took Helen's body ashore to bury it. Then took the dinghy back to Achilles. Then put Achilles on autopilot and sent her off to Milwaukee. Then took the dinghy back to shore and scuttled it. Then walked to the harbor and took the ferry back to Leland.*

*Or maybe the killer rode the dinghy back to the mainland. Dicey, but it could be done if the seas were calm.*

\* \* \*

Burr stood in front of the jury. "Ladies and gentlemen, the prosecution has presented an altogether unconvincing case. Mr. Brooks has tried to tie certain facts together, but the facts he presented don't fit what really happened. I am about to show you why." Burr looked at the gallery. "The defense calls Consuela Rodriguez."

She took the witness stand, still nervous or nervous again. Burr didn't know which. Judge Fisher reminded Consuela she was still under oath.

Burr walked to the evidence table and picked up the 380 Auto, the murder weapon. He walked back to the witness stand and showed it to Consuela.

"Have you seen this before?"

"Yes."

"And what is it?"

"Mr. Tommy's gun."

"Thank you, Ms. Rodriguez. And do you know where this was usually kept?"

"In Mr. Tommy's dresser. In the top drawer."

"Thank you, Ms. Rodriguez."

Burr put the gun in his other hand. "And did Mrs. Lockwood know about this gun?"

"Yes."

"Did she ever use it?"

"Oh, yes. Mr. Tommy showed her how. They practiced out back."

"Really," Burr said, surprised but not really surprised. "Do you know why he had her practice?"

She smiled, not so nervous now. "He wanted her to take it with her when she went places without him."

"Like on her boat?"

"Yes."

"So, it would be normal for her to have it with her when she took the boat out?"

"Yes."

Burr turned to the jury. "Ladies and gentlemen, the fact that Mrs. Lockwood was killed with a gun registered to Mr. Lockwood doesn't mean that he shot her with it. Mrs. Lockwood kept the gun with her on her boat." He looked back at the judge. "I have no further questions."

Brooks stood. He walked up to Consuela and smiled, but she looked scared again.

"Ms. Rodriguez, do you know if Mrs. Lockwood took the murder weapon on her last visit to South Manitou?"

"I think so."

"Did you see her take it?"

"No," she said, nervous again.

"So, you really don't know."

"No, I guess not."

"If she did take the gun with her, Mr. Lockwood would have known, wouldn't he?"

"Objection," Burr said. "The witness can't know what Mr. Lockwood might have known."

"Sustained."

"Thank you, Ms. Rodriguez. I have no further questions."

Burr thought he might be able to turn that around, but he was afraid any more questions might likely make things worse. No matter what she said.

Burr called Lester Dillworth, the beefy charter captain with the beer belly.

"Mr. Dillworth, you're a charter boat captain out of Frankfort. Is that right?"

"That's right."

Burr nodded. "Mr. Dillworth, would you please tell us a little about what you do and where you do it?"

Dillworth leaned back in his chair.

*I hope he doesn't break it.*

"I take people out sport fishing. Salmon, lake trout, steelhead. I've got a Tiara. Thirty-two-foot sport fish with a fly bridge. Name is *It'll Do*. We run out of Frankfort, up and down the coast. We get up to Leland sometimes, not too often."

"Thank you, Mr. Dillworth. And did you see Mrs. Lockwood's boat, *Achilles*, near Manitou Shoals on June 10th of last year?"

"I did."

"Would you please tell us what you saw and what you did?"

Dillworth leaned forward. "June is slow for salmon. They're not this far north yet and there's no scum line for steelhead. So, I like to run up to Manitou Shoals and fish lake trout." Dillworth nodded to himself. "I'd been up the day before and I seen that boat out in the lake. It looked like it was drifting, but I didn't think much of it. There wasn't much wind."

Dillworth leaned in further. His belly pushed through the spindles of the witness box. "We did pretty good up there, so I came back the next day. Just a light wind. No waves to speak of. There's the boat again. Now she's right off Sleeping Bear, sideways to the waves. Drifting in the wind. It don't look right so I come up alongside and call out." Dillworth shouted. "Anybody there?"

*That would wake the dead.*

"I hollered again. No answer. It sure seemed to me like something was fishy, so I tied alongside and climbed aboard."

*Finally.*

"Did you look around the boat?" Burr said.

"I was just gettin' to that." Dillworth gave Burr a peeved look. "Not a soul around."

"Did you find Mrs. Lockwood's purse on the boat?"

"Nope."

"If she had fallen overboard, I don't think she would have gone over with her purse. Do you?"

"Objection. Speculation."

"Sustained."

*Point made.*

Burr scuffed one of his shoes on the floor. "What did you do next?"

"I went to the pilot's station. Keys in both engines. Turned on. Engines in gear. Throttle low. But they weren't running. Autopilot set to 260. About Milwaukee."

"Did you try them?"

"Yeah. They started right up."

"What do you think happened?"

"My guess is they stalled out."

"But there was no one aboard."

"Nope."

"What did you do then?"

Dillworth leaned back in his chair. "I had sports on board and this fishing boat, commercial fisherman, is coming hard at us so we left."

"Could someone have robbed her, then killed her and set the boat out into Lake Michigan? To make it look like she fell overboard but when, in reality, she was murdered?"

Burr started counting to himself. He got as far two when Brooks roared.

"Your Honor, I object. Defense counsel continues to ask the witness to speculate."

"Sustained. Mr. Lafayette, you know better."

"Yes, Your Honor." Burr knew Brooks would object, and he knew Brooks was right, but he also knew the jury was listening. He turned to them. "As I said a few minutes ago, many times the most obvious explanation is, in fact, the explanation. As in this case. Someone robbed Mrs. Lockwood. It went wrong and she was killed. The thief buried the body on South Manitou and sent the boat out in the lake. The engines stalled and Captain Dillworth found the boat." Burr took two steps toward the jury. "It's as simple as that." Then to Brooks, "Your witness."

Burr sat. Tommy nodded at him.

"Mr. Dillworth," Brooks said, "did you have any idea that Mrs. Lockwood had been murdered when you boarded her boat?"

"No."

"She could have been killed by her husband, who made it look like a robbery."

Burr jumped up. "Speculation, Your Honor."

"Sustained."

Brooks stuck his tongue in his cheek. "Mr. Dillworth, you really have no idea what happened, do you," Brooks said, not asking.

Dillworth looked at Judge Fisher then at Brooks. "No, I guess not."

"I have no further questions," Brooks said. He smiled at Burr, then sat at his table.

*That doesn't help reasonable doubt.*

\* \* \*

Judge Fisher adjourned them for lunch and the unhappy group reconvened at Stacy's. Burr swirled a french fry in his ketchup.

"How can you possibly do that?" Jacob said.

"How else would I eat a french fry?" Burr said.

"I don't care if you eat them with your toes. It's the fact that you're eating them. Those things will kill you."

*My guess is something else will kill me first.*

He dipped another one in the ketchup. "It goes nicely with my cheese-burger." At that moment, a dab of ketchup dripped off the fry and onto his tie.

"Damn it all."

Eve, ever at the ready, dipped a napkin in her water and blotted Burr's tie. "The wonder of Scotchgard," she said.

Burr thought the remaining Sisters of Outrage both looked a bit horrified. Tommy was studying his Reuben. Finally, Karen said, "How do you think it's going?"

Burr finished chewing his french fry. "Actually, I think it's going quite well," he said, lying. "I don't think the jury will be able to get past reasonable doubt," he said, continuing his lie.

\* \* \*

Back in the courtroom, the bailiff called them to order.

Burr looked at his brand-new yellow pencil. There were people who would have been better off if Port Oneida Orchards had been sold to the Park

Service. That didn't mean they'd kill her, but it might at least put reasonable doubt in the jury's mind.

At the moment the most likely suspect was Tommy, but Burr's job was to turn a blind eye to his client's misdeeds, however difficult that might be, and it had been getting increasingly difficult.

Judge Fisher entered the courtroom. She sat then looked at Burr. "Mr. Lafayette, you may call your next witness."

Burr stood. "The defense calls Dale Sleeper."

The beefy ranger sat stone still in the gallery, like a bear just out of hibernation.

"Mr. Sleeper," Judge Fisher said, "you have been called as a witness."

Sleeper muttered to himself. Growled, really, and lumbered to the witness stand. Burr walked up to him and smiled.

*I know you don't want to be here, which is exactly why I want you here.*

"Mr. Sleeper, I remind you that you are still under oath."

Sleeper growled.

"Mr. Sleeper, earlier you testified that you are in charge of confiscating the property of private citizens for your pretty little park. Is that right?"

Brooks leapt to his feet. "Objection, Your Honor. These were all lawful purposes provided for in the Fifth Amendment to the United States Constitution."

*He took the bait.* "Your Honor, if a landowner doesn't want to sell their property, and the government forces them to sell it, isn't that confiscatory?"

"We pay a fair price," Sleeper said, awake from his hibernation.

Judge Fisher looked like she wished she hadn't come back from lunch. "Mr. Lafayette, I think confiscatory might be a bit harsh."

"How about condemned?" Burr said.

Brooks, still on his feet, said, "Your Honor, this is old news. The vast majority of the affected landowners willingly sold their property to the Park Service, many of them because they wanted the treasure of Sleeping Bear protected."

*Please.*

"Do you have a point to make, Mr. Lafayette?" Judge Fisher said.

Burr looked up at the judge. "I think I made it, Your Honor." If he couldn't quite convince the jury that Tommy hadn't murdered Helen, he could at least paint the government as the root cause of the murder and muddy the waters once again.

Burr turned back to the angry bear. "Mr. Sleeper, you just said that many landowners willingly sold their property to you. Is that right?"

"Yes."

"And some of them profited by selling to you?"

"Yes, indeed. They were very happy." The bear looked like he'd just found a beehive full of honey.

"And were there other property owners on Port Oneida Trail who were willing sellers?"

"Yes."

"But you didn't purchase their land. Did you?"

"No." The bear heard a buzzing bee.

"And why is that?"

"All of our plans depended on buying Helen Lockwood's farm. It was the centerpiece of our design for the old dock and Pyramid Point. We wanted to show what it would have been like when the first white settlers started to really develop the area."

"And that meant tearing out the orchard?"

Sleeper didn't say anything.

Burr tapped his foot. "Answer the question, please."

"Yes."

Burr looked at the jury and shook his head.

*Now for the meat in the sandwich.*

"Mr. Sleeper, you just testified that there were willing sellers on Port Oneida Trail."

"That's right."

"And did you have agreements with them?"

"Yes."

"And would the property owners have profited from selling to you?"

"Oh, yes." The taste of honey lit up Sleeper's eyes.

"But…" Burr rocked back and forth, heel to toe. "But all these purchases depended on buying Mrs. Lockwood's farm first." Burr paused. "That is, if you didn't buy her farm, you weren't going to buy anyone else's property on Port Oneida Trail. Is that right?"

"Yes." The bear heard the buzzing of bees.

"So, it's possible that one of the jilted sellers could have killed Helen Lockwood so her farm would be sold."

"No."

"I object, Your Honor," Brooks said, on his feet. "Calls for speculation."

"Sustained." Judge Fisher looked down her nose at Burr. "Mr. Lafayette, you know better than that."

"Yes, Your Honor," Burr said, who did.

"So, Mr. Sleeper, did you have a purchase agreement with Joseph Maguire of Port Oneida Vineyards?"

Sleeper nodded.

"And the Larson family. The ones that own the store in Fishtown but also have property on Port Oneida Trail?"

Another nod.

"And a certain Andrew Pretty."

"Yes." The bear spoke.

*Thank you, Jacob. Your research is without peer.*

Burr looked over at Brooks, then back at Sleeper. "And what about Peter Brooks' family? Our prosecutor."

Brooks launched himself. "I object, Your Honor. This is totally irrelevant."

Burr was sure there was steam coming out of Brooks' ears. "Your Honor, I merely asked if these people had agreements with Mr. Sleeper. And they all did."

"I'll allow it," the judge said.

"Mr. Sleeper, earlier I believe you said the formation of this … this park, was the crowning achievement in your career."

"I might have said that."

"So, you would have profited from the purchase of all this real estate. Career-wise."

"I suppose."

"But Helen Lockwood wouldn't do what you wanted."

"No." Buzzing again.

*Now for the kill.*

"So you killed her."

"No!" The bees swarmed around the bear.

"I object," Brooks shouted. "There is absolutely no factual basis for that accusation. It is egregious."

"Your Honor, I withdraw the question."

"Mr. Lafayette. Approach the bench." Judge Fisher wagged her finger at him. "If you make one more comment like that, I am going to eject you. Is that clear?"

Burr nodded.

"And you know what that means." She looked over Burr's shoulder at Jacob. Burr looked back at Jacob, who also knew what that meant.

"I have no further questions, Your Honor." Burr sat, pleased with himself.

Brooks walked up to Sleeper, who looked like he was licking his bee stings. "Mr. Sleeper, who spearheaded the establishment of the Sleeping Bear Dunes National Lakeshore?"

"Senator Phil Hart."

"Our beloved Senator."

Sleeper nodded.

"And Congress appropriated millions of dollars to create America's newest national park to preserve the beauty of our shoreline forever."

"That's right." Sleeper sat up a little straighter.

"And, everything that you did, you did to create the park, preserve our natural beauty. And you did it lawfully."

"Yes, sir," said Sleeper.

"And all of your actions were within the boundaries of the United States Constitution and the laws of the State of Michigan."

"Yes, sir."

Burr thought Sleeper might salute.

"You acted lawfully and you treated everyone fairly and you paid top dollar."

"We did, indeed."

Burr knew he could object to all of this, but he'd made his point and he didn't want to give any credibility to Brooks.

Judge Fisher had clearly had enough of all of them for the day, especially Burr, and dismissed them early, which was fine with Burr. He had important business to attend to.

Burr walked down the courthouse steps. It was only three o'clock, but it was cold. The sky was clear, but the wind blew straight out of the north at about twenty-five. Burr's tie flapped in the wind.

He watched Tommy walk to his car.

*He told me why he went to the island. I don't believe him, but with those puppy dog brown eyes and that floppy black hair, I'd like to believe him.*

Burr climbed into his Jeep, turned the heat on full and pushed the lever to *defrost* while the engine warmed up. By Suttons Bay there was enough heat that he stopped shivering. At 4:30, he parked at the marina in Northport.

"Now, for the important business." Burr rescued Zeke from the dock boy, who only had about half-a-dozen boats and an aging yellow Lab in his care. Boating season was over. It was damn cold, and it was finally too damn cold for Burr to stay on *Spindrift* any longer. He emptied out his icebox, packed his clothes, and locked up the boat. Zeke was worried until Burr lifted him off the boat and onto the dock. The dog ran ashore, found the closest tree, then sat by the passenger door of the Jeep.

Burr loaded his gear in the Jeep, Zeke first, then started back the way they'd come. They pulled up to the Park Place Hotel at dusk, Traverse City's finest hotel and Northern Michigan's tallest building. The desk clerk, after several bribes, agreed to let Zeke be a guest.

Art Deco, vintage 1930s, the Park Place had suites, which Burr couldn't afford but Tommy could.

Burr checked them in and ordered room service. Half-an-hour later, he sipped on a Labatt he'd retrieved from his suitcase while the bottle of Zinfandel opened. He'd fed Zeke dog food with a cheeseburger ala mode. His ribeye, twice-baked potato, butternut squash and garden salad, was in the warmer. "Zeke, I'm going to have a glass of wine before dinner. Maybe two." The dog wagged his tail. Burr poured himself the first. He swirled the wine and took a sip. Chewy with chocolate and raspberries. "Zeke, it is now Zinfandel season." Zeke wagged his tail again. "Tomorrow, we press the attack."

But it was not to be.

# CHAPTER TWENTY-TWO

"The defense calls...." Before he could get Joe Maguire's name out of his mouth, the ever-dapper Brooks cut in.

"Your Honor, the prosecution has just discovered new evidence that may well determine the outcome of this case."

"I object, Your Honor," Burr said. "The prosecutor has presented his case. It is now time for the defense."

"Your Honor, the evidence is compelling and simply cannot wait."

"Nonsense," Burr said. "The defense is throttling Brooks, and he's grandstanding to try and disrupt my case."

Judge Fisher curled her finger at each of them. They walked up to the bench. She looked down her nose at them.

"You two have made this personal. Too personal. This is not about either of you. It's not about your overinflated egos and your high opinion of yourselves. This is about the right of the State of Michigan to have justice and the right of Mr. Lockwood to have a spirited defense." She looked at Burr. "Which he is getting. In spades." She looked at the prosecutor. "Mr. Brooks, I am going to put you on a very short leash." Brooks nodded.

"Your Honor..." Burr said.

"Be quiet, Mr. Lafayette." Then to Brooks, "You may introduce your evidence and call one witness. I will then decide if anything further is warranted."

"Yes, Your Honor," Brooks said.

Burr turned to leave.

"Mr. Lafayette?" she said.

Burr raised his hand and started to walk back to his table.

"Mr. Lafayette, you will look at me when I am speaking to you."

He turned around and looked at an angry Judge Fisher.

"Come here." She pointed at the floor directly in front of her.

It was all he could do to stand where he was told.

The judge wagged her finger at him. "I have tolerated, even indulged, your drama and theatrics. I find you to be a most able lawyer. Just like you were at my father's firm." She lowered her voice. "But you are perhaps the most spoiled, self-absorbed man I have ever met." She leaned over and whispered. "I thank my lucky stars we never married." She sat back in her chair. "Do I make myself clear?" she said, not whispering.

Burr shifted from one foot to the other. "Not exactly, Your Honor."

"You will treat this court, its officers, and particularly me, with respect. Or I will have you jailed for contempt. Do I make myself clear?"

"Yes, Your Honor."

"Sit down and do your best to behave yourself." She pointed to the defense table.

"Yes, Your Honor." Burr sat.

*I made it almost to the end without a judge hating me.*

"Mr. Brooks," Judge Fisher said, "you may call your witness."

Brooks stood. "The State calls Consuela Rodriguez."

She took her seat in the witness stand. The judge reminded Consuela she was still under oath. The housekeeper held her hands together on her lap.

*If she was scared before, now she's terrified.*

"Just a few questions, Ms. Rodriguez." Brooks smiled his 'this is only going to hurt for a minute' smile. Then he walked to the evidence table and picked up a small, clear plastic bag. He held it so Burr couldn't see it. Burr feared the worst. And he was right.

At the witness stand, Brooks stood with his back to Burr but facing Consuela Rodriguez and the jury. He took whatever it was out of the bag and showed it to the terrified witness. "Do you know what this is?"

She nodded. Burr could see her gripping the rail of the witness stand for dear life, her knuckles turning white.

"And what is it?"

"Miss Helen's diamond ring."

Burr craned his neck but still couldn't see the ring.

"Miss Helen's diamond ring," Brooks repeated. "Are you sure?"

Another nod.

Finally, Brooks turned to the gallery. There, in the palm of his hand, a diamond engagement ring with the attached wedding band. It was clear and brilliant and sparkled in the light.

*That thing is the size of a cocktail olive.*

Burr had seen it on Helen's ring finger, but it had never seemed this big before.

Brooks walked over to the jury, his palm still open. "This, ladies and gentlemen, is the diamond wedding ring of Mrs. Lockwood." The jury oohed and aahed. They had never seen a diamond that big before. Burr wasn't sure if he had either. Brooks waited for the oohs and aahs to die down. Then, "She was not wearing it when her body was found. You are about to learn where it was found, and where the defendant..." Brooks pointed at Tommy with his free hand, "...hid the ring."

Burr leaned over to Tommy. "Why didn't you tell me Helen's ring was missing," he said, whispering.

"I didn't know it was," Tommy said, stuttering. "I forgot about it."

*He's lying again.*

"Your Honor," Brooks said, "the State introduces this ring as People's Exhibit Three."

"Mr. Lafayette."

"May I examine the evidence?"

Judge Fisher nodded.

Burr walked up to Brooks and took proposed Exhibit Three from him. It certainly looked like Helen's ring.

*I could pay off my mortgage with this. Nothing will be gained if I make an issue out of this.*

"I have no objection, Your Honor."

"That was easy, wasn't it?" Judge Fisher smiled at him. "Bailiff, please mark this ring as People's Exhibit Three."

Burr sat down next to Tommy. "Do you know anything about this?"

Tommy shook his head no.

Burr wasn't so sure. "Damn it all." He broke his newest pencil, then reached into his pencil box and broke two more.

Eve reached over the railing and tapped him on the shoulder. "Stop that."

*These things have a very short life expectancy.*

"You may continue," the judge said.

"Ms. Rodriguez, would you please tell us what you were doing when you found Mrs. Lockwood's ring?" Brooks said.

"It was in the flour."

"The flour?"

"Yes."

"And what were you doing?"

"I was baking a pie."

Brooks gritted his teeth. This clearly wasn't going the way he had intended.

"Ms. Rodriguez let's start over. I think you told me earlier that every Saturday you bake a pie."

"Yes."

"And you make your crust from scratch."

"Oh, yes. With Crisco." Her eyes brightened.

"Very good," Brooks said, though he didn't care a whit about the pie crust. "And you have a canister of flour in the kitchen?"

"On the counter."

"What did you do?"

"I scooped out the flour. Almost two cups. It was an apple pie, first of the season. From Miss Helen's trees. A double crust."

"And then?"

"On the second scoop, I see something in the flour. I thought it might be bugs."

"But it wasn't."

"No."

"What was it?"

"It was Miss Helen's diamond." She looked at Brooks like he'd just asked a stupid question.

"So, you found Mrs. Lockwood's diamond ring..." Brooks paused while he walked to the evidence table. He held up the bag with the ring in it and shook it at Tommy. "This very ring. In the canister of flour in Mrs. Lockwood's kitchen."

"Yes."

"Ms. Rodriguez, did Mrs. Lockwood always wear her ring?"

"Oh, yes."

"Did you ever see her not wearing her wedding ring?"

"No."

"Thank you." Brooks walked to the jury, the ring in his hand. He held it between his thumb and forefinger right in front of them. "This ring..."

Brooks feigned speechlessness. "This ring. It's… it's as big as a cocktail olive."

*At least we agree on something.*

"Ladies and gentlemen, not only did the defendant murder his wife, he took off her ring after he murdered her." Brooks paused. "Because he was so greedy, he wanted to keep it for himself. He is the only person who has access to the kitchen except for Ms. Rodriguez, and she's the one who found the ring. There can be no other explanation." Brooks pointed at Tommy. "It was despicable. I have no further questions, Your Honor."

Burr walked up to Consuela ever so slowly. He leaned on the railing of the witness stand and looked at her. "You bake a pie every Saturday?" he said, calmly, quietly and full of peace.

"For twenty-three years."

"That's a lot of pies."

"It sure is."

"And a lot of flour."

"Yes."

"Ms. Rodriguez, how big is the container that holds the flour?"

"Big."

"How big?"

"Very big."

Burr bit his lip. He had to do a better job with his vague baker. "Ms. Rodriguez, how much flour do you think the container holds?"

"I don't know. A lot."

"Does it hold a five-pound bag of flour?"

"Oh yes."

"Maybe more?"

"Maybe."

"So, it holds a lot of flour." Burr stood back. "How often do you refill it?"

"Oh, I don't know. Every couple of months or so."

"I see. And how much flour was left in the bin when you found the ring?"

"I don't know. Not too much." She was starting to get nervous again.

"Ms. Rodriguez, isn't it possible that Mrs. Lockwood, for whatever reason, put the ring in the bottom of the flour bin before she went to South Manitou. And for the past year, you refilled the bin when needed and then, this last time, you just happened to find it when you got down to the bottom?"

"I don't know. Maybe."

"You don't know how the ring got in the bin, and you don't know who put it in there. Do you." The biggest nonquestion Burr had asked so far.

"No, I guess not." The pastry chef took her hands off the rails and put them in her lap. Her knuckles weren't white anymore, but her hands were shaking.

It was Burr's turn to walk to the jury box. "Ladies and gentlemen, Ms. Rodriguez may well have found Mrs. Lockwood's ring in the flour bin. But what does it mean?" He paused. "Nothing. It means that she found the ring. That's all. There is no connection between finding this ring and Mrs. Lockwood's murder." Burr looked over his shoulder at Judge Fisher. "I have no further questions."

*It went better than I thought it would, but now we're really in the soup.*

Brooks stood. "Your Honor, in light of this incriminating new evidence, the prosecution asks that Mr. Lockwood's bail be revoked immediately and he be held in the Grand Traverse County jail."

Burr launched himself out of his seat. "Your Honor, finding this ring proves nothing. It has not been connected to Mr. Lockwood. It's nothing more than a prize in a box of Crackerjack."

"A very expensive prize, Mr. Lafayette," Judge Fisher said.

"Your Honor," Brooks said, "the defendant is the only one who had access to the kitchen. He's the only one who could have put it there."

"Unless Mrs. Lockwood put it there," Burr said.

"She never took her ring off," Brooks said.

Judge Fisher slammed down her gavel so hard it tipped over the bud vase. The rose fell on her desk. Water spilled everywhere. She turned away from the jury. "God damn it," she said. Turning back, "I take judicial note of the gravity of this new evidence, but Mr. Lockwood's bail is continued. Bailiff, clean this up."

Judge Fisher slammed her gavel down again, not so hard this time. "We are adjourned for the day." She stormed out.

By the time Burr had collected his papers, Tommy was already gone. He quite needed to talk to his most probably guilty and definitely not very likable client. When Burr left the courtroom, he heard a woman shouting farther down the hall. He followed his ears to the Court-of-the-Star chamber cloakroom.

Karen had Tommy backed up against one of the rolling coatracks, *a la* Burr. Lauren stood off to the side. Tommy's face was flushed.

"I told you. I didn't put her ring there."

Karen screeched at him, "I know what you told me. I don't believe you anymore." She had lost all the color in her face.

"Karen. Screaming isn't helping anything." Lauren put her hand on Karen's arm but she shook it off.

"I wanted to believe you. I really did," Karen said.

"I didn't kill her," Tommy said.

"You did. I know you did." She took a step toward Tommy.

*That coatrack is going to tip over again.*

Karen kept going. "You put her ring in the flour. Helen never took it off. I never once saw her without it."

Lauren took Karen by the arm again and pulled her away. "We need to go."

"No, we don't." She jerked her arm free from Lauren and pushed Tommy into the coatrack. He staggered. The coatrack crashed to the floor again, but Burr grabbed Tommy before he could fall.

As bad as this was, Burr felt a certain peace now that the coatrack had tipped again.

Karen ran out.

"Tommy, I'm so sorry," Lauren said. "She's really upset now, but she'll calm down."

*I wondered how long it would take for them to turn on each other.*

* * *

Burr sat in the bar on the top floor of the Park Place, alone at his table except for his second martini. The bartender had made it just the way he liked it. Burr looked out the window, the lights of Traverse City below, Grand Traverse Bay off to the north, the lights of the harbor blinking at him, red, green and white. He stirred his drink with his finger, took out one of the olives and chewed it slowly.

He'd stayed in the coatroom with Tommy after Karen and Lauren had left. He'd tried to calm him down, but it really hadn't worked. Tommy said he felt more alone every day. It was bad enough that Consuela had turned on him, but Karen was much worse. Burr said that Consuela hadn't turned on him. She was giving evidence, which she was required to do. And neither of them could talk to her about it. That would be witness tampering.

Karen, though, was another story. She had clearly gone off the deep end, and there was no telling what might happen next. "There's something going on here," Burr said to his martini.

The bar was almost empty, but those who were there all looked at him. Burr gave them a wave and turned back to the martini.

*They all think I'm crazy.*

He ate another olive.

*I probably am crazy.*

If only Zeke were here. It always helped Burr to talk things out, out loud. He could talk to Zeke, who didn't really listen, and no one would think twice about it. But if he did it without Zeke, everyone thought he was crazy.

Burr picked up his glass, swirled the ice and ate the third olive. He was sure there was something going on, something that Tommy, Karen, Lauren, or one of the others knew about.

*Was it the missing dinghy? Was it one of the suspects he was going to question tomorrow? Was it something on the boat? The logbook?*

"Damn it all," he said out loud.

All eyes back on Burr.

*I don't care what you think.*

He ate the last olive and ordered a third martini and two shepherd's pies to go.

* * *

Burr tapped his brand-new pencil, the only one he had left. After yesterday's performance, Eve had taken custody of the pencils. He'd have to make do with just this one.

Burr, as always, sat next to Tommy, who looked worn out. He had bags under his eyes and lines around his mouth. The ever-natty Jacob positively glowed through his olive skin. His crisp white shirt looked like it could stand up by itself. But then Jacob hadn't had to do much. Yet.

As for Burr, three martinis always made him a bit foggy the next morning, but like a true warrior, he would rise above it.

As for Judge Mary Fisher, she had yet another fresh-cut flower in the bud vase, yesterday's drama forgotten. But not a rose. It was a New England aster, the last wildflower of the year. A brilliant purple with a yellow center. "Mr. Lafayette, call your first witness."

"The defense calls Joseph Maguire."

Burr watched the ever-so-smooth vintner walk down the aisle, dressed in a navy-blue blazer over charcoal slacks, white shirt and club tie. He looked prosperous, though he wasn't.

The bailiff swore in Maguire.

"Mr. Maguire, you are the owner of the Port Oneida Vineyards. Is that right?"

"Yes." Maguire pulled down his cuffs. His gold cufflinks almost blinded Burr.

"And your vineyard is located on Port Oneida Road, close to the late Helen Lockwood's orchards. Is that right?"

"We're neighbors."

"And Mr. Maguire, you agreed to sell your winery to the Park Service. Isn't that right?"

Maguire's smile disappeared.

"Isn't that right?" Burr pulled down his own cuffs, which didn't dazzle.

"There was sort of an agreement, but it never went through."

"Really?" Burr arched his eyebrows.

"We couldn't work out the details."

Burr walked back to the defense table. Jacob handed him a file. Back in front of the vintner, "Mr. Maguire, I have here a purchase and sale agreement with your winery and the Park Service. It is signed by you and Mr. Sleeper." Burr turned to the gallery, found Sleeper and nodded to him. Sleeper didn't acknowledge him. Back to Maguire, "As I read the agreement, the only reason you didn't sell is because the purchase by the Park Service was contingent on the purchase of the late Mrs. Lockwood's orchard. Isn't that right?"

Maguire sat there.

"Mr. Maguire?"

"I don't remember."

"Please answer the question."

Brooks stood. "Objection, Your Honor. Asked and answered. Mr. Maguire says he doesn't remember."

"Your Honor, the defense would like to introduce the purchase and sale agreement by and between Mr. Maguire and the Park Service as Defense Exhibit One."

"I object, Your Honor," Brooks said. "Irrelevant."

"Your Honor, I am about to show its relevance," Burr said.

"Bailiff, admit the evidence," Judge Fisher said.

"Thank you, Your Honor." Burr handed Maguire the agreement. "Please read this sentence."

Maguire fumbled with it, then dropped it. Burr picked it up. He smiled at Maguire. "I'll read it for you. 'The purchase of the subject property shall be conditioned on the prior purchase by the Park Service of that certain real estate known as Port Oneida Orchards.'"

"I didn't sell my winery."

"No, but you wanted to. And here's why." Burr retrieved another folder from Jacob. "Mr. Maguire, this is the notice of foreclosure on your winery, filed at the Register of Deeds office by Leelanau State Bank. It seems your mortgage is in default."

"How did you get that?" Maguire tried to grab it, but Burr pulled it out of the vintner's reach.

*Jacob, you're a fine fellow.*

Burr, over Brooks' objection and with Judge Fisher's approval, introduced the notice of foreclosure.

"Mr. Maguire," Burr said, "it looks to me like there isn't as much money in grapes as you had hoped. So, you tried to sell your grapevines to Dale Sleeper. But you couldn't. So, you took matters in your own hands. After you killed Mrs. Lockwood, her farm would be sold and so would yours. You'd be a very rich man."

"I didn't kill her."

Brooks erupted. "Your Honor, this is sheer speculation. Counsel is accusing Mr. Maguire when there is absolutely no evidence."

Burr knew Brooks was right, but he wanted to re-muddy the waters, which he most certainly had done. He had to act fast. "Mr. Maguire, where were you on the night of June 9th last year?"

"I...I...don't remember."

"I have no further questions, Your Honor."

Brooks huffed his way up to Maguire. He paced back and forth, exhaled. "Mr. Maguire, have you ever been convicted of a crime?"

"No."

"Have you ever been charged with a crime?"

"No."

Brooks grinned at Maguire. "Have you ever had a parking ticket?"

Maguire turned red. "Yes."

"Mr. Maguire, did you kill Mrs. Lockwood?"

"No."

Brooks walked over to the jury box. "Ladies and gentlemen, it is one thing to have money problems. We've probably all had them at one time or another. It's quite another to kill someone over them." Brooks pointed at Burr. "This man has just made a reckless and unsubstantiated accusation. I ask you to take it for what it's worth and ignore it." Brooks sat.

For his part, Burr didn't care what Brooks said. He didn't care if Maguire killed Helen. In fact, Burr was quite sure Maguire hadn't. It had been almost too much to hope for that Maguire wouldn't remember where he was the night Helen was killed. So far, this was going swimmingly.

*I'm getting closer to reasonable doubt.*

Burr wasn't done muddying the waters. He called Sven Larson, who ran the fishing boat out of Leland, where Burr had bought all things whitefish. Sven and family also owned property on Port Oneida Trail. It was an old farmstead just down the road from the orchards, also subject to a contingent purchase agreement with the industrious Dale Sleeper and just about ready for a tax foreclosure sale. It seemed as though the Larsons were three years behind on their property taxes.

Larson blustered and whined, hemmed and hawed, but finally admitted that what Burr alleged was true.

But the meat in this sandwich was different.

"Mr. Larson, you've admitted that you had a contingent agreement to sell the family farmstead to the Park Service. You also admitted that your farm is due to be sold at a tax foreclosure sale. Is that right?"

"Yes." The fisherman gripped the railing of the witness stand, just like Consuela had, but Larson gripped it so hard, Burr thought he might crush it.

"Mr. Larson, here's what I don't understand. You fish off Sleeping Bear almost every day. You were seen near Mrs. Lockwood's boat the day after she was killed and the day after that as well. In fact, Lester Dillworth said he saw you coming toward Mrs. Lockwood's boat at full speed, when he was already tied up alongside her boat." Burr paused. "You chased him away and then towed the boat in yourself. Why did you do that?"

Larson gripped the railing even tighter, if that was possible. He didn't say anything.

*This is perfect.*

"Mr. Larson, isn't it possible that you killed Mrs. Lockwood, buried her and set her boat across the lake? Then, when you saw it drifting off the dunes, you panicked. You chased Mr. Dillworth away because you wanted to make sure he couldn't find anything that would incriminate you."

"No. No. That wasn't it at all. I thought Dillworth was cutting my nets. I wanted to talk to him about it, but he left before I got there."

"Mr. Larson, isn't it true that you've been convicted of assault and battery."

Larson tightened his grip on the railing.

"You're no stranger to violence." Burr paused. "Are you?"

Brooks jumped up. "I object. This is pure speculation." Brooks ranted and raved again. Judge Fisher scolded Burr again, and he didn't care if Larson had killed Helen or not.

There was one more witness. This one, Andrew Pretty, who wasn't. A florid man who was at least three sizes too big for his rumpled suit that looked like it had been cut from an upholstered chair. As it turned out, Mr. Pretty's family owned a cottage at the end of Port Oneida Trail. It had been in the family for decades. On a bluff three hundred feet above Lake Michigan. Two stories, six bedrooms, four bathrooms, a fireplace at each end, porches all the way around – and just about ready to fall down the bluff and into the lake.

They couldn't move it and they couldn't sell it. Enter Dale Sleeper on his white, government-issue stallion with his contingent purchase agreement. Mr. Pretty had a temper. He'd lost it more than once, and everyone in the courtroom had heard him.

Burr nodded apologetically during his judicial scolding, the waters muddier than he ever thought he could have made them.

"Ladies and gentlemen, the tragic murder of Helen Lockwood was just that…a tragedy. But that doesn't mean her husband killed her. There were many people who had sufficient reason to kill Mrs. Lockwood. If the prosecutor had looked a little harder, he might well have found the real killer." Burr walked back to his table. "Your Honor, the defense rests."

"We will have closing arguments after lunch." Judge Fisher slammed her gavel and walked out.

\* \* \*

The litigants reconvened at Stacy's for what Burr thought would be their last lunch. He was in high spirits after the morning's joust with Brooks. He thought he had closed the gap on reasonable doubt, in spite of the fact that four people had testified that they had seen Tommy on South Manitou the day Helen was murdered. And a fifth person had seen Tommy on the missing dinghy. So, closing arguments and a prompt acquittal.

Burr wolfed down his cheeseburger, no reason to change what worked. Julie gave him another piece of pie on the house. The Sisters of Outrage picked at their food. Burr left a twenty-dollar tip in the cash register to go with their twenty-dollar lunch.

# CHAPTER TWENTY-THREE

"Gentlemen, we are ready for closing arguments," Judge Mary Fisher said.

Brooks stood. "Your Honor, a new witness has just come forward. The prosecution requests that the witness testify before the closing arguments."

*Damn it all. Now what?*

Burr rose, slowly, his cheeseburger not quite agreeing with him. "I object, Your Honor. The prosecution has had ample time to put forth its case. Mr. Brooks already has had one additional witness, which interrupted my defense, but who proved to be inconsequential."

Brooks walked up to Judge Fisher. "Your Honor, there was nothing inconsequential about finding Mrs. Lockwood's diamond ring at the defendant's home. It could only have been put there by the defendant."

Burr joined Brooks in front of the judge. "That ring is nothing more than a prize in a Crackerjack box. It doesn't mean a thing. It proves nothing."

"Your Honor, this witness is crucial," Brooks said.

"Poppycock," Burr said.

"She has just now come forward," Brooks said. "Had I known about her, I would have had her testify much sooner."

"Who is it this time? Joan of Arc?" Burr said.

Judge Fisher drummed her fingers on her desk. Finally, "In the interest of getting all the facts out, I will allow the new witness to testify."

"Your Honor, this is another outrage in a long list of outrages. Brooks is writing his own version of the court rules." He reached up and slammed his fist on Judge Fisher's desk. The bud vase wobbled and wobbled. They all watched it wobble. Back and forth, then it tipped over, spilling water on Judge Fisher's files.

"I am so sorry, Your Honor." Burr reached into his pocket for his handkerchief, then remembered he never carried one.

"Not again," said the aggrieved Judge Fisher.

The bailiff rushed over and mopped up the spilled water with his hand-kerchief. Then he righted the bud vase.

"Sit down, Mr. Lafayette," the judge said. "Mr. Brooks, you may proceed."

Burr sat.

"The State calls Karen Hansen."

Burr jumped in his chair.

*What's going on? I just had lunch with her.*

He snapped his only pencil in two.

Eve reached over the railing and handed him another pencil.

Burr leaned over to Tommy, "What is going on?"

"I have no idea."

The bailiff swore her in. She had on a knee-length black sweater dress with a high neck. Her only jewelry was a pair of gold studs. Her only makeup was a hint of wine-colored lipstick, highlighting her creamy skin. Her frizzy black hair was pulled back in a French bun. Burr thought she looked surprisingly calm, especially for someone who was about to give damning evidence against her brother-in-law.

Brooks went through her background, including her one-third interest in Port Oneida Orchards and her relationship, by marriage, to Tommy.

"Mrs. Hansen," Brooks said, "would you please tell us what you told me? About your sister?"

"I loved Helen. She was a wonderful sister. And friend. After our father died, she was the leader of the family. She ran the orchards. She was fierce. Nothing and no one could stop her. None of us, including Tommy, stood in her way."

"By Tommy, you mean the defendant?"

"Yes." Karen pulled her skirt down, not that it needed it.

"Please continue, Ms. Hansen."

"Helen had a strong will. Nothing got in her way. But she was also a person of large appetites."

*What is going on?*

"Appetites?"

"Sexual appetites. She liked men. She loved Tommy but she carried on with other men."

"You mean she had affairs."

"Yes."

*Are you kidding me? This is terrible.*

He grabbed Tommy by the shoulder. "What is going on?" Tommy didn't say anything.

"How long did these affairs go on?" Brooks said.

"I think it started once they learned they couldn't have children. She never said so, but that's what I think."

"Did she have many affairs?"

"Yes."

"How many?"

"I don't know."

"More than one?"

"Oh, yes."

"More than five?"

*This is worse than terrible.*

"Yes."

"Ten?"

Burr stood up. He knew where this was headed and he didn't like it. "I object, Your Honor. This is speculation."

Judge Fisher looked down at Karen. "If you know the answer to the question, please answer it."

Karen nodded. "I'd say at least ten."

Brooks looked at the jury. "At least ten affairs. At least ten extramarital affairs." Back to Karen. "Did the defendant know?"

"I don't think he did at first, but he did later. Helen made some effort to be discreet. She took most of them out on her boat."

"Did Mr. Lockwood know about these affairs?" Brooks said again.

"We all knew."

"Do you know how he felt about it?"

"I think he hated it. And I think he hated her for it."

"Why didn't he divorce her?"

"I'm not sure. He loved her. She had a hold on him." She pulled her skirt down again.

"Mrs. Hansen, why didn't you come forward before now?"

"At first I didn't think Tommy was capable of killing Helen. He loved her too much. But when Consuela testified about the ring, I knew only Tommy could have put it there. I think he just finally had enough. I think he lost his mind and killed her."

Brooks turned to the jury. "Ladies and gentlemen, four witnesses have testified that they saw the defendant on South Manitou the day Helen Lockwood was murdered. It may well be that he murdered his wife so he could sell the farm and get her share. Another witness has testified that she saw Mrs. Lockwood take her husband back to her boat by dinghy at South Manitou. A spurned and jealous husband could have killed his wife. In a fit of temper. That is what occurred. Money is one thing. Infidelity is quite another." Brooks turned to the judge. "I have no further questions, Your Honor." Brooks sat.

Burr looked at his pencil. He picked it up, then set it down. He didn't want Brooks to see how mad he was.

He approached Karen.

*How could you have just had lunch with me and done this?*

"Mrs. Hansen, how long have you known Tommy Lockwood?"

Karen looked away, then back at Burr. "About twenty-five years."

"Twenty-five years. That's a long time." Burr paused. "Why, after all this time, and all of those supposed affairs, did you just bring this up now?"

"It was the ring."

"The ring." Burr paused again. "Why didn't anyone else bring it up. Lauren Littlefield, your other sister. The housekeeper. She would surely have known. According to your testimony, everyone knew." It was Burr's turn to turn to the jury. "Don't you find it a little odd that everyone knew yet no one ever brought it up. Until now?" Burr stared at Karen.

*This started out so well, so long ago. It was a complicated, well-paying condemnation case. And now we're going to be enemies.*

"Mrs. Hansen, I'm sure you're aware that if, in the unlikely event, Mr. Lockwood were to be convicted of killing his wife, he would lose his share of the proceeds of the farm. Your one-third share would become half."

Karen looked at her lap. "I had no idea."

"But you were the only one who wanted to sell the farm."

"Tommy did, too."

Burr ignored her. "Maybe you put the ring in the flour."

Brooks leapt to his feet. "This is inflammatory speculation."

"Sustained," the judge said.

"Your Honor, Mr. Lockwood wasn't the only one with access to the flour bin."

"Sustained," Judge Fisher said again.

Burr was just about finished, but he thought he might as well find out as much as he could. It was a risk, but at this point he had nothing to lose.

"Mrs. Hansen, as to these alleged affairs, do you have any proof? Did you ever see your sister with any of her supposed lovers?"

"Well... everyone knew."

"Mrs. Hansen, did you ever see your sister with any of the supposed lovers?"

"Well..."

"Answer my question," Burr said.

"No."

"Thank you. And was there say anything written down anywhere about them? Love letters, credit card records, cancelled checks?"

"I think Helen kept track of things. That would be something she would do. I don't know where."

"Why would she do that?"

Karen pulled at her skirt for the third time, as if it was her virtue being besmirched. "I don't know. Ego maybe. She liked to keep things straight."

"Your Honor, I have no further questions." Burr walked back to his table and sat.

"Gentlemen, we will take a ten-minute recess, then you will present your closing arguments."

*That won't work. Not after what Karen just said.*

Burr stood. "Your Honor, in light of this unexpected, surprising and altogether without-notice testimony, I request a one-week recess."

"A week? That's ridiculous," Brooks said.

*It may be a bit much.*

"Your Honor, Mr. Brooks has run roughshod over the court rules. If this keeps up, the next edition will have his name on it." Burr ran his hands through his hair, front to back.

"Witnesses keep coming forward," Brooks said.

"In a pig's eye."

"Mind your manners, Mr. Lafayette," Judge Fisher said. She drummed her fingers again. She rearranged the flower in the bud vase, not that there was much to be done with a solitary flower in a bud vase with no water. Finally, "Mr. Lafayette, we will have closing arguments the day after tomorrow. At ten o'clock sharp."

"Thank you, Your Honor."

She tapped her gavel, careful not to upset the bud vase, and walked out.

Burr walked back to his table. Karen and Lauren were nowhere to be seen. Eve handed him a pencil, which he broke.

"Thank you, Eve."

Burr saw Tommy head out the door into the hallway. He ran after his now likely to be convicted client and caught up with him in front of the infamous coatroom. He grabbed Tommy by the arm and pulled him in.

"Not here," Tommy said.

"Why didn't you tell me?" Burr shouted at him. "I could have done something had I known. You've just punched your ticket to life in prison."

"I didn't kill her."

"But you did take the ferry there."

Tommy nodded.

"How did you get back?"

"On the last ferry."

Burr glared at Tommy. "Did you take the dinghy back from the island?"

Tommy looked down at his shoes. "No. I took the ferry. I just told you that."

"Why didn't anyone see you?"

Tommy looked up. "I have no idea. The boat was packed. I don't know."

Burr looked down at his own shoes.

*They still need polishing, but I look pretty good from the ankles up.*

He looked at Tommy.

"I think that no one saw you because you didn't take the ferry back. You killed Helen. You buried her on the island. Then you sent her boat off toward Milwaukee and took the dinghy back. It was risky, but if there were no seas, you could do it." Burr took a step to Tommy, who backed into a coatrack. It wobbled but didn't fall over.

"No. That's not what happened."

Burr put his hands in his pockets. "What exactly did happen?"

"I took the ferry over. I was going to have it out with her. I knew she met her boyfriends there. I finally had enough. She didn't throw it in my face, but we all knew. Karen was right about that, but I didn't kill her."

Burr didn't believe him. "What did you do?"

"I took the ferry over. I got Helen's attention and she came and got me. There was no one on board except Helen. We had it out, but I didn't kill her. I swear I didn't."

"It would have helped if you'd told me."

"I should have. I never thought it would come out."

Burr took his hands out of his pockets and leaned up against the coatrack. "Do you know who her boyfriends were?"

"No."

*I don't believe you.*

Burr grabbed one of the hangers.

*I could stab him with this.*

Tommy backed away.

"What about the records that Karen talked about?"

Tommy shook his head. "I could never find anything."

"And the ring."

"I didn't put it there."

*This is a fine mess.*

Burr hung the hanger back on the coatrack. Then he pushed the whole thing over. It fell into another coatrack which fell into another and still another. They crashed to the floor, falling like dominoes. The noise was deafening.

\* \* \*

Burr drove back to the Park Place. He picked up Zeke at valet parking, tipped the bellman a ten, then did what he always did when he didn't know what to do. He drove. He rolled the window halfway down for Zeke, who stuck his nose out, still learning about life through his nose. At M-22, where this debacle had started, he turned north.

*Why couldn't this have just stayed a civil lawsuit, a simple condemnation case.* "Zeke, I'd much rather fight over money. It's so much simpler." He sighed.

"And satisfying. Not to mention the money."

Burr looked out at the bay. The daylight was fading. The wind had died and the waves had become rollers, soft easy rollers. Zeke stuck his head all the way out the window when he saw a flock of bluebills skimming just above the tops of the waves.

"It's duck season, Zeke. This lunacy is almost over. We won't miss it. I promise."

The next thing Burr remembered, he was in Northport, walking out of Woody's with a six-pack of Labatt and two sandwiches, ham and swiss on rye. There was no time for the cherry chicken, not now. Zeke ate his sandwich right away.

Burr parked in front of the shed, picked the lock and, armed with his six-pack and flashlight, fumbled around in the shed until he found *Achilles*.

He borrowed a ladder, climbed aboard and sat on the fantail, Labatt in hand. "I'm going to search this boat stem to stern."

Three beers later, he hadn't found a thing. One more beer and he'd need a nap. "It's here. I can feel it." He had a fourth beer. He laid down on the settee and shut his eyes. Then he sat up. Bolt upright.

"I wonder if it's here."

He climbed down the companionway and stumbled in the dark to the nav station. He opened the top drawer. It wasn't there. Not in the middle drawer. No. He jerked open the third drawer. He fumbled through the jumble of papers. There it was. The logbook.

Brooks didn't care about it. He could have entered it in evidence, but when Burr said he didn't want it. Brooks left it on board.

He went back to the cockpit and opened his fifth beer. He held the flashlight in his mouth, shined it on the book and flipped through the pages.

It was just like before. Dates with weather. May 30, SE at 5, clear skies. June 21, W at 10, rain. Then the last entry. June 9, SE at 5, clear skies. Entry after entry. Date, wind and weather. That's all there was. Just the weather on the days Helen took *Achilles* out. Just the weather. He slammed the book shut.

He finished his beer, then crushed the can in his hand.

"Damn it all."

He reached for the last Labatt but thought better of it. He opened the book and flipped through the pages again. Then he studied them, one by one. Line by line. There were at least fifty entries over the past five years, but there were only about six different weather reports. There would be six or seven in a row all the same. Then the forecast would change. They might overlap but not for long. He slammed the logbook shut again. "Maybe that's what it is. Maybe this is it." Burr put the logbook in his pocket and drank his last beer.

* * *

Back at the Jeep, he let Zeke out. While the dog sniffed who-knows-what, Burr ate his own sandwich. It was after seven now, as dark outside as it had been inside. And cold. The October night had a damp chill and Burr hadn't brought his overcoat. He buttoned his suit jacket and took the car phone out of the bag. He plugged it into the lighter, stuck the magnetic antenna on the roof and called Jacob at the Park Place. He prayed for a connection.

The hotel operator answered and put him through to Jacob.

"Hello, Burr," Jacob said. "You might have just come down to my room."

"I'm not at the hotel."

"Where are you? The connection is a bit scratchy."

"This is my car phone."

"Remarkable."

"It's the future," Burr said, who didn't have time to talk about the future right now.

*Who knows how long this thing is going work.*

"Jacob, we have important business. I need you to do something."

"Tomorrow is another day," Jacob said.

The line crackled. "Jacob, we have one day to finish this. If it goes to the jury, we're cooked."

"My dear, Burr, I don't work nights."

"Damn it all, Jacob. Get a piece of paper and write down the dates and weather reports as I read them to you."

"I most certainly will not." Burr heard Jacob put the phone down, but he didn't think he'd hung up on him.

The line crackled again. "Please, please, please. Don't disconnect me. Not now."

"What's that?" Jacob was back on the line.

"Nothing," Burr said. "Jacob, write all this down. It's from Helen's logbook." Burr rattled off the dates and forecasts.

"I guess that wasn't so hard. I think I'll have a nightcap and turn in," Jacob said.

Burr knew that Jacob smoked his nightcaps. That would never do. Not tonight. "Jacob, there's just one thing."

"No."

"I need you to drive to Grand Rapids tonight. Right now. Buy yourself the best room you can find. First thing in the morning, go to the National Weather Service office. Check the records for these dates I just gave you. Write down what the weather was for these dates. Then get back here as fast as you can."

"No."

"Jacob, please. Tommy's life may depend on it."

"There's no death penalty in Michigan."

"You know what I mean."

"This is another of your follies."

"No. No, it's not," Burr said, who thought it might be. "Meet me at Morningside as soon as you can."

"No."

"Jacob, please."

The line crackled and went dead.

"Damn it all." Burr ripped the car phone out of the car and threw it as far as he could. The antenna pulled off the roof and hit him on the back of the head as it flew by.

Burr decided he was in no condition to drive back to Traverse City, perhaps one of the few good decisions he had made in who knows how long. He left the Jeep where it was and stumbled next door to *Spindrift*, Zeke leading the way.

Fortunately, Burr had left a sleeping bag aboard, and after negotiating the dock, he and Zeke cuddled on the starboard berth. There was barely room for one, but it was so cold he welcomed the company.

\* \* \*

Burr woke at first light, dawn streaming in the portholes. He wasn't quite frozen solid. The steak and eggs at the Little Finger mostly righted him. The aging lab wolfed down the to go order on the sidewalk beside the Jeep. "Zeke, old friend, as soon as this is over, it's back to dogfood." The dog looked up at him. "For you, not me."

Back at the Park Place, Burr showered and shaved. He nicked the mole on his cheek, the same place he always nicked himself. "Back to normal," he said.

Burr cut across the little finger, then north on M-22. There were still colors, but they were past their peak, the aspen bare, the birches not far behind, but the sugar maples still had their brilliant oranges and yellows. The wind blew hard off the lake. Burr watched the leaves fall off the trees and skitter in the wind as they fell.

He passed an M-22 sign. "How can such a beautiful road have caused so much trouble?"

At two o'clock, he turned on Port Oneida Road, then into the driveway at Morningside. He passed row after row of cherry trees. Bare, lifeless, ready for winter. A single crow sat on one of the branches.

"Zeke, they'll leaf out in the spring and then they'll bloom." *Or will they? Will Sleeper's men cut them down with chainsaws?*

He parked next to Jacob's Peugeot. "Will wonders never cease." Burr knocked on the farmhouse door. Tommy let him in. Consuela was nowhere in sight, but then he didn't expect her to be there. Not now. Probably not ever again.

Tommy led him to the kitchen. Jacob was nursing a cup of tea, his hands wrapped around the cup.

*He looks cold. And cranky.*

"So good of you to join us," Jacob said.

"I wouldn't miss it."

Burr said no to coffee and sat next to Jacob. Tommy poured himself a cup and sat across from them. "What's this about? Jacob won't say a word."

"I would tell you if I knew. This is another of Burr's silly ideas."

"I think it's a little late for silly," Tommy said.

"Quite right. I'm sorry," Jacob said.

"Did you find the weather reports?" Burr said.

Jacob reached into his jacket pocket and pulled out a sheaf of paper. He unfolded the papers and set them in front of Burr.

Burr looked at Jacob, then Tommy. "Helen had a logbook on *Achilles*. She wrote down the weather for her trips. But when I looked at the weather, really looked at it, it didn't make any sense. It would all be the same four, five or six times in a row. Then the entries changed. The next batch would all be the same. Then they'd change again. Once in a while there was a little overlap before another sequence, but the pattern kept on going. Right up until she was murdered.

"That doesn't mean anything," Tommy said.

"I didn't think so either. At first. But I thought it was too coincidental. So Jacob went to the National Weather Service in Grand Rapids and wrote down the weather for each of the days Helen did."

Tommy looked at Burr as if he was crazy, which he probably was.

Burr took the logbook out of his pocket and opened it up. "But the actual weather doesn't match what Helen wrote down. Maybe once in a while, but most of the time, it wasn't even close."

"The weather is hardly ever what it's supposed to be."

"That's true," Burr said, "but the sequences don't match the real weather at all."

Jacob took his hands off the teacup and blew on them. "Burr, you have lost me, as usual."

"It's code," Burr said. "Code. Each forecast was one of Helen's lovers. That's how she kept track of her..." Burr paused.

"Conquests," Tommy said.

"I'm sorry," Burr said. "She wrote them down in her logbook. When she was about to move on, the weather changed. If she wasn't quite done with one, but had started up with someone new, there was an overlap."

"I don't believe it," Tommy said.

"It was all in plain sight," Burr said.

"I still don't believe it."

"You said yourself, she had serial affairs. This is the proof."

"My dear, Burr," Jacob said, "there's no way to prove this is so, and there's no way to find out who the...the..."

"Lovers," Tommy said.

"...were." Jacob finished the sentence. "All you've done is prove that the weather doesn't match."

"Tommy, do you know any of them?"

"I have a few ideas but nothing certain. Helen was careful."

"So, you think one of them may have killed her?" Jacob said.

"Yes," Burr said, who didn't.

"One of the jilted ones."

Burr nodded.

"What do we do now?"

"We've got until tomorrow at ten to find out. Then it goes to the jury."

"Maybe the jury will find me not guilty."

"Not after Karen's testimony," Jacob said.

Tommy leaned back in his chair.

Burr gathered up the logbook and the weather reports and left.

\* \* \*

He took the long way back to Traverse City, stopping at the Happy Hour for one last cheeseburger and one, just one, Stroh's, then on to Traverse City. He had important business. Business that would tell the tale tomorrow morning.

# CHAPTER TWENTY-FOUR

At ten the next morning, they were all in their places, including Burr's pencil *du jour*. The courtroom was packed. It looked like Leelanau County had turned out in force, including Tommy's neighbors, the Sisters of Outrage – one of whom had caused this debacle – their husbands, and, of course, Dale Sleeper, who might well have the most to gain from a guilty verdict.

"All rise," the bailiff said.

Judge Mary Fisher entered the courtroom, probably for the last time, Burr thought. She arranged the flower in her bud vase, a rose again. Blood red.

*How appropriate.*

The bailiff called them to order.

"We are here today for closing arguments in the matter of the State versus Lockwood. Mr. Brooks?"

Brooks stood. So did Burr.

"Sit down, Lafayette. It's not your turn," Brooks said.

Burr ignored him. "Your Honor, the defense would like to call one more witness."

"Your Honor, the defense concluded its case. Mr. Lafayette said so himself."

Burr walked up to Judge Fisher, who pulled the bud vase toward her. "Your Honor, the prosecutor introduced new witnesses after he had concluded." Burr held up two fingers. "Twice."

"You may question one more witness."

"Thank you, Your Honor." He walked back to his table. "Maybe two," he said, under his breath. His back to both the judge and the prosecutor, Burr reached into his jacket pocket and took out the logbook. He handed it to Jacob and said under his breath, "When I ask to introduce this into evidence, hand it to Tommy. I'll take it *from him.*"

"You'll never get this introduced. You took it from *Achilles* and that's off limits."

Burr ignored him. "The defense calls Lauren Littlefield." He looked her squarely in the eye. She was shocked but met his gaze. She stood. Burr held the gate open that separated the gallery from the litigants.

She sat in the witness stand, smoothed her dress, also black but shapeless, concealing her figure.

The bailiff swore her in. Burr identified her as the youngest of Helen's sisters. She lived with her husband and children in Northport, worked as a nurse at Munson, and did not, under any circumstances, want to sell the orchards.

*Here goes. All or nothing.*

"Mrs. Littlefield, you heard your sister Karen testify about your late sister and her affairs. Is that right?"

"Yes."

"And do you agree with her testimony?"

"Well, I'm not sure." She rubbed her nose. "I never saw her with anyone."

*Such a kind sister.*

"But you heard the rumors?"

"I suppose I did."

"Your Honor, the defense would like to introduce the logbook of the deceased, Helen Lockwood, as Defense Exhibit Three." Burr turned around, making sure Jacob was handing it to Tommy.

Brooks jumped to his feet. "I object, Your Honor. That logbook is sequestered evidence. Counsel has no right to have it in his possession. I ask you to hold him in contempt for tampering with State's evidence."

"Those are serious charges, Mr. Lafayette," the judge said.

"Your Honor, the logbook is not in my possession," Burr said, although it had been in his possession until about five minutes ago. "The logbook is in the possession of my client. There is no police tape around the boat. It is not a secure site. The property of Mrs. Lockwood is, by law, under the custody and control of Mrs. Lockwood's heir, Mr. Lockwood."

"He won't be her heir once he's convicted of murder," Brooks said.

Burr smiled at Brooks. "That will be for another day."

"Stop it, both of you," Judge Fisher said. "You may introduce the logbook into evidence."

Burr did so, along with Jacob's weather reports. Brooks fumed, but there was nothing he could do.

Burr held the logbook in one hand and the weather reports in the other.

"Mrs. Littlefield, I don't expect you to comment on this, but it turns out that the only thing written in your sister's logbook are weather reports, which, of course, isn't unusual for a logbook on a boat. What's unusual is that the weather in the logbook doesn't match any of the weather reports for the days in question. Perhaps not unusual. It is, after all, Michigan." The gallery snickered.

Burr turned to the gallery and waved the logbook at it. He turned back to Lauren. "What this really is, though, is Helen Lockwood's own code. These weather entries in the logbook aren't weather at all. They're a chronicle of Mrs. Lockwood's lovers, one after the other."

Brooks stood. "Your Honor, this is irrelevant. It's nothing more than a parlor game."

"Your Honor, I'm about to show the relevance."

The curious judge leaned toward Burr. "Please do."

"This is a list of Helen's lovers," Burr said. "In code. We don't know who they are. Any of the jilted lovers could have killed Helen. As far as that goes, so could Tommy, the cuckolded husband." Burr looked at the jury then turned back to Lauren. "But that's not what happened, is it," Burr said, not asking.

"I have no idea what you're talking about."

*She's awfully calm.*

Burr was a bit worried.

*In for a penny, in for a pound.*

He put his hands in his pockets. "I'll tell you exactly what happened."

He stood where the jury could see both Lauren and him.

"It was one thing for your sister to carry on with other men. That was between her and Tommy. But when she started in with your husband..." Burr pointed to her fair-haired, boy-next-door husband sitting in the gallery next to Karen and her husband. "That was too much."

*Not a trace of emotion.*

"Somehow you found out your husband was going to meet Helen on South Manitou. You made sure he didn't go, did you?"

*Nothing.*

"You snuck aboard *Achilles* before Helen got there and hid on the boat all the way to South Manitou. You stayed hidden when Tommy had it out with her. Then you had it out with her. You shot her in the forehead. Maybe you didn't plan that part. Maybe you lost your temper. Then you buried her, sent *Achilles* off toward Milwaukee and came home. No one saw you." Burr looked at his scuffed-up shoes. "Why? Because you took the dinghy back to Leland. It was nervy but it was calm that night." Burr looked at his shoes again. "Where's the dinghy, Lauren? Where did you sink it?"

"You're making all this up. I was at work that night. I was signed in."

Burr put his hands in his pockets. "You showed up for work. You were signed in. But you weren't there. Not that night."

"I was."

Burr looked out in the gallery. She was there. Thank heavens. His important business yesterday had been at Munson. He'd talked to all of the OB-GYN nurses until he found the right one.

"Mrs. Littlefield, as you told me, there isn't much predictability to the arrival of babies. You got yourself scheduled on what you thought would be a slow night. And it was. Your friend Nurse Seamands is here in the gallery." Burr pointed at a worried looking middle-aged woman sitting in the back of the courtroom. "She is about to testify that she covered for you that night. Not that there was much to cover for. It was a slow night. You all did that for each other. Didn't you? And you said you'd come back if you were needed. But you weren't. So, you stowed away on *Achilles* and killed your sister. And you had a perfect alibi."

"It's not true," an edge to Lauren's voice.

*Perhaps a chink in her armor.*

"It would have worked if you'd left well enough alone. But I asked one too many questions about the dinghy. You got worried."

"No. No, I didn't."

*The chink is getting bigger.*

"You'd have been in the clear if you hadn't planted Helen's ring in the flour. Tommy never would have put it there. And only Tommy, Karen, Consuela, and you – yes, you – had unfettered access to the house. You planted it where you were sure Consuela would find it."

"It wasn't me." She rubbed her nose again.

"Oh, but it was. I'm about to call your colleague. She's going to tell us exactly where you weren't that night. And then your husband is going to tell us that you caught him and Helen. And he certainly doesn't want to be convicted of murder." Burr pointed at Curt. He had his head in his hands.

"It almost worked, Lauren. Almost."

"I hated her," she said. "I hated her."

"She was the prettiest and the smartest. She got everything she wanted. She didn't love Curt. She just wanted to prove she could have him. But she wasn't going to get him." Lauren gripped the railing just like the rest of them, but she didn't cry.

\* \* \*

At two o'clock that afternoon, the entire staff of Lafayette and Wertheim sat in a booth at the bar at the Park Place. Grand Traverse Bay positively shimmered in the late afternoon sun. Zeke, with the special dispensation that a fifty-dollar bill could bring, lounged under the booth. Eve was on her first Bloody Mary, Burr his second martini. Jacob sipped his Perrier through a straw, sans lime.

It had taken the jury all of twenty minutes to acquit Tommy. He had written Burr a big check right on the spot and disappeared, keeping well clear of the coatroom. Eve had immediately taken possession of the check and put it in her purse. Karen and Lauren had gone their separate ways.

"What happens now?" Eve said.

"Now we deposit the check and pay our bills," Jacob said.

Burr stirred his drink. "And my alimony."

"What happens to Lauren?" Eve said.

"Probably nothing," Burr said.

"She confessed. In front of the judge," Eve said.

"Brooks has to decide what to do. I'm not sure he has enough proof or the stomach for another trial."

"But she killed Helen," Eve said. "She said she did."

"No, she didn't say she killed Helen. She never confessed. She said she hated her sister. And that she wasn't going to let Helen have Curt. She never said she killed her," Burr said.

"But Tommy was acquitted."

"Tommy was acquitted because the jury couldn't get past reasonable doubt. That doesn't convict Lauren."

"Curt had the affair with Helen. He could testify," Eve said.

"A husband can't be forced to testify against his wife. Or vice versa." This from Jacob.

"Where is the justice in any of this?" Eve finished her drink and raised her glass for another.

"Tommy wasn't convicted. I think that's about all the justice we're going to get," Burr said.

"What if Lauren had been called back to the hospital?" Jacob said.

Burr fished out an olive. He chewed it slowly.

"She'd either have gone back or she wouldn't. My guess is she was so incensed, she was going to kill Helen no matter what. She was spitting blood on the stand. But if she'd been called back to the hospital, my guess is she'd have waited for another day."

"That leaves the orchards," Jacob said.

"I'm sure Sleeper still wants to buy them. We'll have a nice run arguing about the value."

"What about the family?" Eve said.

"I think the family has been destroyed. Helen held it together, and in the end, she tore it apart." Burr ate another olive. "The face that launched a thousand ships," he said.

"I beg your pardon?" Jacob said.

"It's from the *Odyssey*," Eve said. "When Helen left her husband for a Trojan prince and fled to Troy, the jilted husband's family sailed a thousand ships across the Aegean to get her back. The few Trojans who weren't killed were taken as slaves."

"I see," Jacob said, who didn't.

"And the park?" Eve said.

Burr picked up a third olive and chewed it slowly. "I think Sleeper is going to finish acquiring the land he wants for the park. I'm not against it. But I don't like the heavy hand of government bearing down on private citizens. Especially when it's administered by bureaucrats."

"Isn't that a bit philosophical for you?" Eve said.

"The constitution gives the government the right to take private property. It's the police power in the Fifth Amendment," Jacob said.

Eve rolled her eyes.

*She's never been interested in constitutional law.*

"But there's also due process. Very few people have the money or the will to stand up to the government," Burr said.

"Except Helen," Eve said. "And you."

Burr swirled the ice in his glass.

*This tastes like another.*

"What about you, Burr?" Jacob said.

"The first nice day we get, I'm going to sail *Spindrift* back to Harbor Springs and put her to bed for the winter."

\* \* \*

Burr didn't take *Spindrift* to Harbor Springs on the first nice day. On the first nice day, he and Zeke drove to the park. He parked the Jeep on the back side of the big dune and the two of them started up.

"Zeke, you're a great friend, but I wish Maggie was here, too."

Burr's shoes and Zeke's paws sank into the loose sand all the way up. Both were out of breath by the time they reached the top. Burr looked out at the lake. The wind blew hard from the northwest. The waves crashed on the beach hundreds of feet below them, whitecaps as far as he could see. The wind blew sand, fine sand, that stung his face. He looked north at the Manitous, then up at the mound of trees and brush that was the sleeping bear, still waiting for her cubs.

"Zeke, she's always waiting. That's probably a good enough reason for the park. As long as they pay for it."

**THE END**

# *Acknowledgements*

To Ellen Jones for her copy editing, sage advice, encouragement ... and deciphering the yellow-pad scratchings that were my first draft.

To Mark Lewison for his copy editing, story editing, unflagging attention to detail, and especially for his enthusiasm.

To Nancy Anisfield, Jesse Melcher, Mark Sherwood, Julie Spencer and Steve Spencer for reading the manuscript. They found countless factual, contextual and typographical errors.

To Jesse Melcher for straightening out my website.

To Kathryn McLravy for creating my website, managing my Facebook page and for driving me all over Leelanau County.

To Bob Deck at Mission Point Press for the book's interior design.

To Heather Shaw and Jodee Taylor at Mission Point Press for all their help with publicity and marketing.

To John Wickham for his cover design.

To Doug Weaver at Mission Point Press for his help in naming the book and for keeping everything on schedule.

Finally, and most importantly, thanks to my wife, Christi, for encouragement, support, tolerance, patience, and most of all, her love.

# About the Author

Reviewers are calling Charles Cutter a master of the courtroom drama and the next Erle Stanley Gardner, author of the Perry Mason series. Although Mr. Cutter has years of legal experience, he is now a "recovering attorney" writing full-time. In addition to the Burr Lafayette series, he has written literary fiction, screenplays, short stories and a one-act play. He is currently working on the next book in the Burr Lafayette series. He lives in East Lansing, Michigan, with his wife, two dogs and four cats. He has a leaky sailboat on Little Traverse Bay and a leakier duck boat on Saginaw Bay.

His books are available on Amazon and at your local bookstore.

For additional information, please go to www.CharlesCutter.com.

*Also by Charles Cutter*

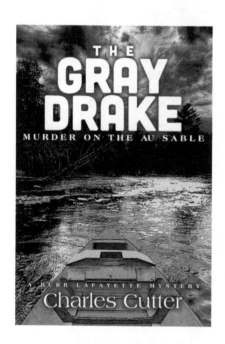

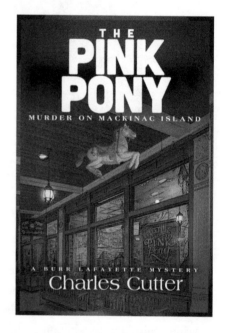